Books by Henry Kane

LUST OF POWER   1975

A KIND OF RAPE   1974

DECISION   1973

THE MOONLIGHTER   1971

Lust of Power

Lust of Power

HENRY KANE

Atheneum   NEW YORK   1975

Cupido dominandi cunctis adfectibus flagrantior est:

Lust of power burns more fiercely than all the passions combined.

TACITUS, *Annals*

Lust of Power

I

THIS FRIDAY night in hot July, Joshua Fitts Kearney, anonymously in bed in a London hotel, thought fleetingly but admiringly about Arthur Upton. Quite a man, Arthur Upton. Old, but young. Seventy-one years of age, but lithe, spry, ageless. Probably the finest constitutional lawyer in the United States, Arthur Upton, but he no longer worked at it: his sights were aimed higher. A wizard at politics—during a prior administration he had been Ambassador to the United Nations—he was now (and had been for the past eight years) the brains behind the enormous political apparatus that would present the junior Senator from New York as his party's presidential candidate, and the convention was only a year away.

Joshua Fitts Kearney was the junior Senator from New York State.

A Congressman for two years, a United States Senator for six years, he was now two years into his second term as U.S. Senator. And the public polls (and the private polls) showed that the dynamic young Senator from New York was not only his party's leading candidate for the nomination, but he was far and away the favorite for election no matter whom the opposition selected to run against him.

Yes, of course. Eight years in the making. With the superlative Arthur Upton at the helm of the apparatus, and limitless funds always at hand. Apparatus. A huge staff, a conglomerate of the best in the business. The best of political tacticians. The best of speechwriters. The best of public-relations advisers. The best of federal, state, and municipal politicos. And the very best of the VIPs of the media. The organization had it all, the best of all, the best that money could buy, but at nucleus they were four; Barney had dubbed them the Big Four and the name stuck. Big Four. There was the Senator, J. F. Kearney. There was the Senator's wife, Kathryn Braxton Kearney. There was the brain, Arthur Upton. And there was the pragmatic executioner of policy, the formidable Barnabas F. X. Wilson. They were it. They were the nub, the hub, the nucleus.

But now, here in bed, in London in the quiet hotel, the Senator's fleeting admiration was peculiar, oblique. He was admiring Arthur Upton's prowess as a pimp. Christ, the very thought was monstrous, rococo, bizarre, anomalous— the distinguished Arthur Upton a pimp. But pimp, in this case, carried no connotation of pejorative. *Au contraire,* by Jesus. It represented a human being of depth and compassion, a human being who understood the foibles and tortures of a fellow human being. Only Arthur Upton knew of some of Josh Kearney's secrets, knew of his carnal aberrations, knew that he required "dirty sex" for the stimulation and satisfaction of his kinky libido. And so when the need was upon him —be it England or wherever, France, Germany, Italy, or even the United States—it was Arthur Upton who covered for him. It was Arthur who secured the hotel suite (or motel room) and Arthur who procured the harlots for hire, always

4

the best and most expensive, and always two. Josh Kearney required two. But they were never repeated; always it was a different pair. (People, you must try to understand. We—I —must be circumspect. I am the junior Senator from New York. I am your paragon, your white-haired boy. I am the Party's Choice for candidate, and the People's Choice for President. Presidents don't fuck, except with their wives. Presidents, unlike you, do not have freaky desires. Presidents, unlike you, do not have sexual peccadilloes.) Therefore the wily, the astute, the compassionate Arthur Upton covers for me. And this evening the wily, the astute, the compassionate Arthur has outdone himself. Christ, look at them there, naked with me naked in my anonymous bed. Look at them, bronze, glistening, gleaming, exquisite West Indians newly arrived in England. Look at them, as I am looking, disporting themselves with themselves because so I have commanded. For now, I am a voyeur. For now, obliquely thinking about Arthur Upton, it pleases me to be a voyeur. But not for long; not for long shall I be thinking about Arthur Upton. Soon I shall issue another command to this lissome, glistening, expensive duo. Soon I shall say enough, disengage, and engage with me. But not yet. For now, it pleases me to lie languid, Joshua Fitts Kearney, the passionate voyeur.

This Friday night in hot July, in the Kearney mansion in Sussex, Arthur Upton sat alone in the drawing room and sipped white wine. It had been a good three weeks, no vicissitudes: the itinerary had gone precisely to plan. The senatorial party had visited with the heads of state—a week in Russia, a week in China, a week in Japan—and the newspapers back home (as Norman Eden faithfully reported) had given the trip excellent coverage. The distinguished, handsome, junior Senator from New York was not only the people's representative in Washington, he was also an acclaimed and renowned international figure. And he kept right on being an international figure because, unlike most of the other Senators in the United States Senate, this particular Senator had the wealth to support his being an international figure. He was the last of the Kearneys, a scion with hundreds of millions of dollars by inheritance. What other Senator could afford to fly to far places in a personally owned jetliner, a ten-million-dollar craft?

And that was good, all of it good: riches made for good politics in these days of our times. The Abraham Lincoln log-cabin syndrome was ancient history; riches made for glamour in these days of our times, and the people loved it. But it was more than glamour, it was a bulwark of protection for the commonweal: the rich have no need to steal. The people had lived through an administration riddled with corruption at the top; they were weary of the peculations, the misfeasance, the malfeasance, the endless duplicity, the double-talk, the collusions and connivance. The great wealth of J. F. Kearney set him head and shoulders above any of that. No need for knavery, trickery, fraud, and deception; his wealth obviated any form of thievery: he had nothing to gain. Further, he was already a proven commodity; the handsome, vigorous, valiant J. F. Kearney was a White Knight. For ten years—two in the House of Representatives and eight in the Senate—he had plumped for the common man, the average man. He had inaugurated bills for the good of the people, and constantly and continuously he pleaded the people's cause.

It was not sham. It was truth. The people's cause *was* his cause. Perhaps this noble drive was a matter of unconscious guilt, the born-with-the-golden-spoon complex, which can work two ways. You are either a profligate spendthrift, a high-living waster and wastrel, or you go the other way, driven, a dedicated philanthropist. J. F. Kearney's philanthropy was politics. He was a White Knight warrior, battling for the people, and the people believed.

6

The people can be fooled, but you cannot fool the inner core of your own apparatus. J. F. Kearney was more than a politician; he was a statesman, a devoted public servant. Of course he was ambitious. He had it all, born to it all; he had all that money could buy, except ultimate power, and the ultimate of power was the Presidency.

In the flux and turmoil of politics, in the churnings of the strife for power, infrequently—too damned infrequently—a great man evolves: Joshua Fitts Kearney was The Man.

Early on, Arthur Upton had not believed. Early on, he had resisted Josh Kearney's importunities to join the cause. Early on, he had remained a practicing attorney, the surviving member of the firm of Kearney & Upton, 350 Fifth Avenue, New York City. That Kearney, the senior partner of Kearney & Upton, had been Earl Kearney, Josh Kearney's father, now nine years deceased of the inevitable heart attack. Early on, when the young Kearney had run for Congress, Arthur Upton, despite importunities, had remained uninvolved, a dispassionate watcher from the sidelines. At age thirty-nine, Josh Kearney had been elected to the Congress, and for the two years of his tenure Arthur Upton had watched and waited, and had become convinced. The rich young Kearney was not another dilettante meretriciously pushing for a seat of power; the young man was driven, dedicated; not an ego-impelled flamboyant politician happily waving narcissistic banners, but a statesman truly devoted. And so, when the party had selected the dynamic Josh Kearney to run for the Senate, Arthur Upton had come over as campaign manager, and he had gone all the way.

At that time, eight years ago, Arthur Upton had been sixty-three, and sufficiently rich to retire from active practice as an attorney. He had come over as chief of staff for Josh Kearney because Arthur Upton had had a dream for Joshua Fitts Kearney, and that dream, eight years later, was now at threshold. Arthur Upton, a widower, his children grown

7

and married, was devoting the rest of his life to the cause, and that cause was now at imminent point. Joshua Fitts Kearney, a product of golden-spoon wealth, was his party's man for the nomination, and once nominated he would be a shoo-in next November. Arthur Upton had spent eight years of his waning life to that purpose. The man would be a good President; Upton sincerely believed he would grow in office to be a great President.

The wealth. From the beginning it had been a serious problem—how much should the public know? It was good for them to know that J. F. Kearney was rich, very rich, so independently rich that he could never be seduced to bribery, extortion, chicanery, dirty tricks. But—how rich is rich? If you go all the way, you can be subject to the groundswell of reverse reaction, envy, jealousy, proletarian rage. Therefore Arthur Upton, the chief of staff, had taken his cue from the campaign people of the political Rockefellers—and so he had instructed Public Relations. Play up the riches, but don't play up *all* the riches. Lord, the riches!

Joshua Fitts Kearney owned a mansion in Sussex, England. And a townhouse on Sutton Place in New York City. And a palatial home in Chevy Chase, not too far from his senatorial office in the Capitol. And a palatial home in Southampton, Long Island. And a palatial home in Key Biscayne in Florida. And apartments in Paris, Rome, Copenhagen, Munich, and Tel Aviv. The junior Senator's wealth was now close to a billion dollars. Should the public know? The Big Four knew: J. F. Kearney, Arthur Upton, Kathy Kearney, Barney Wilson —but should the public know? Should they know of the vast real-estate holdings, the oil companies, the computer company, the shipyards, the immense plexus of interlocking corporations; should they know that four stories in a Madison Avenue building were filled with accountants and lawyers and bookkeepers and financial experts who administered the far-

8

flung Kearney complex? No. The decision had been to play it like the Rockefellers; let the aura prevail, but limit the specifics. Whenever necessary, however, the absolute truth—because no credibility gap, ever, must exist between J. F. Kearney and the general public.

Upton glanced at his watch: five to twelve. At twelve o'clock he would receive his daily report from Norman Eden, the chief factotum of the Senator's office, their permanent man in Washington. Eden called every day, including Saturday and Sunday, at precisely midnight *their* time in whatever country they were. Still looking at his watch, Upton did a rapid computation. What with Daylight Saving, the time along the Eastern Seaboard of the United States would now be five minutes to eight. He shrugged, sat back, sipped wine. The phone rang and he talked with Norman Eden, routine political matters. Then Eden said, "Oh. There was a message on the machine from Harrison Quealy."

"Message from *whom?*"

"Chairman of the New York State Parole Board."

"Yes. Quealy. Why on the machine?"

"I wasn't in the office. Nor was my girl. Quealy called and the machine answered. I have it for you verbatim."

"Nobody in the office? What is it—a holiday for the staff?"

Eden laughed.

Upton said, "All right, let's have it."

"Verbatim as follows. The message. 'Re Dwyer. Parole will be approved. He will be released on November eighth.' "

"Right. What else do we have?"

"That's it for today, Mr. Upton."

"Thank you, Norman."

Upton hung up, looked at the phone, hesitated. Should he call him right now? He knew that Josh was interested in obtaining parole for Simon Dwyer, that he had utilized his political weight in quietly pressuring Harrison Quealy—although Upton had never been told precisely why. Josh Kearney, although appearing to be the easygoing extrovert, was in fact a subtle man and a man of subtle secrets. Upton assumed a nuance of guilt was involved. Before his election to Congress, Kearney had represented Simon Dwyer in a criminal matter, had pleaded him guilty, and Dwyer had been sentenced to serve from fifteen to forty years. Thus, in a manner of speaking, the attorney had been responsible for the client's imprisonment, and therefore the nuance of guilt and the pressure for the earliest parole. But Dwyer had been no more than a minor pawn in the original proceedings: the kingpin had been Vito Arminito.

Upton stood up and paced. *It's after midnight. Do I call him?* He knew Josh Kearney as well as anyone, but how well did anyone know Josh Kearney? It *was* a matter to be communicated, but in view of the sexual circumstances, should he not let it go until morning? Josh was capable of awful wrath: why risk the embarrassment of being the brunt of it? On the other hand, this was a damned important matter to Joshua Fitts Kearney, a long-term task; he had spent years pushing hard (but soft) upon the pious Harrison Quealy; and here it was in hand, a success at fruition. Certainly he would want to know as quickly as possible, and with J. F. Kearney that meant right now, at once, instantly!

It was warm and pleasant in the bedroom in the quiet hotel, the harlots adroit and adventurous. The Senator's head was nuzzled between the copious breasts of one; the other's head was nuzzled within the fork of his thighs. Now both his hands took hold of a firm, bronze, shining tit, and he sucked the purple nipple into his mouth. And down there, the other, as though on cue, commenced her performance: a hot wet mouth engulfed his tumescence, and an artful tongue titillated.

The phone rang.

10

"Kathy? Arthur Upton."

"Well, *Arthur!*" She winked toward Barney. "How are you, Arthur? How's Mr. Man?"

"Out on one of his diplomatic missions."

"To what do I owe the pleasure, Arthur?"

"Change in schedule, dear. Monday the fourteenth. My diary shows a party for the ladies of lib. Cancel it."

"Why?"

"Do it as quickly as possible. Of course, discreetly. Contact the proper people. Put it over for—a week or whatever. I'm sure you can handle it."

"Of course I can. What I'm asking—why?"

"I've been trying to reach Barney. Can't get him anywhere. Any idea where he is?"

"Nope."

"It's important."

"Can it hold till tomorrow?"

"I think so."

"He'll be here tomorrow. For Saturday and Sunday at the beach."

"Good. Give him this message. On the fourteenth, he's supposed to give a speech in San Francisco—the American Legion. He's to get in touch as quickly as possible and cancel. Postpone. They're sensitive; he'll have to think up a good reason. The White House or something. Leave it to Barney. Please give him the message first thing."

"No."

"I beg your pardon?"

"I've been asking you what the heck this is all about."

"We're coming home on that day. You and Barney will meet the plane at Dulles. That's Monday the fourteenth. We'll go to Chevy for a conference. That's it."

"Same question, Arthur. What the heck is this all about?"

A pause. Then Upton said, "It concerns a person named Simon Dwyer."

"Who the hell is Simon Dwyer?"

"He's important to Josh. That's the best I can do for now, my dear. I'm merely transmitting orders from Mr. Man. See you the fourteenth. Best to Barney. Bye, now."

He hung up. She hung up. "King Arthur," she said. "Orders from The Man. A message for you when you come here tomorrow."

"Okay, I came here. It's tomorrow."

"Postpone your American Legion speech. Give a heavy excuse—White House or something. Me, I'm to postpone my women's thing. Instead on the fourteenth we meet the royal party at Dulles. For an important conference at Chevy Chase."

"What about?"

"Simon Dwyer." She squinted. "Now who the hell—"

"You've heard the name before."

"I have?" She tilted her head. "I think—rings a little bell. Maybe because I'm drunkie. But I don't get gongs. How're you fixed for gongs, Mr. Wilson?"

"Simon Dwyer. Jailbird."

"I *am* drunkie—but you're beginning to reach me. Can you give me a little bit more, Mr. Wilson?"

"I don't have much. Now and then, Arthur sort of sketched me in—and I know *you* know. Back when Josh was practicing law, he represented the guy. Criminal rap. Pleaded him guilty. Guy drew fifteen to forty. The way the law works, you come up for parole after you've served two thirds of the fifteen."

"Yes. No gong, but a lot of little stupid bells."

"Mr. Man has been, for a long time, working quietly. Pushing for the early parole."

"Beyond me." She scowled. "So a lawyer wants to do a

bit for a client, he wants to get him out of the pokey-dokey as quickly as possible. All right, that I can understand. But this lawyer, at this time—that I *cannot* understand. This lawyer at this time is pushing toward the nomination for the highest office in the land. Your speech to the American Legion is important. My party for the wheels of women is important. Why must we postpone because of something back there in ancient history? Because of some silly little jailbird named Simon Dwyer?"

Barney shrugged.

"Why," she demanded, "is this *jailbird* that important? Why does Josh have Upton call all the way from England?"

"The ways of politics are intricate."

"So is Mr. J. F. fucking Kearney."

"You just said a mouthful, luv."

"Well, hell, fuck him."

"Yes, ma'am."

"And also Mr. Arthur Upton."

"Yes, ma'am."

"And also Mr. Simon Dwyer."

"Yes, ma'am."

"But all of them, figuratively."

"Yes, ma'am."

She reached, took the cigar from his fingers, laid it in an ashtray. Moved her naked body over his. Kissed his mouth. Smiled down at him.

"And also Mrs. Joshua Fitts Kearney."

"Yes, ma'am," he said.

"Literally," she said.

"You bet," he said.

And then, for a long time, noisily, they said nothing.

This Friday night in hot July, at five to twelve, Ronald Seely came home to the apartment on West 82nd Street in

New York City. He bolted the door, removed his jacket. He made a Jack Daniel's, looked in a mirror, saw unhappiness, nodded sullenly. Dear Lord, what more poignant unhappiness than that of an aging homosexual who is not beautiful? He had never been particularly beautiful, and the aging process did not help. He was fifty-three.

He sank into a chair, licked at the Daniel's. It had been a long, lousy night of pub crawling, but nothing. Many dumb conversations—but nothing. Not unusual, these frustrations, since the death of Bob Wright.

They had lived together for seven years—a good, affectionate relationship, and then a year ago, without hint of prior depression, Bob had cut his wrists and that had been it. A horrible debacle, but it's the damn living who suffer. For Bob it was done, his miseries were over, but Ron Seely had been left alone, lonely, suffering, aging. And so it had been back to the gay bars, and the gay parties, trying to make new friends, but when you're gay and over fifty, mostly you have to pay. Well, hell, he could afford, but tonight he could not even *buy* a lover. Holiday night, the city deserted.

He stood up, sought the mirror again, but this time he smiled, ruefully. Heck, he thought, let's look at the good side, and the good side was all Carleton Armin.

He freshened the highball, thinking about Armin, president of Carleton Armin, Ltd., Investment Bankers. Ron Seely was the executive secretary, and he loved the boss. Eleven years ago there had been that opening—Armin's secretary had quit to get married—and Armin had decided on a male secretary. At that time Seely had been a secretary on the staff of the Mayor of the City of New York, a solid job where his talents were wasted. (But a homosexual is always tentative, and civil service represents security.)

Carleton Armin, important in municipal politics, was a friend of the Mayor, and his requirement had filtered down to the Mayor's staff—and Ron Seely had decided on this one last chance for the gold ring. He had presented himself at Armin's office, taken the tests, and come off, of course, with colors flying. Armin had been impressed with the technical prowess, the education, the personality, but he had been most impressed that a man was willing to surrender the permanence of civil-service tenure. Seely had explained, but then he had added, "I must tell you right now up front. I'm gay."

Armin had said, "So what?" And that had been it.

Eleven years now, and not one regret. The money was great, and the Christmas bonuses bountiful. But it was more than money. It was esteem. Stature. He was more than executive secretary, he was the personal secretary, and he was privy to many secrets. Not all, of course. He knew, for instance, that Armin, tightly married, was a cheater, and he always knew with whom he cheated. So he cheated. So what? As Armin had said about Seely's homosexuality—*so what?* The guy was a good husband and a good father. So he screwed around. Hell, how could he miss? The women flocked like flies to sugar. Tall and handsome. Slim and straight and dark. Forty-eight years of age. I would love it if he was, at least, bisexual. Not Carleton Armin. No, sir. A dedicated ladies' man, strictly heterosexual.

Sipping the highball, he expunged, for the moment, Carleton Armin, and thought about the possibilities of reviving the weekend. Gay-bar prostitutes were one thing, but he had made *some* new friends since Bob's demise; perhaps—*I hope, I hope*—one of them had called this evening. He went to the phone and dialed the service. There was one message.

"A Mr. Thayne," the girl said. "You're to call him back."

"Thank you."

Bernie Thayne was gay, but not for Ron Seely. Bernie was happily married to a lovely man. The call had to be business, and the business Armin's, and since it came on the Fourth, something was up, and whatever was up had to do with Simon Dwyer.

On this Dwyer, Ron Seely had been of special value to Carleton Armin. Mr. Armin had been interested in obtaining an early parole for a Sing Sing convict named Simon Dwyer. Seely had no idea who the man was, but he did have a damn good connection in the office of Harrison Quealy, who was chairman of the Parole Board. That connection was Bernie Thayne, a minor factotum in Quealy's employ. So—many years ago—Ron had put through a call to Bernie, and Bernie had told him to tell his boss to hold his water because a bigger wheel than Mr. Armin was riding that selfsame rail—the wheel being Joshua Fitts Kearney. That took Armin off the hook; Kearney was doing the work for him. Over the years Ron had kept in touch with Bernie—and now the call on the Fourth of July.

He looked at his watch. It was late, but to hell with it. He checked Bernie's number, dialed, and after three rings Bernie said, "Yes?"

"Ron Seely."

"Hi, pal."

"I know it's late."

"Never too late, hah hah. No. Seriously. Not late at all. Listen, I've got news. And you're gonna earn yourself a bonus. Simon Dwyer. In the bag. Parole, first shot. This is strictly inside. Way before the official announcement. But it's a lock, one hundred percent. He's coming out November eight. Now you hit your guy for a bonus, Ronnie. You're goddam entitled, baby. You're giving him first-hand news way in advance. That's it, Ronnie. Good luck."

"Thank you, Bern."

Mr. Armin would want this news immediately, and Mr. Seely knew where to reach him. Not at the duplex on East

67th. There would be nobody home there this weekend. The wife—Marion—was away at their ranch house in the Adirondacks. The son—a student at Yale—was vacationing in the south of France. The daughter—a student at Wellesley—was vacationing in Newfoundland. Mr. Armin was here in New York because Suzy Buford was here in New York. Miss Buford was an airline stewardess—Los Angeles to New York—and this was her weekend free in New York.

This Friday night in hot July, in bed in the bedroom of the sumptuous apartment on Central Park West, the slender man writhed between the thighs of the red-haired girl. Face to face this time, the girl on bottom, the man on top: missionary position. A skillful lover, he ground deeply, relentlessly, and the girl sighed and screamed in recurrent orgasm; finally the man let go, capitulating in explosive climax. Then they lay like that, entwined, panting like animals, locked, until her legs came down from around him.

"God," she whispered. "You're wonderful."

He turned to the bed table, drank warm champagne from a tall goblet. He tapped cigarettes from a pack, offered one.

"No, thanks," she said. "Not yet." She closed her eyes.

He lit the cigarette, adjusted pillows under his head. He loved it, all of it, although he no longer particularly loved the girl beside him. Sex was a joy, a hobby, an excruciating diversion. Sex was an exquisite game, and he had been a game player, a convivial cheater, all through his marriage. In the beginning there had been some small resentment on Marion's part—early-marriage jealousy—but in time it had subsided: she had learned to understand that frivolous side of his nature. Today she could not care less—as long as he continued to remain discreet. At fifty-one, three years his senior, she made no sexual demands; her fires, never hotly burning for sex, were banked. There were other fires. Marion Armin, laughing, charming, vivacious, eminent in New York society, was an active woman of many interests.

Now here in bed, Suzy Buford, twenty-six. He *had* been in love with her, and when Armin was in love he required exclusive possession. An age-old ironical inconsistency: a cheater in love demands fealty from the beloved. He must capture, enrapture, and keep for his own. Carleton Armin, long experienced. His preference was young girls, and he knew how to play the pragmatic game. First, of course, there must be mutual attraction; but given that, then give to them. Give! Money. Things. What they themselves cannot possibly afford. And once they take, you have them ensnared. And since you are married, you must always hold out to them the possibility of your divorce and remarriage. To this new lady of your life.

He had captured Suzy, but he was now engaged in the subtle process of releasing her. Because there was a new one up there on the horizon, a real one. They were rare, the real ones; not the usual pretty ones, the mundane. Suzy had been a real one. Now there was Dolores Warren, who had enflamed his imagination. Fascinating, alluring; very young, twenty-two. Up from Houston, Texas, an actress seeking, hoping, trying. Did small stints as a part-time model, lived on Perry Street in the Village. He had met her at a party given by one of Marion's friends, a charity affair, and there had been that instant, hermetic, mutual reaction. Gorgeous, and coincidentally, like Suzy, a redhead. Christ, her effect. First time in a long time. First time in two years that Carleton Armin was plighting a new troth, and that is damn difficult to do when you are deeply keeping a Suzy Buford.

He thumped out the cigarette. It had been a good day: early dinner, a play, and then here with champagne. He looked toward her. Her eyes were closed. He touched her.

"Sleeping?"

24

"No. Thinking."

"I'm going to say a cliché."

"Say away."

"Penny for your thoughts."

"Oh wow! Would *you* be surprised."

"Tell me."

"Never," she said. Her eyes were still closed.

She was thinking about Arnold Quentin, a West Coast lawyer, young, rich, and recently divorced. On the East Coast she did not cheat; she would be crazy to cheat on the East Coast. On the East Coast there was the possessive Carleton Armin, who provided her with clothes, furs, jewels, and charge accounts at the best stores. He gave her everything you could ever need. Heck, just this apartment! He had provided the furnishings—but just the rent for this pad was seven hundred a month. She could not quite afford that, could she, on her salary as a stewie.

There had been a time when she had thought she would marry him. He had artfully laid it in, and she had stupidly scooped it up. Heck, right now this minute she would still marry him. Rich and handsome and debonair and a marvelous lover—and so marvelously full of shit. Two years his girl, she knew. He was the world's most charming bullshitter. But how can you put him down?—he did it so damn beautifully. An artist, a great artist, a bullshit artist, he was entitled to his due. *I give you your due, you fuck.* By now, of course, she knew he would never give up his Marion and his high-society socializing. And knew that when she was on the West Coast he cheated on the East Coast. But did he, on the East Coast, know that she was returning the compliment on the West Coast? Put up your money, folks. I am betting against.

She cheated. Of course she cheated. In rage she cheated. Hell, she would have raped to cheat in order to even it up

25

with that glorious son of a bitch, but nothing of consequence had happened, not a thing, until Arnie. Dear God, he was so much like Carleton, it was amazing. Suave and smooth with the bullshit and a crazy lover, but younger than Carleton: Arnold Quentin was thirty-four. And giving off with the crap about marriage—just like Carleton in the early days. But this was Buford, trained by Armin, and no West Coast prick would do her in. She had already been *done* in. On the East Coast. Therefore she accepted nothing from him. Nothing! And even held out on the sex. Occasionally, yes; regularly, no. And encouraged his talk about marriage, but he had better come through. It was marriage with Arnie-boy, or he would get the air faster than a flat tire. But—hold up. Give the guy time. Infected by Carleton, don't put the disease on Arnold. Don't tell him to stick the plow up his ass before he even knows he's a farmer. Patience, Suzy, old girl. Nothing happens in one fell swoosh.

"Tomorrow," Carleton was saying, "we'll go up to Westport. Saturday and Sunday, the beach."

"Sounds nice." She opened her eyes, sat up. "May I have that cigarette now?"

He lit it, gave it to her. The phone rang.

"This late?" he said. "Who the hell—"

"My other lover."

"Yeah," he said.

She put the receiver to her ear. "So?" she said.

"Mr. Armin, please." Of course she recognized the voice.

"Hang," she said and gave Carleton the phone. "Your fairy godmother."

"Hi, Ron," Carleton said to the mouthpiece.

"Got a call, Mr. Armin. Bernie Thayne. On Dwyer. It's not yet official, but he'll be coming out November eighth."

"You sure?"

"Thayne called *me*. He said—definite! Yessir, I'm sure."

"Great. I thank you." A pause. "I can depend . . . ?"

"Mr. Armin, Bernie called me *special*—"

"All right. Yes. I thank you, and I thank your Bernie, and it's a great favor, and I won't forget either of you. Now, Ron, I was going to call your service. Where to reach me if you need. Saturday and Sunday, I'll be at the cottage in Westport."

"But for Monday—may I remind you? You have that Tower Stadium board meeting, early Monday." Carleton Armin was the chairman of the board of the Tower Stadium Corporation.

"Yes, Ron, thank you, I know. I'll be driving home Sunday night. See you Monday morning."

"Good night, sir."

"Good night, Ron."

Armin hung up, smiling.

Suzy said, "How much money did you earn?"

"Money?" he asked. Remotely.

"That's your money smile, Father Armin."

"Not money. But very pleasant news." He took the cigarette from her fingers, drew a drag. "Tomorrow morning, remind me. I'm to call a lady."

"I don't remind for the calling of ladies."

"This lady is sixty-two."

"I'll remind, I'll remind. As though you *ever* need reminding, about *anything.*"

His stomach rumbled. "Wanna know something? I'm hungry."

"Wanna know something? Me too."

"How about some scrambled eggs and coffee?"

"Yep. You bet." Kissed him and moved out of the bed.

He admired the glistening, slow-swaying, undulant ass, as she went toward the closet for a robe.

2

ON SATURDAY MORNING the sun on her eyelids awoke Mrs. Olivia Bono Dwyer. For ten years now, it was always so. Since Simon was away, she did not set the alarm. There was nothing to wake up to. No reason, no purpose. When it got light, she woke up.

Stirring in the bed, she heard herself groan. A touch of arthritis. Nothing, really. A bit of pain sometimes happened when she had a long sleep, but once she was up and around, it would disappear. Pain. As you grow old, pain becomes a companion. Stop it, she thought. Stop commiserating. For sixty-two, you're doing darn all right. You're still a fine-looking woman, you've never gone to fat, and you're not sickly. Thank God for blessings.

Out of bed, she removed her nightgown, put on a house-coat, and raised the blinds to the sunny morning. In the bathroom she brushed her teeth and then came out to her first cigarette, a ritual. A nasty habit, smoking before breakfast, but a lifelong habit that she could not break. She crossed to a window and stood looking out at the trees and flowers at the height of their bloom in early July. That was all that was left—her trees, her lawns, her garden, her lovely house in Queens. It was a ten-room house which, thank God—and thanks to Vito Arminito—the Dwyers owned outright. But it was now an empty house. Simon was away, and their one child was married to a fancy doctor in Palm Beach, Florida. Once a week, by phone, she talked with her daughter, and once a year, at Christmas, the daughter and husband came up for a visit. There were no grandchildren.

She lit a new cigarette from the stub of the old one, pulled a chair near, and sat looking out on the lush July greenery. That was all that remained—house, lawns, trees, garden— and that gave her her work. She was a regular, meticulous cleaner; she did two rooms a day and made them immaculate. Then there was the tending to the lawns, the shrubs, the trees, and the flowers of the garden; and of course the normal shopping. In the evenings, there was the television. And some-times, daytimes, visits with friends in the neighborhood— those who still remained friends after Simon had become a convict. Convict! How sad and wrong for Simon Dwyer, dear man, loving husband, intellectual, poet, philosopher. She thought about the early days of their marriage, and that trig-gered recollection, her mind going back, and she was a girl again, so young, a girl again on the Lower East Side of New York City.

Ollie Bono. Buoyant daughter of Salvatore and Angelina Bono, who owned a flourishing restaurant on Broome Street, between Eldridge and Allen, which flourished because it was the favorite restaurant of the most revered man of respect, Don Carmine Arminito, *capo di tutti capi*. How clearly she remembered—back, it must be fifty years—the hush, the reverence, the pomp and circumstance when the old don came in to dinner, sometimes with his son Vito (who, in time, succeeded the father in the honored society). Dead now, Salvatore and Angie Bono, and dead now, the deathless Don Vito Arminito; only the oldest of all, Don Carmine, long deported to Sicily, was still alive.

At eighteen, Olivia Bono, a graduate of Washington Irving High School, was sent off to Northwestern University; she came back a schoolteacher at P.S. 20 on Rivington Street. And at age twenty-five, she was introduced to Simon Dwyer, age twenty-five, and was told that he would be her husband. So it went, back there long ago, a part of a system that is still the system in certain European countries: the parents arrange the marriage. The Bonos had done well by their daughter: Simon Dwyer was handsome and slim and very tall, six feet two. He was an accountant and, of all things, an Irishman, an Irish Catholic.

Irishmen had been rare on the Lower East Side. The Dwyers lived on Forsyth Street, which was a street of demarcation. East of Forsyth were the Jews, the Russians, the Poles, the Ukrainians, and some Irish. West of Forsyth, starting with Chrystie Street and going west, it was all Italian.

Simon Dwyer had been a brilliant young man, an accountant with a degree at the age of twenty. The father had been a cop, killed in the line of duty, and the mother lived on the policeman's pension. There was a sister, two years older than Simon, who was now a snobby widow in Darien, Connecticut. She was Mrs. Walter Hulett and she had little to do with Simon Dwyer; she disapproved of him and the reason for her disapproval was organized crime.

The organized crime was the Mafia, and the Manhattan overlord had been Vito Arminito. He too had started young; he was only eleven years older than Simon; but where Simon Dwyer was merely brilliant, Vito Arminito was an absolute genius. Uneducated, a high-school dropout but an absolute genius, and trained from childhood within the strictures of the respected society. When Don Carmine had been deported, young Vito, at nineteen, had taken over—supposedly a figurehead to be directed from afar by the father. But Vito had quickly become the *capo* and the first real organizer of organized crime. His headquarters, in those days, had been a house on Grand Street.

Don Vito had known Simon Dwyer since Simon was a boy, and when Simon graduated as an accountant, Vito took him under his wing and they grew together. (Vito's marriage gift to the Dwyers was the deed to the house in Queens, free and clear.) For thirty-two years they ruled the roost, Vito and Simon, until the catastrophe ten years ago. An unlikely pair, the Italian Arminito and the Irish Dwyer, but together, from lavish offices in Rockefeller Plaza, they changed the shape of organized crime. And then, suddenly—the whole house fell in on them.

She could not understand how that had happened. They were the best, the cleverest, the wisest—with thirty-two years of trenchant experience behind them: it could not happen. The brilliant powerful Arminito, the brilliant canny Simon Dwyer: it could not possibly happen. But it *had* happened. They had been charged with multiple crimes, indicted for multiple crimes—and they had pleaded guilty. The sentence —fifteen to forty years. Fifteen to forty, may God have mercy—

"What must be, must be," Don Vito had said.

"Forty *years!*"

"Not forty, Ollie." The don had laughed. "Ten. No more than ten. I give you my promise. You will have him back in ten."

Simon had then been fifty-two.

Arminito—sixty-three.

"Don Vito, my God, how can you laugh? Leaving aside

Simon. You. Even ten years—it is the rest of your life. Old. You will be seventy-three."

"Young." And again the doughty old man had laughed. "For me seventy-three—young. We live long in my family, the men live long. The grandfathers and the great-grand-fathers, all past ninety. For me, my people, seventy-three is young. My grandfather made a baby when he was eighty."

But for once Vito Arminito had been wrong. They had gone off to prison together—to the same prison together—to the prison with the musical name: Sing Sing. But two years later the deathless don was dead. Eight years ago he had dropped in his tracks. Dead. Suddenly dead. Mercifully, swiftly. The autopsy had disclosed a cerebral hemorrhage. Cerebral hemorrhage—and he was swiftly gone. And Simon was alone. The quiet Simon—soft, gentle, diffident—bereft of his lifelong friend and mentor. The deathless don was dead and Simon Dwyer was alone.

She stirred in the chair, suddenly longing for the morning coffee. She rose, pulled her housecoat together, killed the stump of the cigarette, and went downstairs to the large, gleaming, spotless kitchen. A creature of habit, she always had the same breakfast, a preliminary breakfast: a pot of percolated coffee and a slice of toast with butter and red currant jelly. Later, her early lunch would be the real break-fast, and always the same: two squeezed oranges for juice, two fried eggs, two slices of bacon, one slice of toast, and more coffee.

She measured the water, measured the coffee, set the pot to perking, and the phone rang. She took the receiver from the kitchen extension, said, "Hello." It was Carleton Armin.

"Ollie, how are you?"

"I'm well. You?"

"Just fine. I want to talk to you."

"Talk," she said.

"Not phone talk. May I take you to dinner?"

Startled, she said, "Today?"

"No." A laugh. "Monday.   Monday all right?"

"Whenever you say, Carlo."

"Carleton."

"Whenever you say, Carleton."

"Monday. Pick me up at my office at five. I'll take you out for a real big splash."

"What are we splashing?"

"Tell you when I see you."

"Right," she said.

"Got to run now," he said.

"Right," she said. "Monday at five. G'bye now, Carlo."

"Carleton."

"Carleton," she said and hung up.

She sat at the kitchen table with her first cup of coffee and her buttered toast with red currant jelly. He was a symbol, Carleton Armin. He represented the dying of the dynasties, the ending of an era, the gradual disintegration of the honored society. In time in America there would be no more Mafia: there would be ineffectual, indiscriminate, stupid little gangsters killing one another. And so it should be, and so the old dons knew it would be, and they prepared their sons. Don Vito Arminito, at the very height of his power, knew already that he was an anachronism, and he had sent his son along other paths.

She munched her toast, sipped her coffee. Who in all this world, except the inside of insiders, knew that the esteemed Carleton Armin was in fact Carlo Arminito, the only son of the redoubtable Mafia chieftain who had died in jail? Nobody knew, except the inside of the insiders—and Don Vito, aided and advised by Simon Dwyer, had laid it out like that.

Early on, the boy's name had been Americanized to Carleton Armin. He had been sent to the St. Paul's School in New Hampshire, and from there to Harvard University. His major had been business administration, and he had taken his Master's in psychology. Then he had come home and the old man had set him up, with a vast amount of money and discreetly recommended clients, as an investment banker. Today he was a big man, among the biggest in the city. His new offices were in a new building on Wall Street, a sixty-story edifice named after him: the Armin Building. He was married to Marion Whitney, whose ancestors went back to Peter Stuyvesant. His son attended Yale. His daughter attended Wellesley. He was a society man in New York society.

He needed power. He was the son of his father—he required power—and his push for power was through politics. (His father had also been a powerful politician.) He himself could not run for office—they would discover who he really was. He was therefore the man behind the throne: the kingmaker. He had helped elect the Mayor of the City of New York and he had sat in as a member of the committee—Don Vito's son—that had selected the Police Commissioner.

He was a good man. His roots went deep, his loyalties were stern. There were those, of course, who knew who he was, but they were the insiders. Ten years ago, when Vito Arminito went to jail, nobody of the "outside" connected Carlo to Vito. But Carleton Armin knew who he was, and he knew who the steadfast Simon Dwyer was, and he knew who was Olivia Bono Dwyer. (She was fourteen years older than he. She had become a schoolteacher on Rivington Street when Carlo Arminito was eight years old.) And that very first month, after Vito and Simon had been consigned to prison, he had sent a check for a thousand dollars. She had brought it back to him, had sat with him in his old splendid office on Broad Street. She had said she did not need the money. Simon Dwyer had been no more than an employee of Vito Arminito, but his salary had been two thousand dollars a week. True, in his young days he had been a big spender, and of course he had paid his taxes meticulously; nonetheless, she had a sufficient nest egg. Two hundred thousand dollars in gilt-edged stocks and bonds. Thirty thousand dollars in her savings bank. And the house that was worth sixty thousand dollars. But Carleton Armin had insisted. He had said that capital rapidly diminishes when there is no steady income. He had said he was doing what his father would have wanted. He had said that he could not visit his father to talk with him—the wise old don had strictly proscribed any such procedure—but *this* procedure, a regular stipend to Simon Dwyer's wife, was the law, the code, and rightfully so. He had said he would have them out of jail—Simon and Don Vito—in the ten years that the father had predicted; he would devote special energies to that purpose. Don Vito was dead. But Carleton Armin was still devoting energies for Simon Dwyer. And a check came through every month, the first of every month, for a thousand dollars. He was a good man. His roots were deep.

She stood up from the kitchen table, poured her second cup of coffee, and with the second cup of coffee she smoked her third cigarette of the morning.

3

O N M O N D A Y , J U L Y 7, in the board room of his
offices on the fortieth floor, Carleton Armin presided
at a meeting of the directors of the Tower Stadium Corporation. It was a small meeting—many directors were away
on vacation—but there were sufficient for a quorum. Tower
Stadium in Flushing had been completed ten years ago,
and from inception it had been a successful enterprise:
baseball in the summer, football in the winter. Carleton
Armin, a heavy investor, had been chairman of the board
from the beginning.

Now he rapped the meeting to order and explained why
it had been convened. Through his myriad political contacts,
he had information from the office of the District Attorney.
A quiet ongoing investigation of the Department of High-
ways had disclosed that certain officials in the department
had accepted bribes in the assignment of contracts. One
such official, granted immunity, had named names. One

such name was the engineering firm of Thompson, Hartley & Smith. And the specific name was the junior partner— J. Ted Smith.

"I don't believe it," somebody said.

"Believe," Carleton Armin said.

J. Ted Smith was a member of the board, a director of the Tower Stadium Corporation. He had not been invited to this meeting.

"He'll be indicted, no question," Armin said. "But it's still a long way off. Won't break until next year. My sources tell me—not until January. That's why we're here now, gentlemen, long in advance. We must vote him off. We must ask for his resignation."

"An indictment is no more than a charge," somebody said. "It's not a conviction. A trial can show him to be totally innocent. That's the law of our land. Presumption of innocence. Hell, the Bill of Rights. Hell, the Founding Fathers."

"Gentlemen," Armin said, "I'm a personal friend of Teddy's, and if this were a closed corporation, I would certainly vote to go along with Ted. But Tower Stadium is not, quite, a closed corporation. More in the nature of a quasi-public corporation. Baseball heroes. Football heroes. Kids who idolize them. A whole new generation has grown up with Tower Stadium. We must not knock their legs from under them. We cannot, and should not, risk even the faintest whiff of scandal in connection with Tower Stadium. That's the problem, gentlemen. We are open for discussion."

The discussion was animated, never loud, but often recriminatory. Nonetheless, an hour later the vote by secret ballot was unanimous: J. Ted Smith would be removed from the board. A committee was appointed to obtain his resignation, and the meeting adjourned, and Carleton Armin returned to his office, and the intercom came alive.

"At twelve thirty," Ron Seely said, "you're having lunch with P. Byron Falk. At your club. I have the research here."

"Research?" The Tower Stadium meeting had drained him. "Oh, yes, of course, the research. But we've been over it."

"I have it here for you—for him."

"Yes," Armin said. "You'll give it to me in the car."

Ron Seely served as chauffeur on the drive uptown to the Harvard Club. He had delivered the folder with the research and Armin had it in his lap. The boss this day was reserved, withdrawn, and Seely was sensitive to the vibes. Therefore he offered nothing, said nothing; silence was the keynote, the linchpin; on this day, on this trip, he offered no chatter, no banter, no office gossip. Nothing. Silence.

Carleton Armin, in contemplation of his appointment with Olivia Dwyer, was thinking about his father. The old man, in the Italian tradition, was given to aphorisms. Long ago that wise old man had confided, "Every fucken big-shot crook I have known, he has got an initial for a first name. Now you think about that, Carlo. How come? Why is it? Why are the crooks ashamed of their fucken first names? Why push it down to just an initial? Watch yourself. Always watch yourself with a guy whose first name ain't no first name at all—it's an initial."

Syllogism. The fact that all the old man's big-shot crooks had had an initial for a first name did not mean that all persons with an initial for a first name were crooks. Like. Take. For instance. J. Ted Smith was a crook, but P. Byron Falk was as honest as a sunrise. P. Byron was president of Lion Mutual Funds, and he had worries, and he damn well had a right to worry, and the Armin Building was one of his worries—which was the reason for today's luncheon at the Harvard Club. Lion Mutual was the principal investor in the Armin Building on Wall Street, and the Armin Building was not renting well. It was, in fact, renting fucking lousily. Which was why Carleton Armin bore a thick folder of research on his knees.

The car pulled to a curb and Seely said, "I'll park in our Kinney and I'll stay there. When you're ready, call me there and I'll pick you up. Good luck, Mr. Armin."

"Thank you, Ronald."

The lunch, of course, was excellent, and then, over coffee, Byron said, "We're in trouble. Do you have advice, young man?"

"My advice is patience."

"We're fast running out of that. I've been staying along with you, son. You're a brilliant businessman, but my board has begun to push me. That piece of real estate has been a hell of a disappointment. The board feels we can correct by reducing the overall rental structure. Scale it down—"

"No."

"You have a strong spine, but there's a difference between a strong spine and sheer intransigence. Carleton, you *are* the largest individual investor, but my board doesn't represent Carleton Armin. It represents thousands of small investors."

"Because they're small, should they get a nothing return for their investment?" He took the folder from his side of the table and handed it across. "Take a look."

"What is it?"

"A dramatic presentation for the people of your board. Weeks of work by my research department. The original facts and figures of the Empire State Building."

"Empire *State* Building?"

"When it was completed—a bust. A white elephant. They couldn't *give* the space away. Like now, money was tight. But they hung in there. And then it began to go. And once it went it soared! These days, a pretty fair piece of real estate, wouldn't you say?"

Falk opened the folder. He slid glasses onto his nose and studied the sheets. "Smart," he murmured.

"Dramatic presentation. All I'm asking—one year. Give me a year with the rental structure as is. If by a year we're not over the hump, then it's all yours. Your board can re-rate; they can do whatever the hell they please."

Falk removed his glasses, smiled. "Dramatic presentation. Damn clever, these Chinese." He nodded, tapped the sheets. "I think this'll do it. Please remember I've been on your side all the way, but when it's mutual funds, you've got to battle a conservative board. I think I can win them over for your year. Hell, what we're *all* looking for—is the best return for our money."

"Now you're talking," Armin said.

At two thirty, on the fortieth floor of the Armin Building, Ron Seely ushered in the principals and the attorneys for the final conference of the day. Armin greeted them and seated them; he had sought them, found them, and brought them together, financial giants badly in need of one another. He had arranged the merger, at a huge commission for himself, and this was the penultimate meeting. It was a long meeting, but it went off well. At four twenty they were logged out, and Carleton Armin sat back, wearily, in his leather swivel chair. He flicked on the intercom.

"Ron?"

"Yessir?"

"Except for Mrs. Dwyer, I'm gone for the day."

"Yessir."

"What time's my reservation at Lafayette?"

"Six thirty."

"Thank you."

40

He stood up, opened a door in the rear of the office, and entered a small, smartly appointed apartment: living room, kitchen, bedroom, and bath. He removed his clothing, showered, and shaved. He redressed, fresh linens, a complete change of attire. In the living room he drank a vodka.

He returned to the office and the tall-backed swivel chair, looked at the desk clock. Still early. He lit a cigarette, smiled ruminatively, thought about Ollie Dwyer. And about Simon, and Vito—and Kearney & Upton, Counselors at Law, 350 Fifth Avenue. They had always been Vito Arminito's lawyers—all the way back to when Carlo Arminito had been a small boy. And when Carlo had grown up to be Carleton Armin, they had been Carleton Armin's lawyers. But they had maintained a break, a space, a divergence—Carleton Armin was on his own, a financier, a Harvard gentleman.

Kearney & Upton had been Vito Arminito's civil lawyers, his financial lawyers—not his criminal lawyers—because Vito Arminito had never been involved in a criminal matter until the trouble. Kearney & Upton, for instance, had represented Vito Arminito in the purchase of the land (with other investors) upon which Tower Stadium had been built ten years ago. But Don Vito's name had never appeared on any of those proper legal papers; it had been Carleton Armin who had signed, and who had become—and still was —chairman of the board.

And ten years ago—the trouble had happened. Ten long years ago—criminal trouble, for the first time. Vito Arminito and Simon Dwyer—suddenly arrested and clapped into jail. And then out on bail, and the series of consultations at the offices of Kearney & Upton. But it had been the young Kearney, the son of Earl Kearney, who had actually represented them. Joshua Fitts Kearney—today Senator J. F. Kearney, the white-haired boy in the run for the Presidency.

But back then, ten years ago, he had not yet been even a Congressman. He had been Josh Kearney, thirty-nine, one year older than Vito Arminito's son. Joshua Fitts Kearney, even then a thrilling speaker, an eloquent advocate, a renowned mouthpiece, a brilliant courtroom attorney.

Carleton Armin rubbed out his cigarette, remembered a meeting at 350 Fifth Avenue, a full-dress meeting, all present: Vito Arminito, Simon Dwyer, Carleton Armin, Earl Kearney, Arthur Upton, and Joshua Fitts Kearney, the trial lawyer of record.

"Josh," the crusty old Earl had said, "don't look at him like that. Don't quiver your delicate nostrils, don't try to stare him down. You are my son—and there sits *his* son. Well, let me tell you something." He had pointed a finger at Vito Arminito. "There but for the grace of God go I. He is Vito Arminito and he controls what is euphemistically called a family—but he controls! The man is a brilliant administrator, and his type of traffic is essentially victimless. What I'm asking is—let's have a little compassion here. He brought up *his* son as well as I brought up *my* son, and he did it alone, the mother died early. But to hell with that. Mr. Arminito does not deal in dope, or prostitution, or loansharking. He deals in gambling. Aided and abetted by the wily Simon Dwyer, Mr. Arminito is Number One, he controls all of the illicit gambling in the Borough of Manhattan. So what? The Establishment has been after his ass, because the Establishment has established him as a major criminal—but I disagree. Control of gambling does not make of you a major criminal, except in the tight strictures of law. But, philosophically, forget it. Prostitution is the world's oldest profession, and gambling is the world's oldest vice, and our hypocritical society places them both beyond the pale. But not *all* of society. There are states in our very own Union that have legalized both, and the same goes for sovereign states throughout the world. I, for one, cannot condemn Don Vito Arminito. One day, some day, gambling, as it is in Las Vegas, will be a perfectly legal activity, and when such day dawns, the Don Vitos of the community will be estimable gentlemen on a par with the chairmen of the boards of IBM and General Motors. But until such day the Don Vitos are illegal, and they must operate illegally, and must enforce their illegal form of justice in their own ways. Josh, what I'm asking of you in conjunction with Mr. Arminito can be contained in one word. What I'm asking is, quite simply—compassion."

On the fortieth floor of the Armin Building, the president of Carleton Armin, Ltd., bestirred himself in his richly upholstered, tall-backed, leather swivel chair. Christ, by God, a eulogy. He himself could not have done better for his sainted father. And then, one year later, the other father, the splendid Earl, was dead in bed of a heart attack. And a year after that the splendid don was dead in jail of a cerebral hemorrhage. And that same year Arthur Upton had closed down Kearney & Upton, committing himself to the career of the white-haired boy, and Carleton Armin had retained a new firm of attorneys.

But you had to hand it to the white-haired boy, the well-born, the biggie-wiggie, the patrician Senator J. F. Kearney. The guy had stayed in there, punching. And what in hell was he punching for? A Simon Dwyer. A nothing, really. An adjunct. An appendage of the volatile powerhouse that had once been Don Vito Arminito. He had been the trial lawyer, but they had pleaded guilty, so why was he punching? Hell, somewhere in there he had to be a good guy. *He is not of my party but I will definitely vote for him for President. Man, would I like to have a piece of that one. But he is beyond my reach. Who in hell can get a finger up the asshole of a J. F. Kearney?*

The intercom crackled.

Ron Seely said, "Mrs. Dwyer."

Armin looked at the desk clock: five twenty.

"Thank you."

He went out to her in the waiting room.

Kissed her cheek. "How are you, Ollie?"

"I'm sorry I'm late. The darn traffic."

"We've lots of time." He led her through to the office and to the apartment in the rear. "A drink?"

"A bit of sherry, please."

He poured a sherry, gave it to her, made a vodka martini, and raised the glass. "Drink, my dear. We're celebrating."

"Oh?" Placidly. "What?"

"Simon. He comes out—November eighth."

"Oh, God." She sank into a chair. "Oh, dear God." The hand holding the sherry was trembling. She sipped, so as not to spill the wine. Looked up. "Are you sure?"

"It's not official, but the word has come through. Definite. In time, they'll announce. Parole granted on first request. When's your next visit?"

"Thursday."

"You'll tell him—but tell him he doesn't know. He knows nothing until he gets the official word. He'll get the word."

"God, I prayed."

"Hell, if God wouldn't answer *your* prayers . . ."

"Don't blaspheme, Carlo."

"Sorry." He checked his watch. "We're going uptown for a French meal. Italian you can make yourself, and better than anyone else. French. The best. We're celebrating. How do you feel, sweetheart?"

"Wonderful."

44

"I told you we'd get him out first crack."

"I thank you, Carlo."

"Carleton."

"God bless you."

4

KATHRYN BRAXTON KEARNEY, lying up to her chin in the warm tub, thought about her house and loved it. Fifteen years; Lord, how the time flies. Fifteen years ago she had persuaded Josh to purchase this house on Sutton Place. Prior, their residence had been a triplex at 812 Fifth Avenue. But when the Sutton Place house had come on the market, she had overwhelmingly insisted and Josh had not demurred. They sold the triplex and bought the house and never once in all the years had they regretted their decision.

She loved it, a charming six-story whitestone just north of easternmost East 57th Street. The lower three floors were the drawing rooms, dining rooms, kitchens, sitting rooms, recreation room, library, music room, writing room, billiard room, and study. The fourth floor had the bedrooms, the fifth floor the guest rooms, and the sixth floor the apartment of the live-in caretakers, an elderly couple, Carl and

Rita Hoffman. The entrance was on Sutton Place South, up seven granite steps to a carved door imported from a castle in Venice. There was a second, rarely used entrance guarded by a steel-mesh gate: the basement entrance beneath the granite stairs. And it was hers, all hers—her house, literally. Josh had bought it in her name: his most expensive gift of their marriage.

Now at two o'clock on the Tuesday after the Fourth, lolling in the tub, she ceased adoring her house and went back to thinking of Barney. Where in hell *was* he? Yesterday morning, from Southampton, they had done their chore for Arthur Upton, and then, during the drive back to the city, she had said idly: "Who in heck *is* this Simon Dwyer?"

"Your wish is my command, me love."

"I beg your pardon?"

"You wish to know—you shall know. By tomorrow you'll know all there's to be known about Mr. Simon Dwyer."

He had dropped her off at the house, and that was the last she had seen of him.

She splashed in the perfumed water. She missed him— almost as much as Hubbell Jackson had missed him. Heck, she had him all the time; for Hubbell he was a treat. Hub would pump and Barney would regale him with stories.

"Tales of the CIA," Barney, wickedly grinning, had once said to her alone.

"Is it allowed? I mean—aren't you breaching something?"

"Who breaches? All lies."

"Lies!"

"Here and there a stray speck of truth. Hell, the guy's a moviemaker. He loves stories, so I tell him stories. And he believes, because I'm authentic."

"Maybe you ought to go out there and be a screenwriter."

"You're here. I like it better here."

A visit. It had been an overnight visit: Josh's sister and

her husband, and Josh's mother. Unexpected, but not unusual. Always, on their way to Europe, they stayed over at the Sutton Place house, whether or not the Kearneys were home. Hubbell Jackson was a film producer; they lived in Beverly Hills. As did Josh's mother. After Earl Kearney's death, she had moved to the West Coast; she preferred the California climate. They had arrived yesterday at four o'clock, and this morning at ten the limousine had picked them up. A vacation in Copenhagen.

She got out of the tub, toweled, pinned up her hair, donned a pink peignoir. Barefoot to the small, round, mirrored elevator, and down to the lower drawing room. At the bar she poured a Campari, sipped, and the bell rang. She went to the door and looked through the tinted, one-way porthole of unbreakable glass. Barney Wilson out there. She opened.

"Well, look who's here," she said.

"Oh, my," he said, appraising her across the threshold. His eyes were coals. "All dressed up," he said.

"Where the heck you been?"

"Working for you."

"Come in. Stop just standing there."

He entered, she closed the door. In the drawing room she sat on a tall bar stool, sipped Campari, crossed her legs. A part of the peignoir fell away, revealing a gleaming thigh.

"Oh, my," he said and turned and went to the drawing-room door and locked it and came back and took her off the bar stool and kissed her. And held her away, at arm's length, and looked at her. Beautiful. Gorgeous. And with the hair up like that, the little ears exposed—so young. Go believe thirty-nine. And the curves, that figure—

"God, you're something."

48

"Thank you."

"Fits you real quick."

"What?"

"That housecoat."

She laughed. "Not a housecoat, boor. A peignoir."

"Whatever it is."

"It's a hundred bucks at Bergdorf's."

"Worth every dime."

"Why?"

"The way it makes you look."

"Makes me *look?*" A frown now at the blue eyes.

Christ, women. Whatever you say, somehow it's wrong.

He said, "I mean . . ."

Her fingers fumbled at buttons, and the flimsy thing drifted down from her. Christ, look at her, look at that body. Look at those breasts, firm, outthrust, nipples pink as a virgin's. Never suckled, those nipples: she had never borne a child. Look at that smooth white belly, the long legs, the round hips, the shapely thighs—

"Which way?" she said.

"What?" he said. "What—"

"Which way do I look better?"

"Honey, you're driving me out of my—"

She stood proud. Insisted. "Which way?"

"This way."

"Thank you."

He grabbed. Pulled her to him. "I love you," he said. Fiercely. "Christ, if you ever leave me, I'll kill you."

"I'll never leave you."

He pushed her down to the thick rug, pulled at his fly, extruded his penis. His knees between her knees opened her.

"Rape," she breathed. "God, rape. Barney—"

His mouth over hers closed off speech.

They fucked.

She sat, cross-legged, Indian fashion, on the drawing-room rug. He lay on his side, Barney Wilson fully clothed, except for his genitals. Funny, she thought. Both naked, it's beautiful. Both dressed, beautiful. But one naked and the other dressed with pudendum exposed, somehow it's obscene.

"Your thing is out," she said.

He smiled.

"Please," she said. "Get dressed."

"Yes ma'am." He zipped up, and then lightly to his feet. And to the bar. Poured a bourbon and drank. Sat on a bar stool, and looked down at her.

"Strange resemblance," she said.

"Me?"

"You look like that Reynolds guy."

"What Reynolds guy?"

"In the movies."

"I don't go to the movies."

"Where the hell have you been?"

"Doing duty for you, me lady."

"We had company."

"Oh?"

"The Jacksons and the old lady. On their way to Copenhagen. Came yesterday and went off this morning."

"Delighted to have missed them. They bore the shit out of me."

"So? What's your story?"

"You were curious about Simon Dwyer. Matter of fact, so was I."

"Called you yesterday evening. Called you this morning. Where the hell were you?"

"Out hunting facts. To assuage m'lady's curiosity." He took her Campari to her.

"Thank you," she said.

"Welcome," he said. At the bar he made a bourbon and soda. "Simon Dwyer," he said. "An accountant connected with the Mafia."

"Oh, come on," she said. "With the CIA—ex-CIA— it's always melodrama. Kathy Kearney here. Not Hubbell Jackson."

"Simon Dwyer," he said. "In jail in Ossining. A fine house in Queens. A nice wife who used to be a school-teacher. A daughter married to a doctor in Palm Beach."

"Lord, how do you *know?*"

"My profession." He made a bow. "And I'm the best in the business, or haven't you heard?"

She stood up. "I've heard." She set her glass on the bar.

"There's more. Rather interesting."

"Hold it," she said. She picked up the peignoir, slid into it, buttoned it. Padded to the door and opened the lock. Padded to the bar, sat, poured the Campari into a tall glass, added ice and soda for a spritzer. "Now I'm all yours," she said.

"Simon Dwyer," Barney said. "A minor figure in the employ of a major figure—one Vito Arminito, a Mafia boss-man. Ten years ago they both got hit by the law—a heavy indictment. Their attorneys were Kearney and Up-ton. Josh was the trial lawyer, but there was no trial. He pleaded them guilty, and they both got socked with that fifteen to forty. The big shot, he died in the clink. The other guy, of course, is still around. All this was before my time with The Man. But you—you mean to say you don't know *any* of this?"

"Hardly any. And the little I do know is sort of *ex post facto*. I know—you reminded me—that Josh has been quietly working for Dwyer's parole. Admirable—an attorney who doesn't forget a client. But as to the actual facts way back then . . ." She shrugged. "Ten years ago, Mr. Wilson, I was twenty-nine years of age, the young Mrs. Joshua Fitts Kearney, doing her own thing. Papa Kearney was still alive, and Josh was a practicing attorney, and I was living my own little life. It's only after Arthur came into the picture, and Mr. Man ran for his first term in the Senate, that I became a political animal. We mature. And under Arthur's tutelage I'm ready. And willing and able— First Lady of the Land. No longer that callow twenty-nine. I am now *Mrs.* Man, and I work at it diligently, because I'm just as damned ambitious as Mr. Man."

"Jesus," Barney said. "You ask a simple question and you get a speech."

"I'm Arthur-trained. Like toilet-trained. Sit me down at a rostrum and I spill over with a speech."

"Mother, did *you* just get your metaphors mixed."

"But why's it important to Josh?"

"Toilets? Peeing on rostrums? What? And since when is this local bar a rostrum?"

"Dwyer," she said.

"Fifteen to forty," Barney said. "I explained it to you the other day. Or didn't I?"

"You did."

"Fifteen to forty. If you're a bad boy in the slammer, that's where you stay for the forty years. If you're good—and especially if there's a heavyweight on the outside pulling wires—you can see daylight in ten. It's ten—and Simon Dwyer is coming out."

"But why's that important to Josh?"

Barney drank bourbon. "I ran into some funny angles, and checked them out. That's what kept me so long. Funny angles, you stay with it. Ever hear of Carleton Armin?"

52

"Armin." She wrinkled her forehead. "I think—yes. Marion Armin's husband?"

"The wife's name—Marion. Marion Whitney Armin."

"I don't know him, but I do know her. On charity things. Lovely woman. Old New York society. Philanthropic."

"She may not know—and we're not about to tell her—but she's the daughter-in-law of a dead Mafioso."

"Honey, I am *not* Hubbell Jackson."

Barney unfurled a cigar and lit it.

"Carleton Armin. Carleton Armin, Ltd. Wall Street. Hell, there's a building named after him. Big in New York politics, and reaching for up. No connections with the mob, clean as a whistle. A duplex at Four Hundred East Sixty-seventh, an estate in the Adirondacks. A son at Yale, a daughter at Wellesley, and—you're right—the wife is old New York. Also, once upon a time, Armin was a client of Kearney and Upton—until Arthur retired to work for The Man." He puffed the cigar. Smoke drifted. "Carleton Armin, paragon, politician, investment banker—his tracks are covered pretty good. But he was born Carlo Arminito, and he's the only son of Vito Arminito, who died in the clink eight years ago."

"Jeepers," she said. "You sure you're not doing a Hubbell on me?"

"I'm not putting the guy down. Seems Mr. Armin has made it on his own, straight and clean—and more power to him."

"Interesting." For moments she was silent. Then she said, "To hell with Carleton Armin. And to hell with the father who died in jail."

"Rest his soul." Barney grinned.

"Simon Dwyer."

"Here we go again."

"My point—what in hell's so important about this convict coming out of prison? Why does Arthur, on orders from Josh, call from London? Why do I postpone my feminists, and you the American Legion? Why must we meet them directly they touch down at Dulles? Why an urgent conference at Chevy Chase?"

"I don't know."

"Beautiful." She laughed, came to him. "Beautiful there's *something* my wizard doesn't know. Well, you listen to me, wizard. To hell with Simon Dwyer, and Josh, and Arthur— all of them. At least until Monday, you and me, we're free. And from now until Monday, you and me, we're going to live it up. I'm going to let you go home and change and rest, but starting this evening we live. You're going to take me out to a grand night club and we're going to eat and drink and dance and laugh. And then I'm going back with you to your apartment and I'm sleeping over. How do you like *them* apples?"

"I love them apples," Barney said.

5

HER HEART CLAMPED. It was always so at the sight of him: that twinge of terrible pity. If ever a man did not belong within walls, a caged animal, it was Simon Dwyer, who loved the sea, the sky, the smell of earth; who, upon the pretense of duck hunting, would take long walks, but never once got around to shooting the rifle; who would drag her to symphony concerts and sit enthralled; a quiet man, a contemplative man, a man who wrote poetry and was shy to show it, even to his wife. Ten years. Ten awful years a caged animal, but now he would be free and she was here to tell him. On this Thursday, July 10, he would finally learn that his agony was over.

She smiled at him coming toward her, and he smiled. He did not look bad, no prison pallor. In ten long years, of course he had aged, but, despite prison, not badly. The stoop was more pronounced, but there had always been a slight stoop; he was a very tall man. The sandy hair had grown thin and the lines around the mouth had grown deeper, but that was it—except for the eyes, large, deep-set, gray-blue. No fire. Prison had put a film over those magnificent eyes. But the pain was there. In all the years he had never once voiced complaint, but the pain of his plight was there in his eyes.

Smiling, he came to her.

The face was smiling, but not the eyes.

"Ollie. So good. How are you, Olivia?"

Always quiet. Never raised his voice. A strange man, my husband; Simon the ambivalent. A man who would bring home a bird with a broken wing, set the wing, and nurse the bird back to life—that man had been the right arm of a Mafioso. A poet who had been a member of the mob. A kind and gentle man who had pleaded guilty to crimes—including the crime of conspiracy to murder. And suddenly here, now, outrageously, she remembered—how passionate in bed, this sweet and gentle . . .

"Ollie. How are you?"

"Just fine. You?"

"Just fine. How's Tessie?"

"Just fine. A grand lady down there in Palm Beach."

She knew of his hurt. It had been *he,* long ago, who had softened it for *her.* He, the poor man, suppressing hurt, had tried to take the hurt from her.

"Ollie, you look so unhappy. Don't say what you want to say; you may say what you *don't* want to say. She's young, Ollie, a good kid, but not the strongest. She can't take it that her father's a convict. She must hide it from her friends, and even from herself. We must, you and me, try to understand. There are deep psychological reasons. . . ."

Today the conversation was light and pleasant, visitation talk, and then she brought it around. "Regards from Carlo."

"Carlo?"

56

"Carleton."

"He hates being called Carlo. Why do you do it?"

"Old habit."

"You're not that old."

"I have news. He gave me news. The parole. There will be the hearing. The request will be granted. You will come out on November eighth."

He looked at her. His mouth moved, but no sound came.

She bit down against tears. "You don't know. You know nothing until they tell you."

He sat there. The poor man sat there.

"November eighth," she said. "You know nothing."

"Jesus." His lips were pale. "God. Oh, Jesus Christ."

Her tears came. She looked away from him, took a handkerchief, touched her eyes. She heard him:

"Are you sure? God, are you sure?"

Now she faced him again. "He said absolutely certain. They will tell you. And you will tell me. And on that day I will be here to take you home. To your house, your trees, your garden. To a *banchetto*, a big fat Italian meal. And to your wife"—she hesitated—"in bed."

He smiled, shyly. "I love you."

And then the man came.

"Time's up," the man said.

Tall Simon Dwyer, stoop-shouldered, went slowly back. Not to a cell. To the hospital, the infirmary, where his name was Doc. And there his young assistant said, "Everything copacetic, Doc. Go sit in the sun, old man. When there's something, I'll call you."

He went out to the patio and sat in a chair tilted against the wall. In jail he was Doc—Doc Dwyer—a tribute to the power and the glory that had been Vito Arminito.

"In the joint, it's the hospital," the don had said. "Only

in the hospital you are not a beast in a *gabbia*. We will live in the hospital."

"How?"

"Because that's where we will work. The hospital."

"How?"

"Vito will manage."

He had managed. The don had the means, the machinations, the outside connections, and a limitless flow of incoming money—plus the most powerful of political contacts. In short order they were workers in the hospital and lived in the hospital and there in the hospital the don had died of his cerebral hemorrhage. But Simon Dwyer, despite the decease of his patron, had been kept on—because he was damn valuable to the harried, overworked prison doctors. They had taught him and he had learned well; he was considered the best first-aid inmate in the whole damn prison. He could quench the blood-bursts of accident or attack; he could clamp and suture and inject the proper antibiotics. And more. He did blood work in the lab, he helped with anesthesia, he assisted in the operating room. The don was eight years dead—but Simon Dwyer was still in the hospital. He was Doc—Doc Dwyer.

On the patio, in the tilted chair against the wall, Doc Dwyer leaned his head back and took the sun.

Dead now, Don Vito Arminito, who had long life in his family. The don had expected to live, like his antecedents, into his nineties. He had talked of that so often—the longevity of the males in his family—that his untimely death had plummeted Simon Dwyer into a deep depression. He had been sick with it—for weeks, months. *But time heals, Olivia. We recover, we survive, we continue, we exist within the walls.* Who would believe? Vito Arminito, a convict. Simon Dwyer, a convict. Put away under sentence of fifteen to forty. As Olivia Bono Dwyer so frequently asked—"How could this have happened?"

For thirty-two years they had never once been touched by law—because Simon Dwyer was a canny planner, and Vito Arminito had full faith and confidence in Simon Dwyer. From the beginning, Dwyer had streamlined the operation, limiting the take to gambling. Let the small fry deal in the dope, the loan-sharking, the prostitution—gambling was the rich base of the business: horses, baseball, football, basketball, hockey—and policy, the numbers game, the inevitable lottery of the ghetto people.

And Vito Arminito had swung it, Vito a feared *capo,* the son of a Mustache Pete (the legendary Don Carmine, who was still alive in Palermo). Vito had bargained and traded, and given away lucrative fields in drugs and sharking and prostitution, sometimes at substantial loss, in exchange for the gambling territories. But it had not been all talk and trade. There are always the stupid ones, the dummies, the intractables. And so for a time, long ago, there had been blood on the streets, the deadly parochial warfare. But in the end Vito had emerged as the overlord of gambling in the Borough of Manhattan. Others controlled the other vices in Manhattan, and others controlled the gambling in the other boroughs, but for the Manhattan gambling Vito Arminito was the boss of bosses.

And the sage Simon Dwyer had elevated the boss of bosses to higher and more proper regions. It was Simon Dwyer who, a quarter of a century ago, had invented "laundering"—the shipping out of dirty money and garnering its return, no matter the loss, as respectable money. And the respectable money was invested in respectable business, and the profits were lawful and legal, the taxes scrupulously paid.

Respectably, they had become VA Enterprises Inc., and

they had the entire twenty-first floor at 75 Rockefeller Plaza. VA was a legitimate holding company that owned various legitimate enterprises. Vito loved the name—VA—one word, but the initials of his name. VA had sixty-eight employees, sixty of whom were legitimately dedicated to legitimate business—the remaining eight were the inner core of the gambling business, and that business was far-flung, recondite, and intricate.

For horses, hockey, baseball, football, basketball, there were small bookmakers who reported to bigger bookmakers, who reported to the top bookmakers, who reported to Vito Arminito at VA Enterprises. For numbers, the runners and controllers reported to their policy bankers, and those bankers reported to the top bankers, and the top bankers reported to Vito Arminito at VA Enterprises. Everybody made money, and good money, from the smallest bookmaker to the lowliest runner, but the big money was regularly delivered, cash money, to Vito Arminito at 75 Rockefeller Plaza. And nobody—no outsider—could put a finger on it, could interfere, could know. It was all inside and there were no outside leaks. For instance, one of VA's companies was Atlantic Electronics, and the best man of Atlantic was permanently assigned to VA Enterprises; his job was to test, day in and day out, for bugs and wiretaps. The alleged reason—to circumvent industrial espionage. In his time he had not once come up with a planted bug, but over the years, four times at widely spaced intervals, he had knocked out attempted wiretaps. And Vito had laughed.

"Crappy little nobodies," he said. "Some cocksucker reformer looking to make a reputation. Don't worry a thing about it, Simon. The big guys are in my pocket."

They were not all in his pocket—but real big guys stayed within the law, too clever to risk illegal bugs or taps. On the other hand, a good many of the big guys *were* in his pocket, in a manner of speaking. Vito was a political powerhouse and many of the big guys owed their office, however roundabout, to the good offices of Vito Arminito. But there *were* big guys after him because they could make a reputation: Vito was a thorn, and when news was sparse, pious editorials nailed him on the cross.

"Shit," Vito would say. "All of a sudden Vito Arminito is Public Enemy Number One. A lot of shit. The bastard that wrote that thing, he bets on the ballgames, and if he's a nut, he bets on hockey, and without me he'd get his ass swindled. With me, if he wins he gets paid. What the hell do they want? Victimless crime." Vito had learned the words. "Victimless crime, which ain't no crime at all. They want to gamble —they get paid a hunnert percent. They don't want to gamble—I'm out of business."

Vito Arminito, grown fashionable. The Lennies invited him to parties, and the Glorias and the Jackies and the Trumans and the Olegs; he was a rare bird for them; a catch, a sensation at the high-society parties; and he loved it; Vito Arminito, big in the ego, loved it, he ate it up.

"I fuckem," he said. "I ain't fooling myself; I fuckem where they breathe. I go because I want to go, not because they want me to go. I can wine them and dine them, if I want, and buy them and sell them. I go because I want to go; the broads are cute, they dress good and they smell good and they talk with the pretty words. I fuckem. And, man, would you be surprised how many of them fancy broads I have really fucked, cockwise. Not so much for me they give the quiff to me; they're looking for a favor for the husband and they goddam know I got the power to pull it off."

He had the power; even from jail he wielded enormous power. As witness the career of J. F. Kearney, now moving up as number one for President. Without Vito, there would not be this number one. When J. F. had decided to run for

Congressman, he could not have had the nomination without the word from Arminito. If Vito had put in the quash, another nice young guy would have got it up the ass. But Vito had not put in the quash; this Joshua Fitts was the son of Earl Kearney, whom the don respected and admired. So the don, from jail, had passed the word, and Joshua Fitts Kearney had received the nomination in a district where his party could not lose.

Jail. Vito Arminito in jail.

How could happen what could not *happen?*

They had done it themselves. Turns take twists: fate is fitful. You do your best, wisely and well, but you cannot foresee every twist and turn. As Olivia would say, "God created man in His image, but man is *not* the image of God."

They had done their best. They had planned it perfectly, wisely, well. . . .

. . . A morning in June. Simon Dwyer, age fifty-one. Treasurer and controller of VA Enterprises. In his splendid office in Rockefeller Plaza. Engrossed. Poring over sheets, working on figures. Legitimate figures in legitimate business. The door opens and closes. Dwyer looks up. His squint is surprise.

"Hi, boss."

"Hi, Si."

Unusual. The boss does not come to the treasurer. If the boss wants the treasurer, he sends for him. But the boss *has* come to the treasurer—so it is impulse. This boss of bosses can restrain impulse unless the trigger is trouble. No doubt it is trouble. It is clearly written on the dark, expressive face. An amazing face. The man is sixty-two, but the amazing face, swarthy, saturnine, is forty. And if you toss him a compliment, he will toss it right back. "Shit, man, that's the way we're born. We age slow. In the blood, in the family.

I will go to ninety, minimum. The old man in Palermo is still screwing his nuts off, I will lay odds." The hair is black, and the black eyes are young and lively. But today, this morning in June, the eyes are murderous.

He sits in a leather easy chair. Crosses long legs.

"Tommy Gianni. A goniff, the fucker."

"No."

Thomas Gianni. Boss of a bank in Harlem. Shrewd, suave, a trusted favorite of Vito Arminito. For nine years now Tommy Gianni has skillfully managed the top-paying policy bank uptown.

"A fucken *ladro*. Would you believe?"

"No."

"Simon, baby, I don't bug you with the street business, but like a year now, I don't like the figures from the Tommy bank. Big, but I figure them figures should be bigger. So I slip in a check, and I check the checks, double-check, triple-check, and Tommy-boy comes out a fucken goniff. Skimming. Picking up pieces. Running a little side bank on the side."

"Jesus."

"How do you *like* that cocksucker? Good for two hundred thou in a *bad* year. But when you got larceny, baby, you got to steal. I pegged him wrong. I used to love the son of a bitch. Handed him that bank because he was tough, he was smart. Turns out too smart. Larceny. A stealer. So he is done. Out. Finished. Tommy is dead."

"You sure?"

"Dead."

Silence. Then Simon Dwyer.

"All right. I'll arrange the hit. Not from you. Not from me. Mario in New Orleans. He's trained some new people, ex-soldiers, beautiful professionals. They'll come up—"

"No."

"You don't want him hit?"

The Vito smile. Good white teeth, all his own.

"No New Orleans. I got a way, it'll do us all good. Call Ollie. Tell her you won't be home tonight. You're working late, you're sleeping over in my joint." Vito Arminito's joint is a penthouse on Park Avenue. "I got things to do this evening; you come over to my joint, like eleven o'clock. We will talk; I will lay it out for you. At twelve o'clock we get company."

"Who?"

"The Buck brothers."

Steve and Danny Boccino, called Buck. What Simon Dwyer is to Vito Arminito, the Buck brothers are to Tommy Gianni. His right hand and his left hand. They are one step down from Tommy in the hierarchy of the uptown bank.

"We will discuss tonight," Vito says. "I don't turn a deal like this without picking the brain of the treasurer." Uncrosses his legs. Uncoils from the chair. "See you tonight, my friend."

Eleven o'clock. Penthouse on Park. Scotch in highball glasses. "Why I held you up till eleven," Vito says, "I got laid. A princess. Wants a favor. Wants her husband to be an ambassador. She thinks I can help."

"Can you?"

"Possible."

"Will you?"

The don laughs. "She was a hell of a good *shtoop.*" Drinks Scotch. "The hell with ambassadors. We got important things to talk. We're gonna wipe out a *ladro.* You're gonna like it."

Vito pacing. A man alone. A widower. A loner. A genius, a master administrator. Knows where and how to delegate authority. The right man in the right spot. Rarely makes a mistake, but when he does, the vaunted ego does not block him. He readily admits and quickly moves to rectify.

"We don't need no hit men from New Orleans. We got the Bucks, and they fit perfect. I'm gonna pay them twenny-five thou apiece, but there's more curves to the deal."

Simon Dwyer listening. Vito pacing a gold carpet.

"Smart, them two. Moved up good and worked out great. In my book, they're next in line after Tommy. Like if Tom croaked from pneumonia, I would give them the bank up there. So now they're gonna get that bank faster. They're gonna find out what happens to a fucken goniff. Twenny-five gees apiece for the hit, but it won't only be the twenny-five gee. They will have extra—what's the word? You are the guy with the words."

"Extra incentive."

"Correct. Extra incentive. And there's more."

"Still more?"

"A lesson for the new bankers. And they will be teaching theirself the lesson. You steal from Vito, you're dead. No matter how close you are to Vito—and Tommy's goddam close—you steal, you are dead. And there's no meet, no talk, no conversation. Just dead!" Vito ceases pacing. Stands by the bar. "I could save the fifty gee. The—the incentive would be enough. But I want them babies to know, when it comes to a hit, Vito is glad to pay. It will help with the lesson." A finger points at Simon Dwyer. "Good business all the way. Tommy is out, the Bucks are in, and me— I got a couple of trusted bankers up there. And they will keep their goddam fingers out of the cookie jar. So? How do you like it, Mr. Treasurer?"

"Sounds good."

"So why them wrinkles in your forehead?"

"It's just—they're not professionals."

"This set-up, we don't need no professional professionals.

For Steve and Danny, Gianni's a duck." Vito freshens his drink. "We will talk it out, me and you and the Bucks. I know how to work it. I will lay it out for them, and you will check me as I go along. Anything I leave out, you will fill in. Okay, start asking questions. They won't be here till twelve o'clock."

A week later. A warm night in June.

At eight o'clock Steve Buck makes the call.

To Tommy Gianni at his mansion in Riverdale.

"You're in a jam. Can't talk on the phone. I'll be there like about ten o'clock. When I ring, you open up for me."

"What the fuck's going on?"

"It's bad, Tom. We gotta talk."

"Okay. Ten o'clock."

Tommy Gianni hangs up. Pours a shot of gin and swallows. Trouble is possible. But from the other thing—not from Vito. Vito thinks he's a wiz, but Vito's a schmuck. Mr. Tommy's been robbing him blind and getting away with it. Of the thousands of slips, Tommy holds off a few, but a few is enough. A small bank on the side. And the winners get paid, no matter how big. So there's nobody to complain. But the other thing—trouble is possible.

Tommy Gianni, an ambitious man. Branched out. Runs a narcotics operation from right here in the mansion. Interstate action. A small operation, but pays off big. He wants two more years, is all. Two more years and out from the Harlem bank and out from the junk operation. In two years there will be enough millions and he will retire. Invested, the millions will produce enough money to live like a king. In two years—

So what's this crazy call from Stevie Buck? Smart as a whip, Steve. And loyal. Has he heard something? Stevie always has his ear to the ground: he's a listener. Could it be some loose ends are hanging out on the narcotics, and

Stevie has heard, and he's coming up for his piece of the action? No trouble at all. He'll get his piece. If he's smart enough to know, he's entitled to his piece. But he'll have to earn. He'll have to run his risk on junk. . . .

In the warm night driving. Stevie with gloves in the stolen car. Behind him, in the back-up car, Danny with gloves, the naked gun on the seat beside him.

Stevie Buck. Smiling at the windshield. Go fuck with a Vito, huh? Jeez, you would think a Tommy's too smart to fuck with a Vito. Tommy a *ladro*. Jeez, go believe it.

Jeez, that fucken penthouse on Park Avenue. Jeez, that fucken gold carpet right up to the ankles. Jeez, go believe Stevie and Danny in the penthouse pad of Mr. Big. And the other one there too. The other Big. The Dwyer. You hear about this Dwyer, but who the fuck ever meets him? Steve and Dan Boccino, that is who. Like Mama says. You go to church, Mama says. You pray to God, Mama says. You want good things in life, you want good things should happen to you, then you go to church and pray to God. And we don't miss, Ma. Me and Danny, every Sunday on the button, you can bet your ass. And you're so goddam right, *Mamma mia*. A break like from heaven, right out of left field. We are gonna take over that fucken bank, Mama, because Tommy's a stealer and he's gonna wind up suddenly dead.

Jeez, the don, how he laid it out, step by step, smart, beautiful. Every word what to say, every move what to make. The main thing, the don says—get him out of the house, far away from the house. "Right there in the doorway, you'll tell him," the don says. "Like a whisper in the ear. His house is bugged, his wires is tapped, and you know why. . . ."

In the warm June night. Stevie Buck on his way to River-dale. How can he know that the don is clairvoyant? How can he know that the don has it all right, although all wrong.

67

Can he know about interstate narcotics? Can he know—
what the don does not know, what Dwyer does not know—
that the house *is* bugged, the wires *are* tapped? Can he know
that Tommy Gianni is under close surveillance? Can he
know that a car containing electronic equipment and three
FBI agents is there near the mansion in Riverdale?

Ten minutes after ten. Stevie parks the stolen car on the
gravel roadway. Out of the car, removes the gloves. Shoves
them into a pocket of his jacket. The other pocket. Not the
pocket with the piece, a flat .38 Colt automatic.

Trudges up the path and up the steps to the door. Pushes
the bell. Tommy opens. Steve takes his lapels and pulls him
close. Mouth at ear. Whispers. "You're bugged. Your fucken
house is bugged. Your fucken phones tapped. You're a
loser."

"Wha?" Tommy whispering. "What the fuck?"

"The don. He's wise. You been milking the bank."

"Oh, Jesus."

"I'm with you, Tom. Not here. We gotta talk. Your car."

"Right."

Down the steps and around the bend to the garage. Into
the big Caddy and out into the night. Behind them, Danny.
Behind Danny, a car without lights.

"What?" Tommy says.

"You're in the shit, Pappy."

"Christ, how do you know?"

"Me. Always on the ear. Got a broad, close to the don,
up there in Rockefeller Plaza. He's wise. Jeez, you ought
to have your fucken head examined. But, thank God, you're
still alive. Because the don, he's got you bugged. Wants to
face you up with what they call the confrontation. Park
somewhere where it's quiet. We got to talk, Tom. Could
be you'll have to run."

"Yeah."

Silence. A quiet place. They park. Tommy turns off the ignition.

"How much time you figure I got?"

"You're fresh out of time."

"No. I mean. If I gotta run." Then Tommy's eyes open big, staring at the gun. "Steve! What the f—"

The bullet hits him in the middle of the forehead. The goddam blood splatters, and then—pandemonium. Under the white moon, people out there with guns. Danny out there, shooting. Stevie Buck, out of the car, crouched, shooting. The first to go down, Danny. A bullet in the belly. Next an FBI man, bullet in the neck. The last is Stevie Buck, hit in the chest. All finished. The rest is mop-up.

Miraculously, they all recover, even Tommy Gianni. The Bucks and the FBI man, total recovery. They have scars from their operations, but that is all. Not Tommy Gianni. He is done, Tommy Gianni. He is paralyzed, senseless, speechless, a vegetable in a wheelchair.

In Danbury Prison the squeeze is on the brothers Buck. Investigation has developed the link to Vito Arminito. The Bucks worked for Tommy Gianni. Gianni ran a policy bank in Harlem, and that bank is owned by Vito Arminito. The Bucks had nothing against Gianni; in fact, the reverse. They were friends and faithful employees. Thus the theory that Vito Arminito, desiring the liquidation of Gianni, utilized the friends as the executioners. A modus operandi not unusual.

Arminito is a big fish. The state has been after him for years, to no avail, because the powerful don knows where all the bodies are buried. But this trip is different. There is a new District Attorney in the county, Franklin E. Jordan, young, incorruptible, and ambitious to be Governor. So a deal is arranged.

The Feds have closed their narcotics case: the Bucks are not involved. The assault on the FBI agent is minor as compared to the attempted murder of Thomas Gianni, and that crime is a state matter. Further, the state, through the Bucks, may be able to get at Arminito. So the Bucks are turned over to New York State; they are transferred to Riker's Island, and the squeeze stays on.

The DA is not interested in the Bucks: they are insignificant pipsqueaks. He is interested in Arminito and he hammers away at the brothers, separate, sequestered; he promises full immunity in return for a confession of truth. But he has no success until a private meeting with Mama Boccino, and it is Mama, fighting for her sons, who conquered the unconquerable Vito Arminito. It is Mama who done him in. It is Mama who made the deal that delivered the don—but she demanded more than immunity. The deal was money, a plastic operation to change the features of the faces, and properly official (and properly moneyed) new identities. Hey, man, mister. Hey, goombah. You wanna do business, that is it. If the fucken state will do all of that, then the fucken state can have the true testimony of Stevie and Danny Boccino. If not, then the fucken state can go fuck hisself.

The state did not go fuck hisself. Or did it?

It was Mama who made the sensational deal: Mama Boccino and District Attorney Franklin E. Jordan. Thereafter the lousy little shrewd little lawyers pinned it down, and tucked it up, and pasted together the despicable legalities, and then Stevie and Danny were brought before the grand jury, and DA F. E. Jordan obtained his indictment, and then in the dead of night Vito Arminito on Park Avenue and Simon Dwyer in Queens were summarily apprehended by the constituted authorities. Summarily! But fucking dramatically!—because tomorrow there are always headlines. Doors were banged, bullhorns were bulled, shotguns were fired, tear gas was tossed, grenades were thrown. Surrounded! Vito Arminito and Simon Dwyer. Rushed upon and arrested! By an army of cops sufficiently armed to assault a citadel. (And all they would have had to do, for the same result, was call on the phone and say, "Cops. We have got an indictment from the DA. Come on downtown and bring along your fucking Kunstler.")

At the arraignment, the defendants are represented by Joshua Fitts Kearney. Who pleads for small bail by reason of the fact that the basis of the indictment is the testimony of known and vicious criminals. And defense counsel is opposed by the pleasant prosecutor, who pleads for high bail by reason of the fact that the accused *are* known and vicious criminals. The judge agrees with the prosecutor. The figure is high, extraordinary. $250,000. A quarter of a million for each of them. Vito arranges for the bonds; the accused are liberated on bail.

The weeks pass.

There are frequent meetings at the offices of Kearney & Upton, and at one such meeting the young Kearney lays it out on the table. "The People have an airtight case. If we defend, we lose. They'll put you away for ninety-nine years. At your age, gentlemen, no matter any possibility of parole, that sentence is tantamount to life imprisonment. Alternative: we plead guilty. We save the People the expense of a lengthy trial and the expense and time consumption of the subsequent appeals. Judges understand. They also understand a jury can bring in a verdict of acquittal. In my con- considered judgment, there is no possibility of acquittal. In my considered judgment, if we defend, we'll get the book.

Therefore, we must seek mitigation of sentence. We plead guilty and throw ourselves on the mercy of the court."

Don Vito looks to the old one, the Earl.

"What say, Mr. Kearney?"

"You heard the considered judgment of your trial counsel."

"The hell with him. I'm asking you."

"You don't have to ask. You damn well know."

"They got us by the balls."

"You've answered your question, Mr. Arminito."

"Okay, we go for the fucken mitigation. Mercy of the court. Ten years. We'll take ten on this knock, but no more." A shrug of expressive shoulders. "What's gotta be has gotta be. We settle. Ten—"

"The length of the sentence depends on the court."

"Court? What the fuck is a court? A court is a judge. There's good and there's bad."

"We'll try to get you before a judge—who's not a hanging judge."

"And I want you to keep on with the postponements. Tower Stadium is almost finished." Tower Stadium in Flushing, Queens. A project by Vito Arminito. He did the deal, got the investors. The chief investor is Vito Arminito. But all the legal papers are in Carleton Armin's name. "I wanna be there on opening day. I wanna see them flags flying. Then, after that—"

"No difficulty on the postponements, Mr. Arminito."

"Okay. Take easy. We'll rap again. Plenny of time for more bull sessions. I will think, and we will talk."

The weeks pass into months, and the months pass.
Rockefeller Plaza. The office of the treasurer.
The door opens and closes. Vito Arminito.
"Hi, Si."

"Hi."

The don in the leather armchair. The young face. The white smile.

"Shipshape?"

"All shipshape. We're out of business. VA Enterprises, past history. Everybody's paid, with severance pay. Next week we evacuate."

"And the week after—the trial." A shrug of the shoulders. "You gotta go with the tide, kid. You can't fight God. Ten years from now we start up fresh. New life, new deal."

"Who says ten years?"

"I say."

"You the judge?"

"Me. I am the judge and the fucken jury."

"I hope," says Simon Dwyer.

Courtroom. People of the State of New York vs. Vito Arminito and Simon Dwyer. On the bench, Mr. Justice Otto Yoder, old, white-haired, fat-faced, flinty. The defendants plead guilty. Joshua Fitts Kearney, Esquire, makes a speech pleading for mercy. Franklin E. Jordan, Esquire, makes a speech denigrating mercy for the venomous predators of organized crime. From the bench, Mr. Justice Yoder makes a speech excoriating the defendants—and twenty days later they are returned to the courtroom for sentencing.

". . . and you will each serve from fifteen to forty years in the state prison at Ossining, New York."

Simon Dwyer aghast. *Fifteen to forty!* With their histories, their backgrounds, the term will go the limit: forty years. At their age, what difference forty or ninety-nine? It is a sentence of life imprisonment.

"Defendants remanded." Judge Yoder raps his gavel. "Court adjourned."

They are taken away, separately.

And do not see one another for weeks.

Until—Sing Sing. In prison garb, in the yard. Recreation period. Their first conversation alone.

"We're dead. We are dead, Vito."

"You look alive to me, my friend."

"You refuse to understand. Smart as you are, you're blocked."

"Not Vito."

"We're going to do the forty years."

"Ten."

"Blocked. You're blocked. They have the probation reports. We will serve the limit. Forty years."

"Simon—always with the numbers, the figures. Simon the accountant."

"These numbers spell finish for us."

"You don't know everything, my friend." And one eyelid comes down in a solemn wink.

True. With Arminito, no one knows everything. In that devious brain there are always pockets of secrets.

"Vito, we're dead. It's taken them a long time, but they've got us. And they'll keep us. They know just who we are; they'll make an example. We're going to do the full term. Forty years."

"Ten. I promise you."

"God, how?"

"Fifteen to forty. For the parole, the important number is the fifteen. Two thirds of fifteen equals ten. The judge, he's smart, he makes it look good with the fifteen to forty. The newspapers are happy, and that fucken Jordan he's happy, he's got hisself a big victory. But the parole works on the fifteen, and we will be out in ten." Again the eyelid comes down in the wink. "I promise you definite. I swear to God. Vito tells you on the word of honor. My friend, with

74

Vito you don't never know everything. So sleep easy, accountant. I promise we are out in ten. Definite. Absolutely. Mr. Treasurer, we will be out in the world in ten years."

And finally, in that first conversation, there in the prison yard, Simon Dwyer understands. Pockets of secrets. Devious brain. There are things he does not tell, and things you do not ask. But Simon Dwyer knows Vito Arminito. When the don says definite, when the don says absolute, when the don swears to God, when he tells you on his word of honor, then somewhere along the line Don Vito Arminito has put in the fix, a locked-up fix, a fix that cannot be traduced. . . .

In the sunshine on the patio. Simon Dwyer in the tilted chair against the hospital wall. Years ago he gave up smoking, but now, for the first time in a long time, he longed for a cigarette. Vito Arminito, the deathless don, dead. It had thrown Simon Dwyer into a morbid sickness, a depression. Why? Had it been the sudden death of a lifelong friend? Or had it been self-concern? With the don dead, would the fix still be in? Of course not. Who in hell was Simon Dwyer? Therefore he had resigned himself. To live out his life in prison, to die in prison. But hoping. Deep in his heart, hoping. While there is life there is hope, the wise men said. Hoping. Perhaps, someday. Some far-off day—

And then, now, today, Olivia. With the news from Carleton Armin. The parole would be granted at the first hearing. Simon Dwyer was coming out. On November 8, Simon Dwyer would be coming out. Jesus, the deathless don. Somewhere, somehow, the fix was still in.

In the sunshine Doc Dwyer stood up from the chair, a folding chair. Meticulously, carefully, he folded the chair and laid it against the wall. And ambled toward the hospital door, Doc Dwyer, the best first-aid man in the whole damn prison. He must shuck himself of the Doc Dwyer, he must shake off the Doc Dwyer, he must return to being Simon Dwyer. As Simon Dwyer, on the outside, there were things to do. The don had sworn him to secrecy until release. And now, here, suddenly, the release is imminent. Imminent? Four months from now—imminent? Damn right, imminent. In view of the next thirty years to be spent in jail, four months is eminently imminent. On the outside, things to do. No more Doc Dwyer; you are Simon Dwyer, you must begin to re-orient. On the outside, things. Big. Money. A cache. A cache of cash. Ten million. Ten million dollars. Ten *million* dollars. Carleton Armin has no idea of the windfall coming to him. Eight million of that ten million goes to Carleton Armin. But two of that ten belongs to Simon Dwyer.

Jesus, God. Simon Dwyer a millionaire.

Sprung in the ten years, as promised by Don Vito.

Released to ease and comfort: two million dollars.

You deserve, Olivia. You deserve, Olivia Bono Dwyer, good wife, dear wife, long-suffering. We will have a peaceful old age. I love you, wife, dear wife, good wife.

Ollie, I love you.

6

MONDAY. July 14. The silver plane high: far below, the gleam of the ocean. A good trip: excellent weather all the way, no bumps, no turbulence. Arthur Upton at his desk, the inevitable glass of white wine at his elbow, putting the finishing touches to a speech that Josh will deliver to the Knights of Columbus on Wednesday. He was pleased with the work. A damn good speech, and it was ready. Today a secretary would type it up.

He looked at his watch, laid away the pen, pushed aside the papers. Sipped wine, stood up, went back to Kearney's rooms. Knocked lightly: no answer. Opened the door to a sitting room, went through to the bedroom, smiled. There he was on the bed, the future President of the United States, in T-shirt and Jockey shorts, slumbering like an infant. Joshua Fitts knew how to avoid jet lag. Anywhere, anytime, he could stretch out, concentrate on sleep, and he

was out of it, away, immersed in the small death, peacefully asleep.

Look at him, the handsome young man, the Senator, the
statesman, the paragon of the party, but a part of him, a good
part, the extraneous part, was the creation of the chief of
staff, Mr. Arthur Upton. "Image," Upton would say. "It is
image that makes the candidate." Joshua Fitts Kearney
had magic initials—JFK—and Upton's press-relations people subtly impressed that similarity of initials on the general public while Arthur Upton molded Kearney in that
image: vigorous, young, strong, dynamic, outgoing. Look
at the biceps in those arms, look at those muscular thighs;
daily, dutifully, Joshua Fitts performed calisthenics in his
private gymnasiums. He would be a striking figure up there
on the platform before the gathered knights of the Knights
of Columbus, and he would render his speech with thrilling impact—because he was under the constant training of
a voice coach provided by the insistent Upton. His clothes
would be right, modern-tailored for the TV cameras; his
manner, his demeanor, even his haircuts were closely supervised by Arthur Upton—with a view toward attracting
the young voters. But the old were not neglected. J. F.
Kearney was sponsoring bills for national health insurance,
so that a middle-income family would not go flat broke in
the event that one of its members was struck with a lengthy
terminal illness. Nor were the blacks neglected; half of the
office staff of Senator Kearney was comprised of blacks;
his chief of the office staff, Norman Eden, was a black. Nor
were the women neglected—there was always the beautiful, ebullient Kathryn Braxton Kearney, unencumbered by
children, a fighter and a proud leader in the feminist movement. Nor were the international aspects neglected; no
member of the Senate was more internationally involved
than Senator Joshua Fitts Kearney.

78

Look at him there, the international man, asleep in his Jockey shorts. A young man, an intricate man, but a good man for the nation. Intelligent, complex, a subtle man, a man of secrets, but a man with the stuff inside him, the makings; a statesman dedicated; a public servant; truly presidential timber, this was a man who could, and would, grow with the office.

"Josh."

The Senator stirred.

"Josh!"

He opened his eyes.

"We're an hour away from landing," Upton said. "Rise and shine, Mr. Man."

"Yessir, maestro."

The Senator sat up, yawned, flashed the famous toothy grin, and swung his legs off the bed.

They touched down at Dulles at 2:15. There was a crowd, and applause as the Senator descended the stairs, and more applause as his blond wife rushed up to him, and the TV cameras ground away, and the reporters asked questions and the Senator replied, and more questions and more replies, and finally Barney shouldered through and the Senator's party was escorted to the car.

Barney drove. Upton sat in front with him. In the rear Josh and Kathy chatted amiably, but no word about the reason they were met. Kathy made no query, and Josh did not offer. So, at a stop for a red light, the irrepressible Barney asked the question.

"What's with the urgent conference, Mr. President?"

"We'll talk when we get to the house."

"You're the boss, Mr. Man."

Eyes crinkling, Barney looked toward Upton, lowered his chin, turned down the corners of his mouth in a benevolent scowl. Upton smiled, and the light turned green. The car slid forward, and Upton settled back. Only Barney would dare. Barney the insouciant, a free soul. Only Barney would shoot away like that, letting go both barrels. The fact that he missed the mark, and was himself cut down by a return volley, seemed to concern him not at all.

Still smiling, Upton glanced at the rugged profile, tight, strong, impassive. Quite a character, our Barney. Thumped where angels did not tread, but damned well knew where he was thumping—or he did not thump at all. Wise, clever, resourceful. Resolutely loyal, absolutely fearless. Look at him. Even the way he drives a car—with style, flair, swagger. All balls, our Barney. The epitome of *macho*. And the smiling Arthur Upton experienced a warm sense of pride. Barney Wilson was his discovery.

Once at pinnacle they had been three: Josh, Kathy, and Arthur Upton, but somewhere there at the top there'd been a lack. Joshua Fitts Kearney, clean-cut, dashing, dedicated public servant, was the people's hope for the new sweep, the symbol of the bright-new-world-to-come. And his lady was the fair Kathryn Braxton Kearney, DAR, a political activist, a highly visible exponent of the feminist movement. And behind the scenes, Arthur Upton, chief executive of the quiet, muted, complex juggernaut that constitutes a private political organization. But he knew there was a lack at the summit; the supreme command was without a general who, when necessary, could mount a lethal offensive (but the weapons of attack must be invisible). Even the cleanest of politics involves the ineluctable "dirty tricks." In the early years Upton had delegated sections of such work to separate individuals—to specific persons as needs arose— but he knew it was no good; a topflight, trusted coordinator was urgently required.

80

It had not been easy. He had sought, scraped, strip-mined for the right man, but there was always a flaw, something, a quiddity that marked the man wrong, until—Mr. Barnabas F. X. Wilson. Five years ago, at the time of their first conference, that amazing young man was thirty-two years of age, but already renowned among the cognoscenti of Washington circles. Upton was equipped with the full dossier.

Born in Lincoln, Nebraska, Barney Wilson had been a high-school football hero who had received a scholarship to Notre Dame; not the usual athletic scholarship, but a scholastic scholarship. And there at Notre Dame, Wilson had been that rare combination: a straight-A student and the varsity fullback. In his junior year he had been approached for recruitment by the CIA. (Upton was aware, realizing how few *were* aware, that the Central Intelligence Agency plucks likely prospects from college campuses as avidly as do the giant corporations; in fact, the CIA publishes a glossily attractive recruiting booklet.) Wilson had accepted the lure and upon graduation, at age twenty-one, he had joined the "company" and been assigned to Plans, the operational division of the CIA and the most dangerous; the agents of Plans were the "spooks," the covert field men. The new spook proved a dazzling success and rapidly rose in rank, and eleven years later, at the time of the luncheon conference at the Sans Souci, Barney Wilson was the executive officer of his division: he was the DD/P—Deputy Director for Plans.

And there at their first conference, at the Sans Souci, Upton talked about Senator Joshua Fitts Kearney, already a golden name; but more, the sagacious Upton jingled some of Kearney's golden coins. Government employees are notoriously underpaid: the conduit for their capture is money. Upton offered $75,000 a year on a long-term contract and Wilson could bank virtually every dollar—because the expense account would be unlimited. Officially he would go in as a vice president of Kearney Computers in New York City; he would then be transferred, on loan, to head up the "operational division" of the burgeoning Kearney machine. Kearney Computers would purchase a house for him in Georgetown, and an apartment in New York, and a car for Georgetown, and a car for New York, and any chit anywhere that Wilson signed would be honored by Kearney Computers.

"But more, much more," Upton said. "You'll be part and parcel of the making of a President, one of us at the very epicenter. And once he's in the White House, you'll be his right hand. That's a hell of a lot of power and glory, young man."

The young man had smiled his mocking smile. "With that kind of power, who needs glory?"

"True. That kind of power *is* glory."

"Untrue. Power can be achieved without glory."

"All right, all right." Upton laughed. "No glory."

The car slid along the blacktop roadway and stopped beneath the cantilevered portico of the marble-pillared house. Doors opened and snapped closed.

Josh led the procession into the house, veered left, marched them to the small drawing room, and went behind the bar. Joshua Fitts the bartender. Unusual. Barney's gaze flickered to Upton, but the old man avoided it. He turned his back on Barney, clambered onto a bar stool, and nodded thanks for the sauterne that Kearney wordlessly poured for him.

"My dear?" Joshua Fitts inquired of his wife.

"A bit of sherry, please."

Josh poured the sherry.

"And you, Barney?" he said. "How do you want it? Rocks or highball?"

"Highball."

Barney watched the boss behind the bar, an extraordinary experience because it was absolutely new—first time. J. F. Kearney was never the bartender and never presumed to be; Kathy made the drinks, or Barney, or Upton, or a servant. Something was certainly goddam up, Barney thought. An old hand at his game, a professional, he was a keen observer of the psychological nuances. The Man was stalling; Joshua Fitts was steeling himself, pulling his nerves together. Barney watched with interest as the boss shoved bourbon into a tall glass, added ice and soda. He did it deftly, his hands were steady. But his mouth was clamped; the compression made lumps at the corners of his jaw.

He pushed the glass to the customers' side of the bar.

"Thank you," Barney said. "How about you? Not drinking?"

Kearney looked at his watch.

Barney knew all the signs: another nervous gesture. "We late for a date?" he asked.

The Man grinned. The famous smile. A mouthful of square white teeth. "I'm going to shower. And change. Be back shortly." And he marched out of the room.

Barney looked to Upton. "Didn't he have time for a shower on the plane?"

"He had time."

"I've never seen him quite this tight. Something is certainly goddam up."

Kathy carried her sherry to an easy chair, sat deeply, crossed her knees, and Barney frankly admired the shapely legs. Upton pretended not to notice.

"Goddam up. Like a kite," Kathy said. "Arthur, do you really think that Dwyer is what this is all about? Do you really think that Mr. Man is that interested in an insignificant convict? Or is he another one of Josh's boxes? Simon Dwyer, an outside box. Arthur, you know J. F. Kearney. You know him and his goddam boxes. A box inside the outside box, and boxes and boxes inside boxes and boxes. Arthur, what in hell is this all about?"

"We'll know soon enough," Upton said logically.

"Lord, you cover him like a warm blanket, don't you?"

"Look out for her today," Barney said. "Bad mood."

"I'm looking out," Upton said.

"Screw you both."

"Arthur," Barney said, "tell us about international affairs." He grinned his mocking Barney grin. "That's the kind of small talk that'll pass the time."

Kathy was on her second sherry, and Barney on his second bourbon, and Arthur was still lingering over his first sauterne when Joshua Fitts Kearney returned, and Barney Wilson thought: Oh, wow, look at this guy; go give him forty-nine years of age, this young *young* man; God bless his heredity; God bless his genes. Striding purposefully, lithely, lean, Joshua Fitts was wearing white slacks, white moccasins, and a white, short-sleeved, crew-necked pullover. Full of beans, this forty-niner, dynamic, volatile, a goddam vitamin ad, a bouncer on the balls of the feet. Tall: a belly as flat as a surfing board. A short nose, high cheekbones, and wide-spaced crazy green eyes. Crazy because they were chameleon eyes; the color changed, depending on his mood. When the mood was good, the eyes were limpid pale green. Bad mood, and the eyes were opaque: a murky dark green. Now, despite the politician's entrance-smile, despite the man's swinging athletic gait as he went again behind the bar—the eyes were opaque: a murky dark green. "I have a story," he said and laid ice into an old-fashioned glass and poured Scotch. A smile. The politician's professional smile. That's when the age showed, when he smiled. The flesh at the edges of the eyes showed deep cracks: the laugh wrinkles of middle age. "A story," he said, looking directly at Barney Wilson. "It may surprise all of you, but this story must be told."

He kept looking at Barney Wilson, and Upton suppressed a shudder. Not good when he's looking at Barney Wilson; not good when he's looking that intently toward Barney. We're in trouble, he thought, and I'm as much at sea as Kathy.

"It goes back ten years," Josh said.

Upton watched the byplay, the subtle interplay between the two men. In some strange way Josh fairly worshiped the other, the darkly handsome, wry, casual, humorous, cynical Barney Wilson. He knew of the man's devotion to duty, his unmitigating loyalty; he knew the man had literally risked his life in the overall cause of Joshua Fitts Kearney. Time and again Barney had proved himself in dangerous, exigent matters; Josh depended on him heavily, fully. Upton watched them, the cuckold and the cuckolder, different in background, character, temperament, but caught, joined, held, locked in the symbiosis of mutual respect.

"Ten years ago," Josh said. "Arthur knows the initial aspects. He was the Upton of Kearney & Upton at that time, and I was the junior partner, the trial lawyer. One of our clients—a man by the name of Vito Arminito—was reputed to be a Mafia boss. He got into trouble, he and an assistant of his, Simon Dwyer. A criminal matter. I won't bore you with the details. Suffice to say the law had them dead to rights. They were indicted on multiple charges; released on tremendously high bail."

"A quarter of a million dollars for each of them," Upton said.

"I pleaded them guilty," Josh said. "There was no alternative. The prosecution had an absolutely airtight case. As we explained to them, if they stood trial they would risk a sentence of ninety-nine years. The one pragmatic recourse— plead guilty and throw yourselves upon the mercy of the court. My dad promised to try to get them before a lenient judge. He kept his promise—Mr. Justice Otto Yoder. They were sentenced to a term of from fifteen to forty years. We made them a further promise; we would press for earliest possible parole." The dark-green eyes grew narrow. "Dead—three of the four of them. Earl Kearney, dead; Vito Arminito, dead; Judge Yoder, dead. Only Simon Dwyer is alive, and he's coming out on November eight."

"So what?" Kathy said. "So some lousy little criminal is coming out of jail. What in hell does that have to do with us?"

Kearney disregarded her. He looked toward Upton. "All of this, so far, you know. But there are things you don't know." He looked toward Barney. "He doesn't know about judicious judicial bribery. He doesn't know about Mafia stash. He doesn't know about Mafia guarantee."

"What?" Upton said. "What the devil—"

"Let him talk," Barney said.

"Nor did I," Josh said. "Not until Arminito and Dwyer started serving their terms. Then my father took me into his confidence. He told me the truth."

"What truth?" Upton demanded. "What in hell—"

"Let him talk," Barney said. He smiled toward J. F. Kearney; no mockery this time in the Barney smile. "Let's start with judicious judicial bribery."

"Arminito," Josh said, "was a powerful political figure. My father and Judge Yoder were old friends, but Arminito knew more about Yoder than my dad did. He knew, or had learned, facts about Yoder that were not public knowledge. Yoder was strapped for money. Yoder's wife had suffered a menopausal collapse, a mental collapse, and all treatment failed. Declared hopelessly insane, she had been committed, institutionalized upstate in an excellent mental hospital. Such hospitals are extremely expensive. Yoder's wife was costing him forty-eight thousand dollars a year, and Yoder's lifetime savings and investments were leveling down to rock bottom. The judge was ripe for judicious judicial bribery.

"Arminito," Josh said, "wanted to be certain of the court's mercy. He talked to Dad, and Dad talked to Yoder. Arminito was willing to pay five hundred thousand dollars for mercy; a half-million dollars in cash for the assurance of mercy. Mercy was resolved to be a sentence of fifteen to forty; at that sentence, parole could be effected in ten years. The parties agreed and the deal was done."

"How?" Barney said.

"Smart," Kathy said. "That Vito, whoever in hell he was— smart."

"I knew nothing of any of this," Josh said.

"Jesus," Upton said.

"How?" Barney said.

"Arminito," Josh said, "insisted upon a face-to-face meeting, and that meeting was arranged for eleven o'clock of a Sunday morning in a suite in the Regency Hotel in New York City. Please remember, at this time the defendants were out on bail. An emissary of Arminito—a proper president of a Cleveland corporation—had signed for the suite. On that Sunday morning Arminito was there first, and then the lawyer came, and then the judge, and they were met. The situation was thoroughly discussed and the consequent promises duly made. Yoder promised a sentence of fifteen to forty; Earl Kearney promised to pull every political wire on the outside while the defendants were on the inside to effect parole at the first legal opportunity. The money was turned over. Five hundred thousand dollars in a valise. Judge Yoder counted it, every dollar. Then he closed the valise and went away. The lawyer and the client were alone. The client said, 'We have more to talk, but not now. I have an appointment for lunch. Please come back at two o'clock, Mr. Kearney.' "

87

Finally, Joshua Fitts Kearney behind the bar picked up the ice-melting old-fashioned glass and drank Scotch.

"So much for judicious judicial bribery," Barney said. And then somehow gleefully: "Tell us about stash, Mr. Man." He laughed. "Hell, let me tell *you!* Never. Never in all my life did I think I would hear that word—stash—from the eminent Joshua Fitts Kearney, our next President."

"One learns," Josh said.

"You betcha," Barney said.

Arthur Upton drank down all of his sauterne. The bartender made no move to refill the glass.

"Stash," Kathy said. "I once knew a Russian hairdresser by name Stash, a charming little—"

"Let the man talk," Barney said.

"Stash," Josh said. "A criminal term, a Mafia term—"

"You betcha," the gleeful Barney said.

"At two o'clock the lawyer returns to the suite at the Regency and the client tells him about stash. Stash—in effect, a form of mad-money. The client educates the lawyer as to the delicate balances in the criminal world. If the criminal who is 'going away' is big enough, he provides himself with stash. A lump of money, a bulwark. Insurance for when he comes out. No matter his distributed savings, his vaults, his businesses, his numbered accounts in Swiss banks—any or all of that, within the realm of possibility, can be dissipated, or stolen, by his very own confederates if the principal is 'going away' for a long enough time—and Vito Arminito's minimum was ten years."

"Right," Barney said. "So? How much was the guy's stash?"

"Ten million dollars."

"Ten," Kathy said, "million dollars! Beautiful! Whoever he was, this Vito Arminito, he was somebody. Naturally.

Good old Daddy Kearney wouldn't be treating with some insignificant crumbum. Hooray for Vito."

Barney said, "How was the stash arranged? There are many ways. Did Vito—"

"Two suitcases packed with one-thousand-dollar bills. The suitcases to be safely secreted. No outsider will know where, not even his son. Because the son, a businessman, could possibly, in a period of ten years, fall into financial difficulty—and a cache of ten million dollars might prove an irresistible temptation."

"Yeah, the son," Barney said mildly. "Mr. Carleton Armin."

Behind the bar, eyebrows converge. A collision. Like two trucks hitting on a highway.

"How the hell do you know whose son is who?"

"Arthur mentioned that this meeting is about Simon Dwyer. So I did a little checking."

"You would." But the eyebrows came up and the teeth flashed the politician's smile.

"I work my job, Josh. That's what you pay me for."

"You always earn your pay, my friend."

"Ten years ago," Barney said. "Vito and the old Earl. The suite in the Regency. They talk about stash. Cash. A cash stash that has to be hidden. But where? What I mean—he's got to tell somebody. Remember he's a Moff-guy, big. Just the stash ten million; that's no blithering idiot. Suppose he croaks in jail. Would he want ten million to go by the boards like that?"

"No."

"So he's got to tell, right? Somebody."

"Right."

"Did he tell your daddy who?"

"Simon Dwyer," Josh said. "No risk. He considered Dwyer absolutely trustworthy; further, Dwyer would not be subject to temptation because he was going into the clink for the same period as Vito Arminito. Simon Dwyer knew the place of hiding, the repository of the suitcases, but, should Arminito predecease him, and should Dwyer come out in ten years—it would be too much for a Simon Dwyer to handle on his own. Therefore Vito Arminito gave Simon Dwyer specific instructions. Should Vito die in jail, then Dwyer was to do nothing, say nothing to anyone until his release. For his own protection—because a part of that money was allocated to Simon Dwyer in the event of Arminito's decease. A bequest. Once released, then Simon was to go to Carleton Armin, who would supervise the recovery of the suitcases—but Dwyer would not lose his bequest. Because Arminito had given Dwyer a handwritten note—a holograph—which Carleton Armin would honor. The holograph provided that in the event of Arminito's predecease, two million of the stash belonged to Dwyer; the remainder belonged to the son, Carleton Armin. Now then—"

Barney raised a hand, palm out. "Hold it a minute."

"Yes?"

"Suppose the other one—Dwyer—also dies in jail."

"That was covered. Simon Dwyer's wife has a sealed letter in her vault, the letter addressed to Carleton Armin. Should both men die in prison, then that letter, containing all the necessary information, would be turned over to Armin."

"Oh, that Vito!" Kathy shook her head. "He covered it all, didn't he?"

"More than you think."

"Here it comes," Barney said. "The guarantee."

"Guarantee. Another phenomenon of the criminal world." Kearney sipped Scotch, set the glass down hard. Now he was talking toward Kathy. "In the normal world there are normal guarantees of performance. Houses have mortgages; if you don't meet your obligation, you're foreclosed. On a large loan you put up collateral; if you don't pay, you forfeit your collateral."

"Yes," Kathy said. Breathlessly. "Criminal world," she said and Barney admired. She was quick, that Kathy. Until now she had been lackadaisical about this whole damn thing; more than lackadaisical—outright resentful. About being pushed and pulled and commanded to another of the countless meetings where, more often than not, the political minutiae bored her to tears. But now, suddenly, realization flooded that excellent mind and she was sitting upright, spine stiff in the easy chair, frowning, eyes alert, all raillery out of her voice. "Yes," she said. "Criminal world. A Sunday in the Regency. Mr. Vito has paid Mr. Yoder five hundred thousand dollars in cash—a purchase price for mercy. He has Mr. Yoder's promise, but what guarantee does he have that Mr. Yoder will keep his promise? And he has the lawyer's promise that he will press for parole. Again, a promise. What guarantee that the lawyer will keep the promise? Yes," she said. "So?" she said. "What was the wise Mr. Vito's guarantee?"

"A tape," Josh said.

"Oh, no!" Arthur Upton groaned.

"Jesus," Barney said. He put away his glass. He snapped fingers impatiently. "All right, Josh. Come on. Let's have it. Tell."

"He informed my father that, in order to insure performance, he had had a tape recorder going all through that morning's proceedings. After Yoder had left, and my father had left, he'd checked it. It was all there on the tape, clear as a bell. He had his guarantee."

"And what did he do with it?" Barney demanded. "Did he say?"

"Yes. During his alleged luncheon appointment—between my father's morning and afternoon visits to the Regency—he had packed the tape recorder into one of the valises that contained the mad-money. They were together: the guarantee and the stash. Then, if all went well, if everybody kept their promise, Mr. Arminito would return to the outside world in ten years. He would recover his stash and destroy the tape."

Silence.

Then Barney said: "Who else knew about it?"

"What?" Josh said.

"The tape. What the fuck else?"

"Nobody."

"Nobody?"

"Arminito and my father. Nobody else. He swore."

"What about Simon Dwyer?"

"Nobody. Not even Dwyer. It was between Arminito and my father. He swore—and I believe. I knew the man." He looked toward Upton. "Arthur knew him. Strict. A strict man. In his own peculiar way, an honorable man."

"If he swore," Upton said, "I would believe."

Barney paced. Pacing. Arms folded over chest, head down. "Why in hell," he said, "didn't you tell us before?"

"What sense? What purpose?"

"Yeah," Barney said. Pacing.

"The key was Dwyer," Upton said.

"Exactly," Kearney said. "You can now understand why I exerted every effort to effect his release at the earliest possible date. As long as that tape exists, I'm vulnerable. If that tape ever came to light—"

"You're dead," Upton said.

"Only Dwyer can lead us to it."

"Dead," Upton said. "Politically dead. If that tape comes to light, you couldn't be elected dog-catcher, let alone President of the United States. Guilt by blood—like guilt by association. Worse. Jesus, can you imagine!" His hand reached out to his glass. It was empty. The hand returned to his lap. "Can you imagine if political enemies got hold of that tape?

The white-haired boy's father turns out to be filth—caught red-handed in the bribery of a New York Supreme Court Justice. But worse. Much worse. The white-haired boy was the lawyer of record, the trial lawyer. Who on God's green earth wouldn't take for granted that the trial lawyer was in on it? No matter his voice isn't there on that tape—"

"Yes," said Joshua Fitts Kearney.

"Goddam yes," said Barney Wilson.

"Yes, not even dog-catcher," said Kathryn Braxton Kearney.

"Oh, Jesus Christ," said Arthur Upton.

"Folks," said Barney Wilson, "we've a lot of thinking to do and talking to do, but not right now. Right now I gotta go pee. Your revelations, Mr. Man, have excited my bladder. Lady and gents, kindly excuse."

"Jesus, oh, Jesus Christ," said Arthur Upton.

"Yeah man," said Barney Wilson. "That's the name of my Lord."

7

O N   R E T U R N   Barney found a shift in the positions of husband and wife. Kathy was behind the bar and Josh was sunk in her easy chair. Upton, as though riveted by a spike in the asshole, was exactly in the same posture on the tall bar stool. "Listen," Upton said, and sipped white wine. All the glasses had been replenished. Including Barney's. Which sat, neglected, on the bar. "Listen," Upton said. The old guy looked bad, but his voice was strong. "In our time, we have had our vicissitudes. Political ups and downs are normal. But *this* down cannot go up. If that tape finds its way into the wrong hands—we are *done!* We pack up, close the books, and go our separate ways."

"A most pessimistic attitude," Barney said. "It's not going to find its way into the wrong hands, Mr. Maestro. The right hands. That's why I work here."

"I admit I'm confounded," Upton said. "How?"

"That's why you hired me. And you're the guy that hired me, Mr. Maestro."

"These are matters outside my ken, beyond my comprehension."

"Okay, people, let's take it from the top. Beyond the good Mr. Maestro's comprehension. A tape—which is now the object of our adoration." He laughed. He was beginning to enjoy. He paced. Slowly. "The tape is with the stash and nobody knows from the fucking tape and Arminito is dead. The next in line is Dwyer, and Dwyer is alive and coming out. If that were it—if that were just it—it wouldn't do us any harm. Dwyer would pick up the stash, find the tape, and play it. Nothing. No harm. It would please him that his boss was smart enough to have arranged the guarantee. Period. He would destroy the tape because the tape could only do *him* harm. It would disclose that the judge who gave him clemency was *bribed* for that purpose. Remember the guy's a convict out on parole. As long as that tape exists, he can be shoved right back into the pokey to serve out the rest of the forty-year term. So what would he do with the tape? He would kill it, destroy it, burn it—immediately. Is any of that beyond your comprehension, Mr. Maestro?"

"No."

"Unfortunately, Dwyer does not have a direct line to the stash. Ten million bucks—it's locked away too good. A repository. As Arminito told Josh's father, too much for a Simon Dwyer to handle on his own. Therefore Arminito gave Dwyer instructions. Should Arminito die in jail, then Dwyer is to go to Carleton Armin for the supervision of the recovery of that stash. And there's our rub, lady and gents. Our rub is Mr. Carleton Armin."

"Why?" Kathy said.

"You tell her, Mr. Maestro. Kearney & Upton. You

know the guy, you've dealt with the guy. The color's back in your face; you're beginning to feel better. So stop sitting like you're nailed to that stool with a spike up your ass. Stop playing the benumbed, stupid, elder statesman. Benumbed? I'm sure; but that's passing. Elder? A matter of opinion. In my book you're young. But stupid? Absolutely not. In *nobody's* book. So *you* tell the lady—while I wet my parched throat." Barney went to his bourbon on the bar.

"Carleton Armin," Upton said. "Politically oriented. Shrewd, strong, young, ruthless, ambitious. A pillar in New York society, a power in New York politics. But straining to expand. He has high horizons."

"Tell her more," Barney said. "And tell Mr. President. Coming from you, it'll be better than coming from me. I am wont—I've been told—to expand my expositions into melodramatics. Tell what would happen when Armin comes upon that ten-million-dollar bonanza—two of which belongs to Simon Dwyer. And—all incidentally—he finds that tape, plays the tape, and hears it. Tell what would happen."

"The money would be nothing. The tape would be all." Upton sipped sauterne. "Armin would realize—in the present national circumstances—the worth of that tape, its vast potential. Josh Kearney is no longer a trial lawyer in New York City. He is the United States Senator who will be the landslide candidate at the next presidential convention—and every poll shows he is the hands-down favorite for election. Possessed of that tape, Armin has a missile pointed directly at the heart of J. F. Kearney. Either Josh abdicates—possibly even resigning as Senator—or the power behind the throne, with all the perquisites appertaining thereto, will be Mr. Carleton Armin." Upton touched fingers to his neatly combed white hair, then clasped his hands tightly. "The sins of the fathers," he murmured. And sighed. A shiver. The slender shoulders trembled. "The perfect

96

blackmail," he said slowly. "The consummate blackmail."

"Never. Not me. I'll never submit to blackmail."

"As long as you're in politics, you're a puppet for whoever controls that tape. Its exposure would destroy you. Out of the delicate area of politics, a private citizen—that's another matter. In effect, no scandal. But in the delicate—"

"Then I'll get the hell out of politics."

"Oh no you won't," Kathy said.

"You bet he won't," Barney said. "Not J. F. Kearney—whose *life* is politics. He's upset. Talking through his hat." Barney laughed. "Or else he's kidding us, or himself; making with the self-pity, the sympathy pitch. Christ, we all know Mr. Man. He's a fighter, and he knows every trick in the book."

"But not this book, Barney. As Arthur said—outside my ken."

"Maybe your ken. And Arthur's ken. And I don't care who else's ken. But not *my* ken. That's why you hired me on, Mr. President. To fight the fights you don't know how to fight. Which doesn't make you any less the fighter. You've got your ways; I've got mine."

"Image," Upton muttered. "In the business of politics, it's all image: the figure that's out there in the minds of the people. Even the right, the best man, without image—nothing. We've spent eight long years creating the Kearney image, and now—"

"Enough," Barney roared. "Enough!" He bounced away from the bar. The blue jaw glistened, the eyes were burning; the smile was a white slash in the dark face. "Okay, people. You've had your funeral, you've said your obsequies, you've lowered the coffin into the pit—only there ain't no body in that coffin, folks. The boy's out here, alive and kicking, and he's going to stay alive, no matter who else dies. We're making a President, aren't we, people?"

"Damn right we are," Kathy said.

Barney pacing. Buoyant. Barney working. The white slash in the dark face is a happy smile. He stops in front of J. F. Kearney. "You laid it out straight and true. You stalled for years, but I understand. When the father pulls a *shtick,* a corruption, the son is reluctant to declare. But now we have it straight and true. Which is the way you've always been with me—straight and true. You've never fucked Barney, no angles, no politician bullshit. A loyalty from you to me. And therefore a loyalty from me to you. Loyalty begets loyalty, right? I love you, Mr. Man," Barney said and strode away, pacing. "From here on out, it's all mine. My operation. I will handle it. Me."

Meekly Upton said: "How?"

Barney pacing. The smile happy. "We have time, thank God, plenty of time for plans and procedures. It's July. The guy comes out in November. Four months." Grinning, he did a little dance, sang: "Who could ask for anything more?"

"How?" Upton said.

Pacing. A slow pace now. The hands are clasped behind the back, the chin is down. "Let's take it step by step," he said, "and all the steps are simple. Four months. Plenty of time for me for preparation. Okay. Step one—on November eight Simon Dwyer comes out. Step two—Simon goes to Carleton to rescue the stash. Step three—Carleton Armin rescues the stash. Step four—Barney Wilson takes the stash away from Carleton Armin. Simple?"

"No," Josh said.

"How?" Upton said.

"He's beautiful," Kathy said.

Barney pacing. The smile is happier. "The proposition at hand—the good guys against the bad guys. They, in a manner of speaking, are the bad guys. We are the good guys. In a manner of speaking." The dark cheeks are ruddy. The smile is euphoric. "Good guys, bad guys—they are after the same quarry. But the good guys have an inestimable advantage, because the bad guys don't know the good guys exist. They don't know about a tape. They have no idea they are in a competition. Therefore they are loose and easy, comfortable within their own operation. Can we miss?"

"How?" Upton said.

"Hijack," Barney said. "In the parlance, Mr. Maestro, the word is—hijack."

Consternation now in the house in Chevy Chase, quiet consternation, but voluble. Talk and cross-talk. Kathy. Josh. And the revived Arthur Upton. While Barney Wilson drinks bourbon at the bar.

"That's your job," Josh said.

"My job," Barney acknowledged.

"Nothing else." The leader was back in the saddle, issuing orders. "You'll put everything else aside. Nothing else. Starting now. Your one job—bring us that tape. I don't care what in hell you spend."

"And use as many people as you like," Upton said.

"No people," Barney said.

"No people?" A grimace from Arthur Upton, still on the bar stool.

"Amended," Barney said. "One people." He pointed at Kathy. "She'll be my people."

"What the devil?" Upton said.

"King Arthur, who's your cloak-and-dagger man?"

"You are."

"She'll be it. My one people. An assistant, a slight helper within the perimeter. Sort of the liaison. Neither you, Mr. President, nor you, Mr. Maestro, can even be remotely involved. You'll both be far away out of it, and you'll stay far away out of it."

Kearney said, "But won't you need people really to help? Won't you—"

"I don't think so. Please remember our unbeatable advantage—the guys on the other side don't know there *is* another side." He left his bourbon, he left the bar. He paced, no longer smiling. "This has to be my job, and mine alone. No—I'm trying to think of an evil word—no confederates. No accomplices."

"But a better word. Or words," Upton said. "Necessary assistants."

"We'd be right back where we started from. We'd be right back there to—blackmail."

"I don't understand," Upton said.

"Mr. Maestro, when it's politics, you're the superb professional. In this kind of thing—I'll omit the superb—*I'm* the professional. I want to skip over the quicksands that amateurs fall into."

Kearney said, "A poet, our Barney."

"Look, Mr. Man. This is going to be a dirty job. When it comes down to the final action—an awfully dirty job. I'd like to keep it in the family, but without even the family knowing all of it. I don't want to spread it. This has to be my job, what I was hired for. I believe I can do the job without accomplices, and if I can I will. Because, accomplices—you get stuck in the same mud. Once there are strangers in on it, then *they* know things we don't want them to know. That's the amateur's game—the paradox of the amateur's game. Trying to scramble out of one form of blackmail, they fall into another form of blackmail. Not me. I'm a pro. I'll accept one people as liaison. Will you work with me, Kathy?"

"I'll be thrilled."

"She'd be thrilled," Upton said.

Kearney said, "He's Barney."

"I'm Barney. This is up my alley, my operation exclusive. You and the professor, I want you to stay far away out of it. My job of work. I'll be spending a hell of a lot of money, but that'll be me. Unconnected with you. Barney Wilson, vice president of Kearney Computers. From time to time, you'll get reports of the work in progress. Okay? Are we understood?"

"Whatever you say," Kearney said. "I have full confidence."

"Then you'll stay out of my hair. I'll do my thing while you do yours. You run for President. Me—I promise you that tape."

"Plus ten million bucks," Kathy said.

"To hell with ten million bucks," Kearney said.

Of course, Barney thought. When you're a tornado, what's a small breeze? The guy is a billionaire. A billion is a *thousand* million. What is ten compared to a thousand?

"It happens it goes with the contract," Kathy said. "I mean if he gets the tape, the money comes with it. The stash and the guarantee—they're locked together." She raised her hands, wriggled fingers. "Cream of the jest," she said. "It will be Vito Arminito's posthumous contribution to J. F. Kearney's campaign fund."

She liked her joke. She laughed at her joke.

None of the others laughed at Kathy Kearney's joke.

8

H E   H A D   S P E N T   a lovely week at the ranch house in the Adirondacks, a week of fishing, hunting, riding, swimming, and enjoying Marion. He always enjoyed Marion, although no longer sexually. Married for twenty-five years, they had not indulged in physical intercourse for the past five years, and even prior to that the sex had become sporadic. By nature a varietist, his carnal appetite for his wife had dwindled with the years. But, good husband, he had performed the occasional conjugal duty until he had realized that she, good wife, was doing exactly the same: reluctantly performing a duty. And so, gradually, tacitly, the sexual partnership had dissolved.

But for all else he loved and enjoyed his Marion, a laughing, eager, handsome woman, active, deeply engaged in her causes, always the center of her group. Group? Make that groups!

Marion was a lodestone. She attracted people; they gathered about her, charmed by her sparkle, her eleemosynary drive, her vibrant optimism—and she always found the rich ones. Even out here in the bosky blue-green hills, her groups came—for dinners, for picnics, for barbecues—and she always hit them up for stiff checks. "Giving is living," she would cry. "We are lucky. We are well. But out there—" She would wave her hands. "There is so much suffering! We must help. God, if not us!" And laughing, she would shake them down. "Deductible, it's deductible," she would cry, and grab the check, and kiss the giver, and praise the donation. They loved her. They all loved her. Carleton Armin loved her.

It was at one of her groups that he had met Dolores Warren. A society party in a ballroom in a townhouse several months ago, April in New York; a party for the benefit of cerebral-palsy research, one of Marion's favorite charities. Dolores had come with the legendary Abner Moffit, for forty years Broadway's most consistently successful play producer. Carleton had liked that: the fact that she graced the arm of an elderly gent. Smart, a smart kid, she knew what side of her bread to butter. And he had liked her; God, he had *loved* her. A redhead, but not a redhead like Suzy Buford.

Suzy *looked* like a redhead: the hair red-gold, the eyes green, the skin marble white, and a dazzling open smile. This one was different. The red hair was auburn, russet, chestnut —a color called titian when he was a boy. Straight hair, shining, parted in the middle, hanging to the shoulders and framing a heart-shaped face. A closed face, mysterious, lovely, a witch's face. Small pointed chin, small mouth, small nose. And enormous eyes. Dark, long, almond-shaped, a witch's eyes, languid, slumberous. And he knew—a prescience. This was a child who was born old.

The long, languorous eyes, resting on him, had engulfed him. Drawn him out of himself and into her. Carleton Armin, heart pounding, lost. Swimming within deep, dark, limitless eyes. And his response had been typical Carleton Armin. He had offered her a canapé from the buffet table.

"No, thank you," she said. A voice like the eyes. Deep. A slow whisper of a voice. Languid.

"Not hungry?"

"Not for a canapé."

Slender arms, naked arms. Simple sheath of clinging dress. Silk-smooth, swarthy, slender arms. And up there, far away on a dais, an orchestra. Strings. Eight fiddles, two cellos, a clavichord, and a harp. Clavichord and harp!—leave it to Marion's friends. No percussions, no drums. No brass, no horns. And now, as though on cue, the strings drifted into the perfect music for this insane moment. Nostalgia. They were playing an oldie: Hoagy Carmichael's *Stardust*.

"Would you like to dance?"

"Yes," she said.

"Know the song?"

"Yes."

"*Stardust*. An old favorite of mine."

"It's a new favorite of mine."

He took her.

They danced.

In the great room, among all the people, alone. Dancing. To the slow rhythms of *Stardust*. A nude woman in his arms. Not prescience now: he knew, he could feel, holding her, pressed close. She was naked underneath the simple sheath. And *he* was naked, his *feelings* were naked; his hardon between her swaying thighs was prodigious.

"Love you," he whispered.

"I know."

"Crazy."

"Not crazy. I love you," she said. Dancing. Slow rhythm. Old Hoagy's old *Stardust*. "From the moment I saw you,"

104

she whispered. "It happens. People. Whirling. Orbits. From somewhere, somehow. Whoever you are, you have happened, we have happened."

"Don't kid me, baby."

"I'm not."

Of course she was. The gorgeous little bitch was playing with him, having fun, chaffing, sending him up. But was she? Chemistry. The vibes. What he was feeling in his loins. What he was feeling in his heart. The mad planets of astrology. Happens. It can happen. From somewhere. Somehow.

"I mean it," he said. And at that moment he did.

"I love you," she said.

"You're crazy."

"We're crazy."

"Honey, don't put me on."

"I'm not. Tomorrow, maybe. Another time, maybe. Now, no."

"What's your name?"

"Dolores. What's your name?"

"Carleton Armin."

"Marion's husband?"

"Mr. Marion."

"I've heard about you. You're a richie."

"Is that bad?"

"Good. I love richies."

"Is that why you love me, witch?"

"I didn't know who you were, Mister."

"Not much you didn't."

"I didn't!"

"I believe you."

"Go fuck yourself."

"I'll call you. May I call you?"

"Yes." She whispered her number at his ear.

"You did that too fast. It didn't register. I won't remember. Do it again, please. Slowly."

"You'll remember," she said.

He had called her, and had called *on* her in the tiny apartment on Perry Street. And had taken her out on the town, the best spots, the in spots, enjoying her, enjoying the witch, but not touching. He was attentive, adoring, seeking her, sensing her, his antennae reaching. But no touch, no sex. Time, there was time: this one was not for a fast grab. This one he wanted, felt, desired: she would be Suzy's successor. He wanted full possession of this one, born old, languid, smoldering, reserved. Smiling that witch's smile. That little smile. The little white teeth. This one he wanted to own, all his.

They talked. Conversation was their sex.

Each feeling the other, antennae quivering.

He told her about himself—what he wanted to tell her. She knew he was Marion's husband, Carleton Armin, banker. And he told her of the inner self—what he wanted to tell her. Told her he was seeking. In early middle age, seeking. Like the last hurrah, before sinking away into old age. Love. Seeking. A need, a desperate desire. He was an old hand at the game; he did not touch, he talked, confessed. Told about his marriage, by now a flat disaster. Two kids in college. Divorce somewhere in the offing: the marriage continues out of habit, inertia. If he requested, Marion would be quite willing to consent to a divorce. But, thus far—no reason, no purpose for such request.

He knew how to touch, before touching sexually. The first time he came, he brought a single rose. The next time, six roses. The next time, a dozen roses. The next time, a bottle of champagne. The next time, a basket of champagne. The next time, a gift of costume jewelry. The next time, more expensive costume jewelry. The next time a modest but expensive wristwatch from Cartier. She loved things. He was delighted that she loved *things*. Of course he never mentioned Suzy Buford.

But he held off on the sex. Playing the game. He knew the game. He was showing interest. Deep interest. In her, her being, her soul. He knew she was ready, he knew he could have her, he knew he could take, but he held off, playing the game. She was a witch, born old, but she *was* young. He showed sincerity, convincing her he wasn't after her ass. His balls ached, but he held off. He wanted this one, this strange one, this deep one, this witch, but he wanted her all for his own, he wanted to own her, and he knew how, he knew his game. They talked.

She told him about herself, her story. Houston, Texas. The mother was half Mexican, half Cherokee Indian; the father was a red-haired Swede, a plodding, hard-working man, the manager of a supermarket. Five kids, Dolores the oldest. Texas University, majored in drama. Many boy friends, of course, but never in love. On graduation, at age twenty-one, she had cut out: up to New York for a crack at the career. She had kissed Mama goodbye, and Papa goodbye, and her four little brothers. Quietly Mama had given her a going-away present: eight hundred dollars that Mama had saved during Dolores's lifetime. And Dolores, in New York, had made do. She was a good actress; in time she would get her break. Here and there, until now, bit parts; and money, here and there, when her agent sent her out on modeling jobs.

On their last date—before his visit with Suzy and then up to the Adirondacks—their talk had gone in root deep.

"You need a patron," he said.

The small smile, the little teeth, the whispery voice. "What Texas girl in this naughty city doesn't?"

"The pressures have to be off. You should be going to

acting school. That's a catapult. A good acting school—the teachers themselves have terrific connections."

"Well spoken, Sir Carleton. Yes. That would be the name of the game. But who can afford?"

"You."

Thin eyebrows scowl. "How?"

"A patron."

A laugh. Lovely. A throaty laugh, melodious. "You wish to recommend a patron? They've *been* recommended. Like Abner Moffit, who recommended himself. Dolores Warren here. I don't go to bed for career. I don't sell it. I wasn't brought up that way. Like Mama used to say—don't sell it. Because you'll be selling yourself down the river. Love? That's another story. But pick a rich one, Mama would say. You're entitled, Mama would say—you're a cockeyed beauty."

"I wish to recommend a patron."

Now the laugh was derisive. "Like who?"

"Me."

Silence. The great eyes sucked him in.

"When I get back," he said, "we'll talk about it."

Ranch house in the blue-green hills. Sunday. During the week he had talked with her on the phone: he would see her Tuesday evening. Now this Sunday morning Marion walked him out to the car.

"You really should stay longer. The weather's so beautiful."

"I wish I could," he said. "But tomorrow Seely goes off on vacation."

"When he gets back, you come back."

"Of course." He kissed her.

"Anybody in New York wants me"—she laughed—"tell them they can't have me until September. I return the day after Labor Day. G'bye, darling. Drive carefully."

108

He drove carefully, thinking about Dolores Warren. "When I get back," he had told her, "we'll talk about it." When I get back, I'm going to fuck you, baby. Our game will enter its second stage. The first stage was establishing myself. Not a pig. Not a grabber after the flesh. A man deeply interested in you the person. Second stage: we start screwing. Third stage: I get rid of Suzy and move you up to Central Park West, and then you're all mine, sweetheart. Exclusively.

In the sunshine on the highway, he fidgeted in the seat. And laughed aloud. A chortle. Carleton Armin. Forty-eight years of age. Worldly. Sophisticated. Alone in the car, driving to New York. With a pain in his pants, an erection, a suffocation. He took one hand off the wheel, zipped down, and opened up. And laughed again. Carleton Armin, investment banker. In his air-conditioned car on the highway to New York. With his cock out.

On Monday afternoon he went up to Tiffany's and bought a pin, a sunburst, little diamonds surrounded by little rubies on a background of gold petals. He had not discussed price and was surprised when it was only $850. Only. $850 would pay the rent on Perry Street for six months. He asked them to wrap the velour-lined box in plain white paper, and took it back with him to the office. Seely would be gone for a month.

Tuesday he stayed late, shaved and dressed in the apartment in the rear of the office. He tore three checks out of his checkbook, folded them, and placed them in his wallet. He slipped the Tiffany package into a pocket and went down for a cab. He arrived at Perry Street at a quarter to eight and she opened immediately after he rang.

"Hi."

They did not kiss. He had established a routine which she had accepted. He had known her since April and they had never once kissed. Christ, he suddenly thought and smiled. Does she think I'm too old? Or impotent? Or—gay? Gay! It gave him an idea. He knew where he would take her after dinner. She would love it.

"Hungry?" he said.

"Yes," she said.

He took the little white-wrapped box from his pocket and placed it on a table.

"What is it?" she said.

"A box," he said.

"Box?"

"A gift."

She flew to it.

"No," he said.

He was Carleton Armin. He knew how to play his game.

She was Dolores Warren, intrigued by this strange man, but always off balance: never knowing, never certain, never quite understanding.

"Not yet," he said. "Later. When we come home."

"I'll be dying all evening."

"You won't die," he said.

They had dinner in the Four Seasons, and then he took her downtown to East Village, to Club Mirage on Fourth Street, where all the performers were female impersonators. In the well-filled smoky room, they drank champagne and watched the entertainment—singers, dancers, a chorus—and she could not believe they were males, every one a male.

"They're just too beautiful."

"You're too beautiful. I love your eyes."

"Do the eyes show I'm a little drunkie on the champ?"

"Champ?"

"Champagne."

"Oh, these hip kids."

"Let's go home."

"What's on your mind?"

"You damn know."

"I will venture a guess." He laughed. "Boxes?"

"Box," she said. "Singular."

"Let's go home," he said.

And then in the apartment on Perry Street she said: "Now?"

"You may take one giant step," he said.

She tore away the white paper, saw the Tiffany emboss-ment. She opened the box, gasped. "Oh my God," she said. She took out the pin, stared at it, licked her tongue over it, and then ran to him. Her arms encircled his neck and she kissed him. First time; they kissed. His hands hung at his sides, but the kiss was deep.

She moved back from him, stood looking at him. And he knew she knew. The witch knew. Their time had come. And from that moment this evening she was the ruler of the reign.

"Stand there," she said in that hushed whispery voice. "Just stand there as you are."

He stood.

She brought the pin to the table, left it there, and came back to him.

"I want you to see me," she said. Hushed. The whispery voice.

She unclothed. Stood naked before him. Then she raised her arms, clasped her hands, and turned. And kept turning. Like a mannequin on display, revolving.

"Oh my God," he said, and remembered those had been exactly her words before she had licked her tongue over the sunburst.

God, unbelievable, this flawless body revolving. Coffee-colored—*café au lait*—gleaming. She was all tits and ass; the rest of her so slender, warm-skinned, childlike. Slender legs, slender arms; below the armpits the stripes of her glistening ribs. A European woman, a European-shaped woman: full, strong, powerful breasts, and a great, vast, shining mound of round, protuberant ass.

She ceased revolving. Smiled that languorous witch's smile.

"Do you like?"

"I love."

"Don't move," she said.

She undressed him. Removed his clothing piece by piece and he stood naked, tumescence upcurved, huge, a throbbing scimitar.

"Gorgeous." The voice was different, deep, a rasp, an animal sound, feral. "Jesus God, what a gorgeous prick. Oh, Jesus!" And down. Sank to her knees, a genuflection, an adoration, worship of phallus, an obeisance. Her hands gripped his thighs, her long nails bit in, and she kissed the tip of the penis, and took in the head, and her teeth were gentle at the rim of the corona. Then she rose and led him to the bed.

She kept him on his back, kissing his forehead, his eyes, his mouth, his ears, his neck, and down along his body, the nipples of her breasts lightly touching, and she kissed his belly, and his thighs, and down to his feet, sucking each toe, sucking between the toes, and then up again slowly, up to the genitalia, licking at his balls, taking one testicle into the hot mouth, and then the other testicle, and then both, and the whole scrotum was surrounded inside her.

He lay rigid. He was an old-fashioned man, a stabber, a fucker, he was not a man to be pinioned on his back. For him oral sex was the foreplay, the opening gambit, the titillating lead-in to the ultimate pleasure, but that ultimate pleasure was the cock in the cunt, the fuck, the fucking! But with this one he remained on his back. He sensed her need, and did not interfere.

And then she was there, she was at it, she was at his prick, licking, the oscillating tongue at the tender underside of his penis, licking, licking, as he writhed upward, and then the moist hot mouth was over it, and took it in all the way, engulfing, engorging, sucking, deeply sucking, and her head began to bob up and down, ever more swiftly, taking it all into her, and releasing, in and out, in and out, deeply all the way, sucking him, milking him, and now he was cooperating, rearing into her, stabbing upward, moaning, groaning, and she sucked him, ate him, milked him, until, UNTIL—

He lay on his back, limp, exhausted.

And she came up to him, smiling that witch's smile.

"Thank you," she said and kissed his mouth and nestled in the crook of his arm.

They lay.

Lay, resting.

Then talked; placid talk after love. She told of her dreams. Actress. She was good. She knew. She had the talent, the drive, the fire. One day the break would come; she would soar, she would conquer New York. He agreed. He admitted he knew little of acting talent, that was not his field. But drive and fire—that was necessary in every field. To stay in there, to stay with it, to keep punching; in time the break would come. Luck. Necessary in whatever the endeavor. But you must be *there* when the luck hits, you must be ready. Not once did he mention the word patron.

And then her hand was moving along his body, touching, lightly, chest, belly, and down to pudendum, and her fingers encircled the thick rise of his hardness, and her breathing quickened. "You're a man," she whispered. "God, you are all man!" And the man took over. Carleton Armin, old-fashioned man in bed, straight fucker, aggressor. He caressed the marvelous tits, sucked nipples, moved up, kissed her fiercely and prepared to mount her—but her hands were gripped at her vagina, a barrier to entrance.

Gruffly, "What's the matter?"

"No," she said.

"Why? Wha—"

"I—I've never."

His frown was deep. "I don't believe—"

"It's true."

"Are you trying to— Are you telling me you're a virgin?"

Long, dark, smoldering eyes. "Technically, yes."

"I don't believe it." He shook his head. "Something with religion? Is that it?"

"No."

"Then what?"

"Just—I've never been in love."

"The first time you saw me you told me you loved me."

"Loved you. But not *in* love. Not yet."

And then the slow small witch's smile was on her mouth, and she turned from him. Turned her body and lay prone. Face down, breasts down. And her knees moved up, and hunched under her, and the great gleaming cloven moon was presented. And her hands reached back behind her, each hand at a half-moon pulling, until the pink-glowing rosebud was revealed.

"There," she said, voice muffled by pillow. "Do it there. I love it there. Do," she beseeched. "Do it to me, lover. Do it to me there."

When he awoke in the morning she was still sleeping, heart-shaped face in a cloud of titian hair. He dressed and went out of the bedroom. In the little living room, he took one of the blank checks from his wallet, filled it out for five thousand dollars, and laid it on the table near the pin from Tiffany's.

Then, quietly, he opened the door and clicked it shut behind him.

In the cab to the office, he smiled his satisfaction. Carleton Armin, patron. Still smiling, he lit a cigarette. Five thousand dollars was a large hunk of money all at one crack. It could startle her; she might, possibly, return it. She was a strange one, breathtakingly beautiful, inordinately wise in the ways of sex, but withal a virgin. And the mother had admonished her not to sell herself. Well, he thought, we'll see. If she returned the check, he would take another tack. But a money tack. He was an old hand at the game. Money does it all the time. Some way, somehow, cash money. Money ensnares.

She did not return the check. The next time he saw it, it came with his bank statement, a canceled voucher. And so he knew he had her. He did not, yet, own her—because there was still Suzy to get rid of. Time: that would take time. He was Carleton Armin: he took pride in his sense of compassion. Suzy Buford had served him well. She deserved respect and attention.

9

BARNEY WILSON, busy. Busy Barney. A hell of a lot to do, but plenty of time to do it. Preparations. Got to work. Got to keep at it. Got to lay in the early preparations. This was going to be a rough, tough, ugly job, far uglier than his colleagues could ever imagine. They were the effete, the elite, up there in the political stratosphere. Check that. Cut effete. Elite, okay. They were rough and tough, the elite, in their own way, but they had no idea of the killing job he had before him, and he was not about to inform them. The most important job of his life. Upon its success depended the making—or the unmaking—of the next President of the United States. He was willing to die on this job, and it damn well could happen, and he knew he would have to kill on this killing job, but that's the way it goes, folks. We all have our purpose in life. And on this job, my purpose, folks, is to give you your next President.

It had its compensations: three compensations. First, he

was back in action, real action, and he loved it. Next, he was relieved of the tedium of the political speechmaking. And last, but not least, Kathy, upon consent and advice of the elite, was wholly available for the duration of the job; at his beck, at his call. Kathryn Braxton Kearney, his peripheral helper. And she goddam *would* help. Perhaps Josh Kearney did not know it (or didn't he?), but Barney Wilson knew. The willowy Kathy had a core of iron inside her. She was strong, deeply wise, ambitious, and as implacable as any of them, including Barney Wilson. Of the Big Four—whether Josh realized, or Upton—the lovely, lissome Kathy was the biggest. More power, baby.

He closed down the house in Georgetown. His base of operations, of course, would be New York City. And so in late July he visited with Dwight D. Hickey, president of Kearney Computers.

"I need some favors," Barney said.

"Whatever I can do," Hickey said.

"I'm the vice president out on loan."

"I know who you are," Hickey said.

"Like this," Barney said. "I need an office in the Armin Building. I'm Bernard Brown."

"No sweat on the Armin Building. It's still plenty empty. Who's Bernard Brown?"

"Travel agent. A small, personally operated travel agency. I used to work here, but my sideline was travel. I quit to go out on my own in the travel business. You vouch for me, Kearney Computers vouches for me. I'm a hundred-percent guy."

"No sweat."

"How long will that take?"

"A few weeks. What else?"

"How do you know—else?"

"You said favors. With an s at the end."

"Yeah." A Barney grin. "Bernard Brown needs an apartment on East Sixty-seventh Street. Far east. Around Four Hundred East. A complex of modern apartment houses up there. That's where she wants it."

"She?"

"Me. The same Bernard Brown. The apartment is for, well, like Mr. and Mrs. Bernard Brown. Dig?"

"No."

"It's part Bernard Brown, but mostly me." A Barney wink. "I'm a bachelor. You were once a bachelor, or don't you remember?"

"A long time ago."

"I've got a chick who wants to live there. She picked the area, she insists. I'm a biggie; for her, I'm a biggie. So she's depending on me. I'm depending on you."

"That's a heavily populated area. That one *is* sweat."

"Dwight, my boy—my dear, dieting, Anglo-Saxon boy who dyes his hair—you are Dwight David Hickey. President of Kearney Computers. You have a wife and four kids and more money than all six of you can ever spend. You're tired of sitting in that swivel chair, thinking about your stock options. You want up, you want honors—you expect to be a Cabinet member in the next administration. So show me, kid. Show *me!* Or else you'll have your ass in that swivel chair for the rest of your days. Show me you can move a small mountain. Show me some fucking ingenuity. If not—if you can't perform on a small deal like this—forget about being a minister of state."

"What in hell do you want me to do? Evict somebody?"

"Sure," Barney said. "If necessary, evict somebody. You're Kearney Computers. You have the pull, the money, the political clout."

"How much time?"

"Plenty. Three months. But that's the outside. I want that apartment—the latest—by November one."

"I'll try."

"Not enough."

"I'll do my best."

"I want better than your best."

"This is goddam fucking blackmail."

"Correct," Barney said. "J. F. Kearney's our next President. You're penciled in for a Cabinet seat—but you can be penciled out. That's it, my friend. Move the little mountain. You know where to reach me. I'll be waiting to hear."

He visited with Lyle Carter at the Carter Agency on West 57th Street. Lyle had been one of his older boys at Plans. Retired from the "company," Lyle now operated a discreet detective agency in New York City. A great big bear of a man, he hugged his ex-boss, clapped his shoulder, insisted on taking him out to lunch. And over lunch Barney arranged for round-the-clock surveillance on Simon Dwyer and Carleton Armin for an indefinite period commencing November 8. No mention of Kearney. Barney Wilson's private affair.

"Your best people," he said. He laughed. "I'm giving you enough notice, aren't I?"

"You'd have my best in any case." Lyle had been making notes. "You'll want the daily reports delivered to your apartment?"

"No. They'll report to you. I'll call in every day and you'll tell me."

"Right."

"One thing more."

"Sure."

"Armin. At that Four Hundred address. It's a duplex, but I don't know the apartment number. I want it."

"Right."

"Also the names of some people who live in that building."

"How many?"

"Three. Preferably single females. Names and apartment numbers."

"When do you want this information?"

"Next few days."

"You got it."

"I'll call you."

He opened a checking account under the name Bernard Brown. He deposited thirty thousand dollars. Bernard Brown c/o Dwight D. Hickey, 14 Rosewood Drive, Scarsdale, New York. He called Hickey, told him he'd moved in with him, and told him why.

"You think of everything, don't you, Barney."

"If not me, who?"

"Yeah, right."

"How we doing on the Armin Building rental?"

"It's on its way."

"The other thing?"

"I'm working."

"I'm depending," Barney said.

Carrying a bag, he visited with Emanuel Berman of Manny's Radio and Television on Fulton Street. Manny Berman sold radios and televisions and stereos and cassettes and tape recorders, and his employees repaired radios and televisions and stereos and recorders, all of which was a good business, but Manny Berman's chief source of income was the United States government, because Manny was an electronics genius: Manny was number one with Central Intelligence.

"Hi, pal," he said to Barney Wilson.

"Hi, pal," Barney said to Manny Berman.

He was a bandy-legged little guy with a bald head and thick-lensed spectacles.

"What can I do you for?" Manny said, grinning with false teeth.

Manny was going to do him for plenty. Barney knew what he wanted—the latest—and knew it would cost him an arm and a leg. He paid the arm and leg, and came away with a heavy bag. But it contained the best: the stations up there in outer space did not have better. He had the finest little transmitters, the bugs, the best. And for the phones he had New York Telephone Company discs, genuine equipment from the phone company, but within *this* equipment were implanted tiny bugs, minuscule. And the bag contained two exquisite receivers, talkers and tape recorders, on a high band, ultra-high-frequency. It had limited distance—no more than a mile—but it delivered absolute clarity. He was aware of the restraints and was preparing for the UHF restraints: an office in the Armin Building, an apartment close to Armin's duplex.

Barney Wilson came home with his booty, to his pad in Kips Bay, and to Kathy Braxton Kearney awaiting him. Pad in Kips Bay. Bachelor apartment. Three rooms beautifully furnished. 333 East 30th Street. Between Second Avenue and First. A garage in the bowels of the building. Apartment 11-F.

"Got the stuff," he said. Happily. Proudly.

"Of course," she said. "You're Barney."

"Jesus. Stuff. That guy is a wizard. Lemme show you."

He opened the bag. He showed her. He explained.

"I don't understand a word," she said.

"Okay. All right," he said. "Take it from me. This is stuff. The best. Beautiful."

"You're beautiful."

"You're beautiful."

He kissed her.

She kissed him.

"Look," she said.

"What?" he said.

"We're in an interim period."

"Yes. Interim."

"I'd like to go down to visit my folks."

Folks. Her VIP folks. Her mother a stout matron; the father in a wheelchair after a stroke. But pure American folks. In an ancient crumbling mansion outside of Yorktown, Virginia. In a stately mansion, stately folks, poor as fucking churchmice. But very important VIPs. On both sides the ancestors were from the beginning. Came over on the *Mayflower*. Landed at fucking Plymouth Rock. Josh Kearney was no dope. His wife was pure American. DAR. One of her antecedents had been a signatory of the Declaration of Independence.

"For how long?" he said.

"A couple of weeks. All right?"

"Of course," he said. "Give them my love."

"They don't know about you."

"Give them my love anyway."

"All right, I'll do that. Love from a stranger."

"I'm a stranger?"

"Always. You're a stranger."

She kissed him.

He kissed her.

And lifted her, and carried her to the bedroom. And took her. And she took him. Love in the afternoon. Love from a stranger. But which of them was the stranger?

Kathy went away to Virginia, and Barney called Lyle Carter. "How we doing, friend?"

"Armin. The apartment is Twenty-three-C."

"Thanks. Any luck on the females?"

"Got a pencil?"

"A ballpoint pen."

"Three females. All single."

"You're beautiful, Lyle. You are the best."

"Wait till you get my bill."

"I pay. Have I ever quibbled?"

"*You* are the best."

"We are both the best, right?"

"Right."

"Fuck us both. If you've got the girls, gimme."

"Bertha Stanton, Twelve-A. Carla Booth, Twenty-six-G. Beverly Cherner Janos, Fifteen-L."

"Very good. Thanks. You shaping the surveillance?"

"Man, with the advance notice you gave me, if I couldn't shape that, I'd be a real turd, right? Ha ha."

"Yeah, turd, ha. I'll be in touch," Barney said and hung up.

On a Tuesday, August 19, he received a call from Dwight David Hickey. "In like Flynn," Hickey said. "A nice little office, waiting room and inside room. Go down tomorrow to the renting office and sign. A year's lease."

"Where's the renting office?"

"Right there in the Armin Building. They'll know who you are, Bernard Brown."

"I'll want you to furnish it for me. Most important, a big solid desk. With drawers that lock."

"It shall be done, Mr. Brown. It's a nice little corner office. Forty-fourth floor."

"How we coming on the other matter?"

"A nibble. I'll let you know."

"Let me know now."

"You're a tough man."

"I'm the easiest. What's the nibble?"

"There's a sublet at Three-eighty-five East Sixty-seventh. Two small rooms, living room and bedroom. Available October one. A young couple. The husband has a new job in Seattle, Washington. They're going to leave it furnished—but they want seven thousand bucks for the furniture."

"Okay. Don't *hondle* on the money."

"It's not the *hondling*. It's that it's already practically sublet to a young couple coming in from St. Paul, Minnesota. A renting agent here in town is handling it. He needs a bribe to come out from under."

"Well, bribe the fucker."

"We're working on it."

"Sounds good. Don't miss."

"I'll let you know. I'll be in touch."

"Yeah, you do that," Barney said.

On Wednesday he went down to the renting office in the Armin Building. He looked over his office on the forty-fourth floor and signed the lease, paying three months' rent in advance. That same day Hickey sent over the carpet people for the floors. On Thursday the furniture arrived, and the phone was installed, and the gold lettering went up on the outer door: BERNARD BROWN. Centered beneath that, in smaller letters: TRAVEL. And also on Thursday a locksmith affixed a deadlock to the outer door, and one on the door to the inner office. On Friday, Barney Wilson–Bernard Brown came to his splendid new office, carrying a valise. He placed discs and bugs in the top drawer of his huge desk, and also laid in a tall slender wallet of chamois-encased picklocks. He locked the drawer, and from the valise took out the UHF receiver. He looked at it lovingly, kissed it. These were marvelous instruments that Manny Berman had provided. Voice-activated, the tape spun when there was sound at the transmitters. No sound at the bugs and the machine lay dormant. The tape could take twenty-four hours of voice-activated conversation. Push a lever forward and you could clearly hear the conversation as the tape recorded; push the lever backward and the machine was silent while the tape recorded. He placed the receiver in a lower drawer of the desk, locked the drawer.

He spent the weekend as a guest in the house in Chevy Chase. He answered questions and told about some of his initial preparations in New York City.

Back in New York on Monday, returning from lunch to the Armin Building, Bernard Brown, by mistake, got out of the elevator on the fortieth floor. He saw with satisfaction that the entrance portals to Carleton Armin, Ltd., were two floor-to-ceiling heavy-wood doors, now of course widely flung open, revealing a blond receptionist at a steel-blue desk in a vast, steel-blue-carpeted reception room. Far beyond the receptionist were the entrance portals to the offices proper. Two floor-to-ceiling heavy-wood doors, closed.

Bernard Brown worked late that evening, but moved about, observing the habits of the charwomen. On Tuesday a drawer of his desk contained a slender flashlight. On Tuesday he worked late, but moved about, observing the habits of the army of charwomen. On Wednesday he worked late, and knew the habits—those habits that concerned him. By eight thirty they were through on the fortieth floor. By ten they were through on the forty-fourth floor, apologizing to Bernard Brown, who was a late worker.

On Thursday, Bernard Brown worked late, very late, keeping an eye on his watch. At eleven o'clock, pockets filled with bugs, discs, flashlight, picklocks, he went down by the stairs to floor forty. He opened the massive outside doors, closed them behind him. The beam of the flash showed him through the steel-blue-carpeted reception room to the other heavy-wood doors. He opened, closed, flicked on lights. Who could see through two sets of wooden doors? Further, who was looking? Flicking lights, he made his way to the master office. Hey, something! Big. Beautifully appointed; even a tall steel-blue safe. A single door at the rear. He went through it and laughed. A cozy little apartment. This Carleton Armin knew how to live.

Quickly now, Barney working. In the apartment, and out in the office. Screws off mouthpieces from telephones, extracts discs, replaces them with his discs. Plants bugs where they will never be discovered. He knows how. Barney Wilson, working at his trade. Experienced. He has been working at his trade since age twenty-one.

Finished. Done. Going out, flicks off lights. Locks the inner doors. Locks the outer doors. Up by the stairs to the forty-fourth floor. Locks away unused discs, unused bugs, flashlight, picklocks. Closes up shop, and downstairs he signs out.

"Got your car tonight?" the night man asks the new tenant.

"Yes."

"You don't really have to," the night man says. "I mean —any time you work late—I can call you a cab. Be here like in five minutes."

"You're very nice."

"Aim to please."

You bet, thinks the new tenant. Night men are special people who deal with special people. Aim to please. There's always Christmas, and Christmas is only four months away. This night man is a big, burly fellow. His name is Max. He prefers to be called Mac. The new tenant is quick to pick up on nuances.

The night man, with his big key, unlocks the door. "Good night, Mr. Brown."

126

"Good night, Mac. Thanks for the offer of a cab."

"Any time," Mac says.

Bernard Brown drives home.

The Wall Street end of the operation is in operation.

Routine, now. Deadly routine. Essentially meaningless, because nothing can pop until November 8. But in these early days of the Wall Street operation he is at the office at nine in the morning and stays until six in the evening, and he knows more about Carleton Armin than anyone else in the whole goddam world, and is bored shitless with the maneuvers of the making of money. But it's clean money. Carleton Armin is a clean businessman. On the politics he is not so clean, but compared to the Washington politicians, he is positively spotless-sanitary. On the other hand, Arthur Upton had him pegged right—right down there to the marrow of the bones. The guy had a need for power, a drive for power—an obvious, innate, inchoate *lust* for power. If ever he got hold of that Earl Kearney tape, it would be goodbye Josh and hello Carleton. But he would never get hold. Not as long as Barney Wilson was alive.

There were compensations: small flickers of amusement sparked the boredom. We're all human, aren't we? Solidly married, the guy was a cheater. He cheated on his wife with a Suzy Buford, whom he was keeping, and cheated on Suzy with a new one whom he was not yet keeping, a Dolores Warren. He juggled them like a stage magician. Saw Dolores when Suzy was away, held off Dolores when Suzy was in town—Suzy was an airline stewie. The juggling act figured to get more complicated when the wife returned. She was spending the summer at their ranch house in the Adirondacks: she was coming home the day after Labor Day.

Boredom downtown. Breaking in the necessary routine. Sitting and listening. Or going away and coming back and listening to the tape. And at six o'clock, wiping it clean and setting it up for the next day. Downtown: money business and monkey business. But uptown was still wide open. He called Hickey, and kept calling Hickey, and kept getting the same response: "I'm on it, I believe I'm getting there, I'll let you know."

And then on September 15—a Monday—a call. Maiden call. The first incoming call on Bernard Brown's wire. It was Hickey. Who else?

"We got it, kid. You're the next tenant up there."

"You're the next Secretary of Commerce. What?"

"You've an appointment, day after tomorrow. Twelve o'clock noon. Bolan Agency, East Eighty-sixth. Ask for G. B. Bolan. He'll take you over to the flat for a look-see. If you're satisfied, you'll sign the sublet papers right there."

"I'll be satisfied. I'm already satisfied. You just satisfied me."

"Bring a check for seven thousand made out to Bolan Agency. That's for the furniture. Also bring fifteen hundred dollars in cash. That's the personal payment to G. B. Occupancy—October one."

"Good show, Mr. Secretary."

"You're Bernard Brown, travel agent, Wall Street. You live with me up in Scarsdale."

"Till October one. Then I live at Three-eighty-five East Sixty-seven."

"Right."

"God bless," Barney said.

On Wednesday, September 17, at high noon, Bernard Brown presented himself at the Bolan Agency. G. B. Bolan was lank, pale, balding, cavernous. Black suit, white shirt, black tie. He looked like a funeral director. And sounded like a funeral director: a deep voice, pious, sonorous, hollow.

"I'll take you over right now, Mr. Brown. The present tenants, Mr. and Mrs. Purnell, they both work. So the apartment's empty for inspection. All the papers are in order. Just require your signature. This way, please."

He took up his attaché case. They went out to his car. He drove slowly, carefully, but at 385 East 67th Street he parked at a fire hydrant near the entrance to the building.

"Keep an eye on the heap," he said to the doorman. "I won't be too long."

"Yessir, Mr. Bolan," the doorman said respectfully.

They rode up to the tenth floor. The apartment was 10-C and was furnished better than Barney had expected. He had expected a *shlock* deal, seven thousand bucks for some rickety sticks—extortion for the sublet in a modern high-rise. The furniture was quite nice, solid; there was even a liquor cabinet. Low-ceilinged, compact rooms: living room, bedroom, and a tiny closet of a kitchen. The bed in the bedroom was excellent, big and bouncy. Barney smiled. Hickey had said a young couple. For a young couple the most important item of furniture is the bed.

"They're leaving everything, Mr. Brown. Towels, linens, dishes—everything. A rising young executive, Mr. Purnell. Transferring to Seattle. The firm is supplying the Purnells with a fully furnished garden apartment." Bolan chuckled. "Cheaper than moving the stuff by transcontinental van."

"Yeah, right," Barney said.

Bolan opened the attaché case, handed over a typewritten sheet. "The inventory," he said.

"Yes." Barney pretended to look it over. "Very good."

More papers from the attaché case.

"The subleases in triplicate, Mr. Brown. Their signatures are already appended and witnessed."

Barney took a check from his wallet and placed it on the

living-room table. Bolan looked at it, nodded. "Thank you," he said politely and placed it in the attaché case.

From inside his jacket Barney produced a tall white envelope. "The honorarium," he said.

"Thank you," Bolan said. Politely. But he was not too polite to count. It was an easy count. Fifteen one-hundred-dollar bills. He replaced the money in the envelope and tossed it into the attaché case. Clipped a pen from a pocket and clicked out the point.

"You will sign each one of the triplicate."

Bernard Brown signed and G. B. Bolan signed as witness. Barney retained one of the leases; the other two went into the attaché case. "Ah, keys," Bolan said. "These are duplicates. I'll leave the originals with the doorman on October first."

"Not really necessary. I'll probably change the locks."

"As you wish." Bolan closed the attaché case. "I've arranged to have the phone transferred to your name as of October first."

"You're very kind."

"The Purnells will be out by the thirtieth. You have right of entry on the first. You'll send the rental checks to Bolan Agency, the address is on the lease." He extended his hand and they shook. "Good luck, Mr. Brown. Anything at all— don't hesitate to be in touch with me."

"You're very kind," said Bernard Brown.

On October first, a windy morning, Barney Wilson, and the inevitable valise, came to Bernard Brown's new apartment. He took Manny Berman's second receiver to the bedroom and placed it in the bed table, a graceful commode with fluted swing-out doors. The receiver fitted beautifully. Barney patted the table, closed the valise, and stalked about the apartment, examining. Everything in order, everything in shape.

Towels, linens, a fresh bar of soap in the bathroom. Everything clean, shining: Mrs. Purnell had taken trouble. The kitchen drawers contained utensils, clean, shining. One upper closet had dishes, another had cans of food. A lower closet had pots and pans. On the gas stove sat a percolator, clean, shining. He opened the refrigerator. A Tip Top bread in its cellophane sleeve, a closed container of milk dated SEP 30, a see-through sealed package of ham. Good people, these Purnells. Nice people.

In the living room he checked the phone book for a nearby locksmith, and called, and told the man what he wanted.

"Be there in a half-hour," the man said.

"Thank you," said Bernard Brown.

He opened the liquor cabinet and laughed. The racks on the inside of the doors held many glasses, tall, short, all clean and shining, but the cabinet contained a single bottle, an obviously old bottle—a fifth of Canadian Club, an old virgin, its seal unbroken. They were good, nice, clean, considerate people, the Purnells, but drinkers they were not.

The locksmith arrived, installed two secure heavy dead-locks, made his jokes, turned over the keys, received his money, and went away. And Barney Wilson went out into windy October, found a neighborhood liquor store, and came back with a heavy package: three bottles of bourbon, three bottles of Scotch, a bottle of vodka, a bottle of gin, a bottle of brandy, a bottle of sweet vermouth, a bottle of dry vermouth. He threw the cord and wrappings down the incinerator and placed the bottles in the cabinet, all except one: bourbon. He poured into a shot glass, and swallowed. He poured again and raised the glass in a toast to himself. The first stage of the uptown operation was in operation.

10

OCTOBER 6. Monday in Washington. The Hill. The Capitol. It is 2:15 and the galleries are crowded. The word has gone out—leave it to Arthur Upton. The young people are there, fighting for the old people, and the old people are there, fighting for their rights. They are the forerunners, these young and these old, they are the vanguard, but, as Arthur Upton knows, the vanguard must lose. They are out there, and they have always been out there, the beautiful losers of the vanguard. Vanguard. Definition of terms. Those of the vanguard are before their time, and those who are before their time are losers. Sometimes, when their time comes, those who are remembered rise up to martyrdom. Or sainthood. Or are despised as shouters in the wilderness. What is a martyr? What is a saint? What is a man—mortal—in the history of history? Once upon a time, in the history of history, there was a Judas, a mortal man. Judas, predicted by Jesus: necessary to the Son of God. Without Judas—sinner, mortal man, thirty pieces of silver, kiss of death—there would be no betrayal, no arrest, no trial, no crown of thorns, no crucifixion, no resurrection, no redemption, no Christianity as written in the history of history. Judas, weak of flesh, sinner, mortal man —predicted by Jesus as the betrayer.

Did Jesus know? Jesus, who knew of the humanness of humans. Did Jesus know that his necessary betrayer—feckless as all mortal man—would be forever despised? Judas of the Judas kiss—no touch of sympathy for human imperfection, never a breath of compassion for Judas Iscariot. Did the Lord know that this mortal man, weak of flesh, in the history of history would live forever in the mouth of Satan? Did the Lord Jesus know—

Arthur Upton in the gallery among the vanguard. Arthur Upton, theologically wool-gathering, while down there the man is making his speech. Arthur Upton, amid the vanguard, but also amid the press. Upton's people have alerted them and they are here. The press. Not a vanguard. Not fighting for anything except for the headlines of their profession. They are here in the gallery, and down there on the podium the junior Senator from New York is speaking on behalf of the bill he has offered, a doomed bill. Down there on the podium the handsome Senator thrillingly speaks.

". . . we neglect our senior citizens. Our alleged Social Security is the worst in the world. It is neither social *nor* security. These persons have paid—and their employers have paid—over a lifetime of work. It is supposedly a form of insurance, but it is no insurance at all. The present law imposes a penalty. In order for our senior citizens to collect their rightful benefits, they must have no gainful employment; they must be virtually retired. This is wrong. This is manifestly wrong! Why should insurance—paid-up insurance—impose preconditional penalties? Must we retire our older persons— many of whom may be in their very prime—in order that they receive the benefits legally due them? I say no! I say absolutely not! Their insurance has been paid over a lifetime. Its benefits should inure at the time they are due—just like the benefits from *any* insurance policy—no matter what the beneficiary is doing or earning at the moment such benefits legally accrue. But my bill goes further. It reduces the age at which such *additional* benefits will accrue to the aging citizens of the United States. Sixty! For man or woman—sixty! At age sixty, their Social Security will pay them the stipend of their insurance, the benefits to which they are rightfully entitled, whether working or not working. . . ."

Cheers from the gallery. Applause. A standing ovation. And Arthur Upton, standing, applauding, knows nothing will help: this bill will die in committee. But we are not concerned with this particular senatorial bill. We are concerned with *image!* We are concerned with the making of a President. The newspapers will carry the speech, the substance of the speech. With some it will be a front-page story; all will certainly comment editorially. Image! Statesman, leader, the dynamic young Senator fights for the people.

October 9. New York. 3:00 p.m. A call to Carleton Armin.
"Who?" he says to the switchboard.
"Miss Warren."
"Put her on."
"Carleton?"
"Hi."
"Look, I just got a call from Abner Moffit. About that thing on the seventeenth. He'd like to take me. I told him I'd call him back."
Armin smiling. Wise witch. Always tries to be circumspect over the office phone. "Seventeenth?" he says. A small frown. "What?"
"You're going. You and your lady. You told *me.*"
"Oh, that! At five o'clock, cocktails, buffet, and chatter

at Jerry Darcy's townhouse. Then by bus—by festive bus-loads—on to the opera. A gala, at three hundred bucks per person. Benefit for palsy, which is number one with Marion. Next month, for palsy, she goes to Switzerland. For a full month. A world meeting of the panjandrums."

"Pan—what?"

"Big shots."

"Look, I don't care about Switzerland. I'm asking about the seventeenth. Me. I mean, is it all right? I mean, if not, just—"

"Of course it's all right. My goodness, why not?"

"Well, I—"

"You want to go, I assume."

"I'd love it."

"Then call Moffit and tell him. Period, new paragraph. Anything else?"

"Thanks."

"For what?" A laugh. "Talk to you later."

October 17. New York. 3:10 p.m. A call to Carleton Armin from Marion Armin.

"Start moving, dear husband."

"Yes, ma'am. Just clearing my desk."

"I don't want any delays."

"There won't be a one, my love. I'll be out of here in ten minutes. I'll be home before four."

"You're going to have to dress, you know. If I sound like a shrew, forgive. It's just—I promised Jerry we'd be prompt. Gosh, if *we're* not prompt."

"And prompt we'll be, dear love. Five on the button. We'll be there at five, I promise."

October 17. New York. 6:00 p.m. The apartment of Barna-bas F. X. Wilson at 333 East 30th. High excitement but on low voltage. Kathy watches as Barney places discs and bugs in a small, black, doctor-type bag. Then he looks at his wrist-watch, points at the phone.

"Your move, Madam."

"Yessir, Commander."

She dials the number of the Armin residence. The phone rings and rings: then the service answers. Kathy pretends she does not realize it is the service.

"May I talk to Marion, please?"

"They're not at home. Who's calling?"

"Oh. When do you expect them?"

"I don't know. This is the service. Your name? A message?"

"Never mind. Thank you. I'll call tomorrow."

A disconnect, abrupt, before Kathy hangs up.

She hangs up. "Not at home," she says.

"Imagine that," Barney says.

"A Jerry Darcy cocktail party." She had heard the tape: he had played the tape for her in Bernard Brown's office on Wall Street. "And then the opera," she says. "In festive busloads."

"Okay. You ready for *our* festivities?"

"At your service, Commander."

He slips into a dark topcoat, dons a somber snapbrim—and she laughs at the hat. He never wears hats. Now he takes up the little medical bag. "How do I look?"

"Like a doctor. A doctor on a house call." Her laugh is sexy. "If a doctor like you made house calls—he'd sure have a heck of a lot of female patients."

"Let's go."

He points at her mink coat, lying across the back of the couch. He had specifically requested that she wear a mink.

At the corner of First, he hails a cab. They get in, he gives the address. She lights a cigarette, and he reviews the procedure, the entrance procedure: emergency.

The doctor and the mink-clad lady are on their way to Ms. Carla Booth, 400 East 67th, apartment 26-G. Ms. Booth has swallowed an excessive number of Nembutal capsules and then, of course, called her friend to tell. The friend is this mink-clad lady. The friend called the doctor, and here they are. That will be the story, if necessary, to get by the doorman. The doctor and the lady will go up, and in time they will come down, and the lady will slip the doorman a fifty-dollar bill (which now reposes at the tip of her purse). All is well with Ms. Booth; the bribe to the doorman is for the prevention of gossip. Please say nothing to anybody—which is nothing new for the doormen of the fashionable swinging East Side. In the immense buildings that house literally thousands of tenants, intrigue and pay-for-silence is the norm.

"That's our contingency measure," Barney says. "I don't think it'll come to that—which is why we're going at sixish. At sixish, there's a hell of a lot of going and coming. Your mink figures to be the passport. At sixish, I don't think we'll be stopped at the border for visas and interrogation."

There were *two* doormen, but Barney turned out to be right on both of them. The first, the outside man, rushed out to open the cab, and the inside man did not even have the opportunity to open the inside door. A couple were coming out, and the gentleman of the couple graciously held open the door, and the inside doorman smiled benignly while ogling Kathy's mink. Doormen are as expert as the fur buyers at Bergdorf's, and Kathy's gleaming outer garment was utterly unimpeachable.

In the elevator, Barney punched the 23 button and smiled his Barney grin. "We saved the fifty, didn't we?"

"Lord, aren't you nervous?"

"Nothing to be nervous. Something to be nervous, I wouldn't have brung you."

"I'm shitting."

"That's mouth talk. Anytime it gets down to the nitty—my money's on you."

"Me? The weak lady?"

"If you're weak, I'm a eunuch."

"Brother, you're no eunuch. I *know*."

"Sister, you're not weak. *I* know."

They came out to broad, long, thickly carpeted corridors. They found 23-C and Barney rang.

"Suppose somebody answered."

"Simple," Barney said. "Wrong number. I'm a doctor looking for Carla Booth."

Nobody answered. Barney's picklocks opened and they entered.

"Lord," she said. "Lovely. That Marion has taste."

"Glad you like," he said. "I'm not interested. Sit down," he said. "Take easy. Want a drink?"

"Would you dare?"

"There's nothing to dare. If you want, I'll serve you. Then we put away the bottle and put away the glass. Our people aren't due back until after eleven."

"How about servants? Don't they have any?"

"A woman. She comes at ten in the morning, leaves at five in the afternoon."

Kathy sat in a tufted armchair. She wrapped her coat closely around her. "You mean"—she chortled—"you'd really serve drinks?"

"Honey, this is all now apple pie. The one lousy little possible problem—the doormen. Which is why I brought you and your mink coat—the friend of the suicidal Booth. We're past the doormen. Now we're the guests of the Armins. *Do* you want a drink?"

"No. But absolutely—no!"

He removed his topcoat, removed his hat. Disappeared

up a circular stairway. Came back grinning the Barney grin.

"You're right. A gorgeous pad. Separate bedrooms up there."

"One more question."

"What?" He sounded irritable.

"Cloak-and-dagger and stuff and all. Aren't we supposed to wear gloves?"

He laughed. A gutsy Barney laugh. Not irritable.

"Gloves are for not to leave fingerprints. Who cares here about fingerprints? Who's ever going to think about fingerprints? What's going to be disturbed? You sure you don't want a drink—courtesy of the Armins?"

"I don't want a drink. I *do* want a drink. But after we get out of here."

He opened the little medical bag. Went upstairs and downstairs. Unscrewed telephone mouthpieces, removed New York Telephone Company discs, replaced them with New York Telephone Company discs. Then he planted his bugs—in the foyer, the drawing room, the bedrooms, the recreation room, the library, the study. "We're done," he said. He zipped up the little black bag. He put on his topcoat, put on his hat. He locked up and they went down in the elevator. The inside doorman opened the inside door. The outside doorman blew his whistle for a cab.

In the apartment he put away the little black bag, put away the picklocks, flung away his hat. "Okay," he said. "Where do we eat?"

"You're the commander."

"Celebration," he said. "How about the Persian Room?"

"We couldn't get in. Not without a reservation. You know who's singing there, don't you?"

"Who?"

"The gal with the boobs—the Divine."

"Oh, good. Great. Come on. Move it."

"Without a reservation? We'll be on the outside looking in."

"Barney Wilson here. I know the maître. The fifty that was supposed to go to the doorman—that fifty'll go to the maître. And so, no loss. We'll be even up."

"Barney the businessman."

"Yep, that's me."

"Think it'll work?"

"Honey, when you know the maître and you've got a fifty to spare—it'll work. And if your fifty doesn't work, then I'll add a fifty, and for a hundred that maître will not only work —he'll turn handsprings leading us to the table that his flunkies will set up."

They ate, they drank, they enjoyed the Divine. But at ten thirty Barney said, "Time. Back to work. We gotta go test the equipment."

And so out into the October night, and a cab to Bernard Brown's apartment, and inside Apartment 10-C Kathy said, "This is quite nice. Cozy."

He hung her coat away, and his coat, and led her to the bedroom and snapped on the light.

"Oh, my," she said. "What a great big bed you have."

"Better to—" He seized her and kissed her.

Then she drew away from him. "What time do you think your thingamajig will start talking?"

"My guess, not too late. Remember they started out at five. I'd say—before midnight. And no need for any long listen. Once I verify we're receiving, we're in business. No real interest until November eight. We're certainly not interested in the home life of Mr. and Mrs. Armin."

Blue eyes narrow. "I'm interested in a little home life with you."

Dark eyes laugh. "This home is as good as any." He yawned.

She smiled. "Do I detect a lack of enthusiasm?"

"You detect fatigue. I get up too damn early. These Wall Street hours don't agree with me."

"How long will it be—Wall Street?"

He shrugged. "How long will it be—here? Till we get a line on something. I put a lot of bugs in that apartment, but they're only two people, there won't be too much overlap. He's my focus, that Carleton Armin. Because Dwyer *must* go to Armin. Once I get a line on what they're up to, then I pack in Wall Street and pack in this joint."

"And then?"

"Can't predict. But I'll get that tape for Mr. Man, or croak in the attempt."

"Don't say that."

"What?"

"Croak."

"Okay, I won't say croak."

He opened the fluted doors of the bed table, took out the receiver, and placed it on top of the table. He pushed the lever so that the machine would talk while the tape recorded. He touched on the bed lamp and snapped off the overhead light. He removed his jacket, hung it on back of a chair. He pulled off his tie and his shirt. He kicked out of his shoes. "Would you like a drink?" he said.

"No, thank you."

"Mind if I do?"

"Mind if I shower?"

"Be my guest," he said.

He went to the living room, made a bourbon, drank. He turned on the TV, watched for a few minutes—the tail end of a crime show—and turned it off. He went back to the bedroom, and she was in bed, the cover pulled up to her chin.

"You're so beautiful," he said.

"Thank you, kind sir."

He took off his pants, socks, T-shirt, and shorts. Took a cigar from his jacket, lit it. Stood there, naked, smoking his thin cigar.

"Lord, you're a powerful man," she said.

"Fullback," he said and laughed. "Notre Dame, once upon a time." Yawned. "Christ, I'm sleepy."

"Come to bed," she said. "Sleep. When the thing talks, I'll wake you."

He looked for an ashtray. No ashtray in the Purnells' bedroom. Padded to the living room, came back with an ashtray. Laid the cigar in the ashtray and there it died.

"Shower," he said. "If it talks, call me."

"Yessir, Commander."

He showered, toweled, brushed his teeth.

Came out and into bed. Naked to naked.

Her warm hand was on his thigh. His penis tingled.

"It didn't talk," she said.

"Christ, I hope it's working. It's only, y'know, a machine. What time is it?"

She looked at her wristwatch on the bed table.

"Eleven twenty."

"Where the fuck are they?"

He kissed her. They clung, body to body.

"I love you," he whispered. "You are it. Only you. Forever."

"I love you," she whispered. "You only. Forever. I'm so sorry."

"Sorry? What sorry? Why sorry?"

"All those years in between. Lord, why couldn't I have met you—before him?"

"Two sides to that."

She heard his chuckle, the Barney chuckle. Cynical.

"What sides?" she said.

"Before him we were nothing, both of us. Me moving to a government job, and you moving nowhere. Kathryn Braxton, DAR, first people, old Virginny, Radcliffe, stylish and beautiful, but poor as a fucker. But you met him, and you got him, and you moved up into the millions. You have it all. And the next step is the ultimate—First Lady of the Land. Suppose we could push it all back—go back in time—*would* you have wanted me, rather than what you have? The truth."

"I—I don't know. I know I want you. I know I'm glad—God!—that I have you."

"Joshua Fitts Kearney. Mr. Man, the next President. A politician, but a truth-tell with me. Never fucked me, never slipped me an angle. I'm old Notre Dame, Barney Wilson, the All-American prick, conventional, conservative, I go by the rules. Loyal. I am loyal. Mr. Man never lied to me, never pulled any political bullshit. I believe he believes in me, and I believe in him. I believe he would never cross me, and therefore I would never cross him. In his own way he's a crazy man, but who ain't crazy? He has me, he owns me, I believe in him, I worship the son of a bitch. Barney Wilson the prick. When I get truth—real truth—I give back truth. I am Mr. Man's man, and I would die for him."

"But you screw his wife."

"But not screwing him. Ostensibly our secret—but he knows. Therefore, screwing the wife—whom I love—I'm not screwing him."

"What about *his* secrets? He is a man of secrets."

"Not with me. Never with me; he knows his Barney. Maybe even with Upton. Possibly with you. But never with me, because he's wise, he knows his Barney. We're loyal, one to the other, we shoot straight. If not—if I didn't know it as I do know it—I wouldn't let you remain with him. It would be a matter of money—millions. And somehow I'd get those millions, and you'd divorce him and marry me."

"You're beautiful."

She turned to him, and he to her, touching, embracing, and his penis, undirected, slipped into her receptive vagina, and they lay like that, just holding, kissing—and the receiver spoke—and he moved out of her and lay on his back.

It spoke. Clearly. Perfectly. Voices as though right here in the room.

The Armins were home. Talking about Jerry Darcy, the cocktail party, the buses, the opera, and the woman said, "I was most impressed with Abner's young lady. Did you notice?"

"No."

"An exquisite. Absolutely an exquisite. I'm trying to think of her name. Oh, yes. Dolores Warren. Remember?"

"No. In all that gang, probably we weren't introduced."

In bed Barney Wilson laughed.

On the receiver Marion Armin said, "Dark. Slender. Very beautiful. Carleton, you've an eye for beautiful young women."

"There were, my dear, many beautiful young women."

In bed Barney laughing.

In bed Kathy asking, "What's so funny?"

Above them, the receiver talked.

In bed Barney said, "That's some Carleton Armin."

"What—Carleton Armin?"

"Smooth. Plays his cards like poker. The one he's denying having noticed—she's his new girl friend. And with her he's not only cheating on the wife, he's cheating on the old girl friend. A double-header going there, but he plays it sweet and cool. Got to watch your step with him." Sleepily. "A cool customer, our cheating Armin."

"Who are we to criticize cheaters?"

144

"Who the hell's criticizing?"

His hand reached up to the lever, and the receiver ceased speaking. "That's some Manny Berman," he murmured. "Gorgeous equipment."

She touched him. Lewdly. "We've got some gorgeous equipment right here."

He smiled, his eyes sleepy. And she moved to him, kissed the sleepy eyes, kissed his mouth, bit his lip, and her hand went down seeking, and found it, his sword, upright. Sword? A cannon! And swung over him, spread herself over him, high, her knees at the outsides of his hips, and sank down slowly, cunt ensnaring, fully, deeply, a sheath to his sword. Sword? A cannon! And fucked him, fucked the cannon, fucked that marvelous cannon that filled her, fucked, rocked, squirmed, oscillated, ground down on it, pleading, crying, panting, coming, coming on that big thick prick of a cannon, anointing it, leaking herself onto him, hearing his breathing, hearing her own feral hissings, hearing their sounds, the physical, animal sounds, the farting, plopping, body sounds of love, fucking, fucking and marveling, marveling at this marvelous man who knew how to hold it, cannon immutable, unyielding, as she came over it and onto it and into it, climax after climax, until, at last: "Now! NOW!" And only then it exploded, shooting its heat into her, and she fell on him, lay on him, her parched throat sobbing, her spittle drooling on his face.

She moved from him.

She lay, looked at him.

Sleeping. He was already asleep.

She pulled the pillowcase from her pillow, used a corner of it to wipe his face. Sleeping, he smiled. She kissed his lips, lightly, birdlike touching. Asleep, he smiled.

She lay. On the pillow without the pillowcase. Lay. On her

back. Legs stretched, belly taut, heart pounding. Kathryn Braxton Kearney, fully fucked, exhausted, and marveling as always at her marvelous lover. Dear God, what would she ever do without him? Somehow she had found him. In their long search, somehow they had found each other. She loved him. He loved her. Dear God, I thank you. I thank you for my Barney. Barnabas F. X. Wilson. Lord, an extraordinary name.

She lay, and her belly eased, and the thudding heart returned to normal rhythm. Lay awake, alert, ruminating. I am Kathryn Braxton Kearney. I have a lover whom I adore. I have a husband. Once I had neither. Once upon a time I was Kathryn Braxton who was graduated from Radcliffe at age twenty and came up to New York to seek fame and fortune. With Mother's blessing and a letter from Father to a man of distinction at *Time* magazine. Got a job as a *Time* researcher and became a young New York lady about town. Under Mother's watchful faraway eye. Mother, however, did come up for frequent visits, and to talk to friends about a proper match for her nubile daughter, whose credentials were peerless—except that the family had no money.

Peerless family, old America. *Mayflower* on both sides, and Mother's side even had a signer of the Declaration of Independence. Father, until a stroke had made him an invalid, had been a country lawyer. After his stroke, the family had lived on the dividends of inherited stocks and bonds. They did not starve. It was a comfortable income, but not riches. Mother firmly intended that daughter Kathryn would have no such lack. But it was not Mother who had made the match.

An older brother, Ben Braxton, was a chemistry professor at Washington & Lee. Ben and wife Margie had come up to New York for Christmas Week, had been invited by one of Mother's friends to a Park Avenue party; almost as an afterthought, sister Kathryn was also invited. Sister Kathryn had been reluctant, but brother Ben had persuaded her, and there at that party she had met Josh Kearney. Nobody had made the match—no matchmaker.

Kathryn Braxton, never married. Joshua Fitts Kearney, never married. The lady was beautiful. The gentleman was handsome. The lady was a scion of distinguished lineage. The gentleman was a scion of spectacular wealth. And there was even more, a rapport, a subtle commingling of personalities, subliminal comprehension. They fitted. God, did they fit. A perfect fit. This plug in this socket could light all the lamps. And so, seven months after that first meeting, they got married and lived happily ever after.

Kathy Kearney naked. In a strange bed. In a strange apartment. Lying near the man she adored. Kissed his shoulder, and turned from him. Kathy Kearney, no longer a child outrageously flirting at a Park Avenue party; no longer the insouciant researcher at *Time* magazine. Kathy Kearney, age thirty-nine. Tempered, molded, wise, a woman—climbing. They complemented one another, both ambitious, steadily climbing. J. F. Kearney the Congressman. And then the first term as Senator, his reputation growing nationally. Second term as Senator, and the reputation international. And now, soon, the final plum. It. The end. Ultimate. Optimum. The top of the mountain. Joshua Fitts Kearney, President of the United States. Kathryn Braxton Kearney, First Lady of the Land. Soon. Their time was almost at hand. . . .

II

NOVEMBER. A mad month. On the northeast coast November in the fall is as capricious as April in the spring. Today it is warm. The sun shines hotly as the Buick purrs along accustomed roads. Going home. Olivia Bono Dwyer taking her husband home. Smiling. Both her hands firmly on the wheel. In the passenger seat Simon Dwyer, both hands folded in his lap. It is the eighth of the month, a Saturday in November.

"Beautiful." Olivia stared straight ahead, watching the road through the windshield. "For the homecoming, like an omen. Like a day in spring."

"Yes."

"You're so quiet."

"Have I ever been one for nip-ups?"

"No." She laughed. "Never. But I mean. Today. Our day. So special."

"Yes," he said slowly. "It's new. After so long, new. Sitting near my wife. In a car, looking out. The trees. Beginning to be bare. Holding on, conserving themselves to live through the long winter. Sitting with my wife. Looking out. At the trees, bushes, the sky. Just breathing. The sweet, clean air. Free. Outside of walls. After so long, it's all so new. Can you understand?"

"Yes." Her voice caught. "I can understand." She had to hold back from crying.

They were silent.

The Buick purred. Accustomed roads.

She had been driving these roads for ten long years.

"I cooked," she said.

"Yes," he said softly. "You told me."

"Cooked all night. A feast. You'll have to be careful. The stomach. You're not used to rich food."

"I'll be careful," he said.

"A feast. *Banchetto*. A dinner for the homecomer. I hope you'll be hungry."

"I'm hungry already."

Silence. She thought he was thinking about the dinner, a feast, *banchetto* for the homecomer. Whatever, she respected his silence. He was Simon Dwyer, a man for silences. Dear God, especially today.

He sat, looking out through the open window. Breathing the clean, sweet, free air. Watching the barren trees flashing by. Not thinking about dinner. Thinking about stash. Thinking about Carleton Armin. Thinking about eight million to Carleton, and two million dollars to Simon—Simon and Olivia, who would live out their lives in comfort, in peace. Thinking. He was thinking about the manila envelope in Ollie's vault. It contained the blueprint, and Vito's handwritten bequest to Simon Dwyer, and the envelope addressed to Carleton Armin—to be turned over to Carleton in the event that both Simon and Vito died in jail.

The don was dead, but Simon was alive. Alive and well, and riding home in Ollie's Buick. And according to the doctors in the hospital, Doc Dwyer would remain alive for a long time.

"Good old Irish constitution," the doctors said. "An iron constitution. You will live forever."

Manila envelope. There were *two* manila envelopes. He was Simon Dwyer, accountant, a careful man. He had made photostats of the blueprint and the letters. Just in case. In case Ollie died while he was in prison and stupid lawyers took over the vault. He had made photostats, placed them in another manila envelope, and brought that to his sister in Connecticut for her vault. His sister in Connecticut, who despised him. Mrs. Walter Hulett, widow lady, haughty, supercilious, but bone-marrow honest. She would not *dream* of touching that manila envelope unless, as instructed, Vito Arminito died in jail and Simon Dwyer died in jail and Olivia Dwyer died outside of jail. They were all alive—except the don. In time he would go up to Darien and relieve his sister of the guilt that lived in her vault. But not yet. Because Doc Dwyer was still Simon Dwyer, accountant, careful. Suppose, after he gave the blueprint to Carleton, it got lost. Or got burned in a fire or something. There would still be the duplicate in the vault in Darien. Therefore, not yet. He would not remove the envelope from his sister's vault until—

"Envelope," he murmured.

"What?"

Ollie driving. Her eyes on the road.

"In your vault, the envelope," he said.

"What about it?"

"It's there?"

"Where else would it be?"

"Yes, where else?" A little laugh. "Ten years. Weren't you ever curious?"

"No. Like a curtain in my mind. In more than ten years—in a lifetime—have I ever mixed in my husband's business? Have I ever asked, have I ever pried? An envelope in the vault. You told me not to look—unless the don was dead and you were dead. He's dead. You're alive."

"God, I don't deserve you."

"You deserve me."

"An angel."

"A Sicilian woman. A wife. You are my husband. I could not have better. You are the best, the best of men."

"I love you," Simon Dwyer said.

They were home at three o'clock. He changed to slacks and a turtleneck sweater. He went out and walked on the lawns, touched the trees, inspected the garden. He came back to a house redolent with aromas of food. The dining-room table was set—with their best: a damask tablecloth, their china dishes, crystal glasses, gleaming silverware.

"Lovely," he said.

"A *banchetto*," she said. "For the homecomer."

She mixed a martini for him, poured sherry for herself.

He sipped, said, "Ah, good," went to the phone and called Armin's apartment. A woman answered.

"They are not at home, sir. Who's calling?"

"Mr. Dwyer. Did they say when?"

"They should return at six o'clock."

"Thank you."

They ate. Ollie's wonderful food. With red wine in crystal glasses. "You are the best," he said.

"Cook? Or wife?"

He looked at her. His eyes were shy. He said, "I'm going up for a nap."

"Yes," she said.

She wrapped away uneaten food, placed the dishes in the

sink, and went up to him. He was in bed, covered, two pillows under his head. The gray-blue eyes flickered over her. She undressed, right there in front of him, proud to show how well she had kept herself for him. She went into the bathroom, showered, and then came to him. He was nude under the cover.

He took her, gently. Her beautiful man, her passionate man. He was sixty-two, but as firm and eager as ever. She could feel his need, his tumultuous desire. God, a man without a woman for ten years. And yet he was kind, patient, and considerate. Ravenous. Insatiable. But slow and gentle. And then they were lying on their backs and she was weeping, quietly. She could not restrain herself. She wept. And he smiled that gentle smile, held her, and kissed her eyes.

They were still in bed when the phone rang. It was five thirty. She answered, said, "Yes, just a moment," put her hand over the mouthpiece, whispered, "Carlo," and gave him the receiver.

"Carleton?"

"Simon! How are you? Good to have you back."

"Good to be back."

"Called you earlier. You weren't home yet."

"I called you at three."

"I know. I was out with Marion. Shopping. She's leaving for Europe on Wednesday. A month in Switzerland. We just got home, and I was told you called. Everything all right?"

"Yes."

"Need anything? Anything at all?"

"No. But I'd like to see you."

"Any time at all."

"Monday."

A moment's pause. "Monday's impossible, Simon. I'm tied up all day, and in the evening there's a dinner party."

"Tuesday?"

"Tuesday'll be fine."

"Eleven o'clock all right? Your office?"

"Excellent."

"Carleton."

"Yes?"

"It's important. Very important."

Again a brief pause. "If you say so."

"I'm saying so."

"I'll clear all decks. We won't be interrupted."

"Thank you."

"See you on Tuesday."

"Goodbye, Carlo."

Simon Dwyer gave his wife the receiver and she hung it up.

She chuckled. "You forgot yourself. You called him Carlo."

"I didn't forget. In fact, I was reminding him."

"About what?"

"About who he is. About who his father was. And about who I am." Simon Dwyer sighed. "Tuesday morning, first thing, we'll go to the vault."

She nodded. "Then I'll drive you into town."

"No. I'll go alone. I'll take a cab."

She looked disappointed.

He said, "It's business."

"I thought—that kind of business was over."

"Not entirely. A few simple things to attend to. And then that kind of business will be over forever."

Senator Joshua Fitts Kearney and Arthur Upton were in town for the weekend. This weekend commenced on Saturday, November 8. Barney Wilson grinned while shaving—in preparation for dinner at the house on Sutton Place. An important date, November 8—sufficiently important for the clan to gather. And at seven thirty they were gathered, sipping cocktails in the downstairs drawing room.

"November eighth," Upton said.

"A Saturday in the year of our Lord." Barney's mood was waspish. The do-nothing routine was scraping at his nerves.

"What's happening?" Kearney asked.

"Don't you know, Mr. Senator?"

"I do *not* know, Mr. Wilson. Because my Mr. Wilson firmly advised that I keep my fingers out of this pie. Therefore, neither officially nor unofficially have I made inquiries."

"Correct," Barney said. "And you will keep on not making inquiries. As a once-upon-a-time lawyer, you have done your thing for a once-upon-a-time client. You laid in a little weight with Harrison Quealy. And your office was informed that Mr. Dwyer would get his parole first crack out of the box. Finished. You did your thing and you're no longer interested. Hereafter you know nothing about nothing from anything. Especially, you know nothing about a Bernard Brown. That goes for all of you. Remember it. You know *nothing* about a Bernard Brown."

"The commander speaks." Kathy laughed. "When the commander speaks, the crew obeys."

"Is he out?" Upton asked.

"As a matter of fact, Senator, you don't belong in New York. Neither you nor King Arthur. You don't belong at the site of the prospective activities. You belong in Washington, or Europe. Anywhere. Only your old lady belongs."

"The commander speaks," Kathy said.

"Is he out?" Upton said.

"He is out," Barney said.

"How do you know?"

"I have people. On both of them. On Dwyer. On Armin. I call in. They tell me."

"I thought you said," Upton said, "no accomplices."

"They are not accomplices. They are private people working privately—for me on a private affair. They are outside people on an outside matter. When it gets to the inside—I'll be alone."

Kearney said: "He's out? Definitely?"

"He's home. In his house in Queens."

Upton said: "What happens now?"

"They go for the stash, and so do I. They know nothing about a tape, and they know nothing about me. They will do their thing—easily, pleasantly, no looking-over-the-shoulder, no anguish, no competition. And all the while I'm on top of them, in the catbird seat. In my business, nothing can be sweeter. I've got them by the well-known nuts, if you'll pardon the expression."

"I don't care how," Upton said. "I don't care what you do, or how you do it. Paramount. Imperative. Number one. *We must have that tape!*"

"King Arthur," Barney said, "we *will* have that fucking tape."

"You must—"

"I will—"

"Must—"

"Will—"

"Gentlemen," Kearney said. "Gentlemen, please."

A knock on the door. Kearney called: "Come in."

Carl Hoffman. In regalia. Full butler's regalia, including the striped pants. "Dinner is served," Carl Hoffman intoned.

Under his breath Barney muttered, "Jesus, this formal shit."

No one heard, except Kathy near him.

"Commander," she said, "you're a naughty man."

At ten o'clock Barnabas F. X. Wilson paid his respects and took his leave. Routine. The fucking routine. The dull, day-by-day, daily routine was wearing him down. On Wall Street he sat and listened to money deals and the masterful juggling of two sweethearts and a wife. At six o'clock he would erase the tape and set it up for the new day. Then at night to Bernard Brown's apartment, where he would listen to social affairs and lady-chatter, and sometimes an Armin call to Dolores Warren or Suzy Buford. Then he would erase the tape, set it up fresh in the machine, and go home. Always home. He never slept over. Because he had no change of clothes in Bernard Brown's apartment: there was nothing of Barney Wilson in Bernard Brown's apartment except booze and the UHF receiver.

This Saturday night he arrived at Bernard Brown's apartment at twenty minutes after ten. He flung away his topcoat, poured a bourbon, and drank it. He made a highball and took it to the bedroom. He pulled the receiver from the commode, touched the button for talk, and listened to the tape. He heard the morning nonsense in the Armin household, and the early-afternoon nonsense, and then nothing. On Wednesday, Mrs. Marion Armin was going to Zurich, Switzerland, to attend a month-long meeting of the World Conference on Cerebral Palsy, a gathering of doctors, researchers, and the representatives of charitable institutions from every civilized country. Mr. Armin had gone out with Mrs. Armin for shopping. Thereafter, on the phone, Dwyer's brief talk with Armin's maid. The next he heard was dialing—and then Carleton Armin's conversation with Simon Dwyer.

At last! Jesus, finally we're in business!

He reversed the tape, and played that segment over and over. He paced, listened, rubbed his hands. We're in business!

Then he let the rest of the tape go, listening to Armin household nonsense. He erased the tape, replaced the receiver in the commode. He drank down his highball, put on his coat, locked up, and went home.

156

On Tuesday, Simon Dwyer would be in Carleton Armin's Wall Street office at eleven o'clock.

On Tuesday, Barney Wilson would be in Bernard Brown's Wall Street office by ten o'clock.

Maybe, by Christ, earlier.

Correct. Check that. Make it Tuesday at nine.

12

ON TUESDAY MORNING at 11:05 the buzzer made its small sound on Carleton Armin's intercom. He touched a key. "Yes?"

Ron Seely said, "Mr. Simon Dwyer."

"Show him in, please. And Ron—"

"Yessir?"

"No calls. No interruptions. I'm not in to anyone—until Mr. Dwyer leaves."

"Yessir."

Armin clicked off. He rose, came round the desk, stood waiting.

Ron Seely opened the door. Simon Dwyer entered. Seely closed the door behind him.

For moments they stood there: the tall stooped man holding a manila envelope, and the tall dark man smiling his greeting.

Then: "Simon! You look great. Honest—wonderful."

158

Shyly. "Thank you."

The dark man went forward. They embraced. Armin kissed the man's cheek.

"How are you? Everything? Your health?"

"They tell me I'll live forever."

"Good. Good." A graceful gesture toward an armchair. "Sit down, Simon."

"Thank you." Dwyer sat, the manila envelope on his knees.

"May I get you something? A drink? Coffee?"

"Nothing, thank you."

Armin went round to the desk and into the swivel chair. "I can't get over how well you look. I mean—"

"It wasn't too bad. I wasn't—well, an ordinary convict. I lived in the hospital—with privileges. Don Vito. He was a man who knew how. He arranged. For himself, for me."

"Yes. Leave it to my father."

"It is why I'm here. To talk about your father."

"Yes," Armin said patiently. "About my father."

"About money. A large amount of money."

Dwyer smiled at Armin's change of expression. Where the planes of the face had been placid, suddenly they were tense. Where the eyes had been bland, patiently humoring an old man, now they were alert, excited.

"Stash," Simon Dwyer said.

"Please." Armin looked embarrassed.

"What is it, Carleton?"

"I—candidly, I thought you were here to talk about a job. And there damn well *would* be a job for you here. And at damn good pay."

"Stash," Dwyer said.

Armin lit a cigarette. "This is the first I've heard."

"Weren't supposed to hear."

"Why in hell not?"

"A great deal of money involved. For your father to start

all over. He didn't expect to die in prison. Long life in your family. Male longevity. Your grandfather—"

"Still alive."

"You were a young man when we went away. Your father had provided for you. Carleton Armin, Ltd. A businessman, an investment banker. But a businessman can have reverses. If that happened to you—badly—and you knew about the stash, you might be tempted."

Armin inhaled cigarette smoke, nodded. "Wise. A wise man. How much money, Simon?"

"Ten million dollars."

"Ten!" A low whistle. "Ten—" The dark eyes gleam. Then briskly, "Who else knows about this?"

"Nobody. Only me. And I—"

"Just a minute."

"What?"

"He didn't expect to die, but he did. With that kind of money around—why didn't you get word out to me?"

"Same reason as before."

"But what difference would it make? The don is dead and I'm the son. I can't be tempted to steal a stash that *belongs* to me."

"Not entirely. Two million of that ten is mine. The don advised me, in the protection of *my* share, I was to say nothing until I got out."

"But, Christ, suppose *you* died in prison."

"Provided for. If the don died and I died, Ollie was to bring a letter to you. A letter that recited all of the circumstances. She was to bring you the letter and this manila envelope."

Simon Dwyer opened the manila envelope. Of the three items it contained, he handed over two: Vito Arminito's handwritten bequest to Simon Dwyer, and the letter to Ollie.

Carleton Armin read them rapidly. He placed the sheets on

his desk. He took a last puff of his cigarette, tapped it out in an ashtray.

Simon Dwyer said: "You will honor your father's writing?"

"Of course."

"Of course," Simon Dwyer said. "You are the father's son."

"Let me ask you something."

"Please," Simon Dwyer said.

"Two million to you, eight million to me. Right?"

"Yes," Simon Dwyer said.

"But only you know. No one else in the world. Which means—ten million all to you. So why are you here?"

"Two reasons." The thin man in the armchair smiled a thin smile. "Major and minor. May I give you the minor first?"

"You're doing the giving, old friend."

"Minor," Simon Dwyer said. "The money is hidden in a difficult place. I need your help to get it."

"I would say—wouldn't you?—that you could accomplish that kind of help for less than eight million dollars."

"Yes, I believe possibly I could. So now may I give you the major reason?"

"You are the giver, my friend. Literally, in this case, and figuratively."

"Honor," Simon Dwyer said. "I am of the old school. I was brought up under the wing—as were you—of Don Vito Arminito, a man of honor. In intimate matters, in close matters, in *real* matters, men of honor do not cross, double-cross, or triple-cross. Rather, they would die. I desperately want my two million dollars. But I would die—I mean die to death—to protect your eight million dollars."

Carleton Armin in his swivel chair. A prickle in his scalp, a tension in his spine. A bite of tears in back of his eyes.

"Wanna know something, old friend?"

"What?"

"I would die to protect your two million dollars."

"Yes. Yes, you would. You are the father's son."

Armin stood up from his swivel chair. Strolled to the door and turned the lock. A gesture. A symbol. Nobody could possibly enter. Out there Ron Seely was a lock. And before anyone could get to Ron Seely there were locks upon locks: many human beings. But turning this lock was an act of tradition. In the old days the men of honor lived (and died) within the tradition of their symbols.

He glanced at the man in the armchair. The thin smile was broader.

"Just for the hell of it," Armin said and returned to his tall-backed swivel chair. He flicked lint from a sleeve. There was no lint. Flicked at imaginary lint, flicking away sentimentality. Said gruffly, "Ten million. Where is it?"

"Tower Stadium."

"Where?"

"Tower Stadium."

"Tower!"

"Please, may I tell it my own way?"

"Please, your own way."

Armin lit a new cigarette. For moments he held the lighted match, then blew on it and dropped it into the ashtray. Opened his arms toward the man in the armchair. "All yours," he said.

"Tower Stadium," Simon Dwyer said. In the quiet, flat, dry voice. "Ten years ago. Under construction, then. At the tail end, completing construction. Under the auspices of the George B. Ralston Construction Company. I don't know if you remember."

"I remember."

"Don Vito had pushed that contract to George Ralston, and now in return he requested a small favor. Downstairs. Under the concrete stands there would be the many rooms, the offices, all encased in concrete, and now in the final process of construction. The don wanted a little vault within that concrete, but, like, a secret. It would be a small matter for George Ralston, the working chief, to do it by himself.

"We came there early that morning, and George did it— with only me and the don watching him. He was a heck of a great engineer, that George, a strong man, active; he knew his business. We watched. He used wood shorings to make a small vault within the concrete—and then Don Vito himself inserted the two suitcases."

"Two suitcases?"

"George didn't know. The don knew, and I knew, and now you know. Two suitcases containing ten million dollars in cash money. Don Vito put the suitcases in, and George added more wood in front to close the vault, and poured concrete, and then called in his workers to complete that wall of smooth concrete. In time, according to the architectural plans, those walls would be wood-paneled, and that room would be the board room for the directors of Tower Stadium."

"Holy Christ—the board room."

"George gave us a blueprint. A little X, marked in red ink, showed the exact place. George was paid for his work. He did not have to be. Your father had got him the Tower Stadium job—George certainly owed him the favor. But the don was not a man to accept favors for free. In return for that morning's work, and of course the promise of secrecy, your father paid him forty thousand dollars—which went to George's widow. Because on the night of that day, George Ralston was killed, struck down by a hit-and-run driver."

"Yes," Carleton Armin said. Quashed his cigarette in the tray.

"Necessary." The solemn voice did not change timbre. "We were going away for a minimum of ten years. A long time. George could get curious. Your father could not let the stash of his life depend upon George Ralston's curiosity. But

Don Vito was an honorable man. He did not have to pay. George would have done the work for free. Nevertheless, the don, early that day, paid over forty thousand dollars. Which would go to the widow. Please. Can you understand the workings of your father's mind?"

"Yes."

Simon Dwyer stood up. Took the blueprint from the manila envelope, and spread it on the desk. Touched a finger to the X, the red-ink mark.

"There it is. Pinpointed. Ten million dollars. You're the chairman of the board. You can give the order, legally. They drill through and you have it."

"No."

"What the hell?"

"No."

"Why?"

"I'm afraid you've been away too long. Sit down, my friend."

Simon Dwyer went back to the armchair. He sat, crossed bony knees. "What?" he said.

"By what right would I give that order?"

"You are Carleton Armin. You are the chairman of the board."

The dark eyes glittered. "Chairman of the board. Board! There are other directors on the board. I am not alone, sole. I cannot dictate." Carleton Armin leaned back in the swivel chair. "Much to do," he murmured. "Much thinking to do." He smiled at the man in the armchair. "That kind of order— drilling through the wall of the board room—why? Why suddenly am I drilling through a wall of Tower Stadium? No matter what outlandish excuse I could possibly give, there would have to be people present—the very workers—and certainly somebody representing the management. Legally. You said legally. Legally, this kind of operation would have to be supervised. All right." He laughed. A rough laugh. "Let's say I get away with all of it. They drill through. Two valises. Under supervision, we open. *Ten million dollars in cash!* How did I know? Why did I order that drilling in the first place? Whose money is it? How did it get there? By what right can I make claim—"

"Yes." The flat voice broke. A tinge of a sob. "Away too long." A thin hand wiped at the face. "You think. So long. Over the many years. But it does not expand. It contracts. You oversimplify." The thin hands gathered in the lap, fingers enclasped. Tightly. "What do we do?"

"We will do." Carleton Armin sat forward. "But, I'm afraid, *not* legally. I will have my eight and you will have your two." He smiled at the man in the armchair. "What will you do with your two, my friend?"

"Retire. Ollie and I—we will live out our old age."

"Old age? Shame. Sixty-two. You said in the best of health. Plenty of fruitful years ahead. Retire? You're crazy."

"Two million dollars—I retire."

"Be a damn shame to waste a brain like yours. A little rusty after ten years in the can, but rust wears off. I run a big business—"

"I intend to retire."

"As you wish. I'll get you your money and you will retire." He stood up and went near to his father's friend. "Go home, Simon. Rest easy. You have two million dollars—as good as in the bank. I'll take care of this, I'll arrange it. Expensive, it will be damn expensive, but that comes out of my end. Hell, you just brought me a gift of eight million dollars. Go home, my friend. We will have our money. I'll keep you informed, step by step, all the way."

Carleton Armin alone. Pacing. In the massive office. On thick carpet. Stops at the desk. Rereads his father's holo-

165

graph, and the letter to Olivia Dwyer. These writings we do not keep. These writings contain incriminating information. We are not criminals. We are Carleton Armin, Ltd. Slips the sheets into the shredder. Quick crunch of snapping blades. Chopped. Information decimated. Takes up the blueprint, innocent blueprint with a little red X. Slides blueprint into manila envelope. Smilingly turns the dial of the steel-blue safe. Opens the thick, fireproof door, lays in the envelope, shuts the door, and twirls the dial.

Pacing. On the silence of carpet. The name in back of his mind is now at the front of his mind. Antonio Glendo. The only one, of course. The dear and distinguished friend of the dear, distinguished, and departed Vito Arminito. Don Antonio. Now seventy-six years of age. Mafioso of the old school. Godfather. Man of honor. Who, despite his years, is still active and lively, and immensely powerful. And immensely feared. Don Antonio Glendo. Holds daily court, enthroned in a huge armchair, in the rear of his son's restaurant in Lower Manhattan. Nicola's Grotto on Bleecker Street. To which restaurant, at least once a year, Carlo Arminito makes pilgrimage. Not for business. Carleton Armin has no business with Mafiosi. Respect. At least once a year Carlo, son of Vito, makes the respectful journey of homage. To sit with the distinguished friend, the friend of Carlo Arminito's distinguished father. Matters of honor are like matters of church. There are matters to attend, no matter you are Carleton Armin, investment banker, exemplar in New York society, husband of Marion Whitney Armin, a direct descendant of Peter Stuyvesant.

Husband of Marion Whitney Armin. Consulting his desk directory for the phone number. Takes up the receiver.

"Yes, please?"

"An outside wire."

"Yessir."

Dial tone humming.

Armin dials. A thick voice answers.

"Nicola's."

"May I talk with Mr. Glendo, please?"

"Which?"

"Antonio. Carleton Armin calling."

"Just a minute."

Then a thicker voice, phlegmy. "Carlo!"

"Hello, dear friend, how are you?"

"I am fine."

"I should like to see you, Don Antonio. A matter of importance."

"Tomorrow. For the *figlio* of Don Vito—may the soul rest in peace—I have all respect. You will come to lunch. Twelve o'clock. I will push off all others."

"Not tomorrow, Don Antonio."

"Did you not say—importance?"

"Tomorrow my wife is going to Europe. There is packing, and I will take her to the airport. But the day after, *per favore*. Thursday. Is it possible?"

"*Sì*. You will honor an old man for lunch, *figlio mio?*"

"I'll be there promptly at twelve."

"I will await."

"*Grazie.*"

"*Prego,* Carlo. Give an old man's respect to the *moglie*."

"*Grazie.*"

"*Addio.*"

Carleton Armin hangs up. Looks at the receiver. Lifts it again. Dial tone. Still the outside wire. Dials Dolores Warren. Makes a date for Wednesday evening. And Friday evening. But not Saturday, not Sunday. This Saturday and Sunday are Suzy Buford's weekend in New York.

*   *   *

Kathryn Braxton Kearney, responding to a call from Barney Wilson, came to his apartment at seven o'clock. His greeting was brusque: a brush of a kiss at her cheek. He took her coat, but did not hang it away; he flung it away. "We're beginning to pop," he said. "We're beginning to happen. I brought the receiver from the office. I'll bring it back tomorrow morning. I want you to hear. Would you like a drink?"

"If you have the time," she said.

He made a drink for her. Nothing for him.

His eyes were fiercely exultant.

"What in hell?" she said.

"Business. We're beginning to be in business. Sit down, baby. Sit your ass down, sweetheart."

She sat. He busied himself with the recorder, racing the tape until he had it where he wanted it. Then he stopped it. He made an elaborate bow. She admired him, she loved him: Barney Wilson in action. Big, brawny, handsome, gleaming. Bouncing. Crackling. An electric aura surrounding him.

"Ladies and gentlemen," he said. "The next voices you will hear—Simon Dwyer and Carleton Armin. Simon came to Carleton at eleven this morning. Then you will hear a telephone conversation between Carleton Armin and Antonio Glendo."

"Who is Antonio Glendo?"

"Shut up."

She loved him.

"Yessir, Commander."

He switched on the sound. She listened to a conversation between Simon Dwyer and Carleton Armin. Then she listened to a telephone conversation between Carleton Armin and Antonio Glendo. When Barney turned off the tape, her lips were compressed, her face pale.

"Are we in business?" He laughed, teeth flashing.

"I—I'm frightened."

168

"Why?"

"I don't know. I think because, somehow, I sense—violence."

"Violence." His voice grated. "Integral to the human condition. The animal part of the human nature." A mocking frown. "Don't you think you're capable of violence?"

"I—don't know."

"I know. I know you. Superior, refined, cultivated, personification of the well-bred, the gentle gentry. Well, shit, lady. Let them put your back to the wall and you'd come out spitting death."

"It's nice to be aware of your high regard."

"Look, I'm not putting you down. Honey, my job of work in life—the human animal. The shrink studies his specimens in the office. Me—my job—the field worker. I study them in action. We all have an underside, luv. Animal violence. All of us. Some are more quickly capable of animal reaction, some less. You, my dear, in my opinion—more."

"Thank you for your opinion, Dr. Wilson."

"That'll be fifty bucks, Madam."

Coldly. "If the session is over—"

The Barney grin. "How the hell did we get started on this?"

"Who, please, is Antonio Glendo?"

"Tony Glendo. Top Moff. The last of the *real* big boys in New York City."

Finally, Barney Wilson made his drink. Bourbon in a tumbler, a splash of soda, ice. He took it to a chair, sat near her.

"Tony Glendo. A heavyweight. The best of connections. He'll supply the operators. Tower Stadium. Remember that Armin's the bigwig, chairman of the board. An outside job, but an inside biggie. Okay, let's figure it." A grin. "Barney Wilson here." He drank down a good deal of his drink, set away the glass. He threw his head back; the eyes squinted.

He spoke slowly. "Rule of thumb—you keep the personnel down to minimum. The more men, the more mouths. Too many mouths, one is liable to blab. Three. This job—three will do it. Wheel man, electronics man, and a construction-type hood that's good with a jackhammer. And all of them, of course, very good with guns."

"What's a wheel man?"

He drank his drink. He went for a cigar, lit it, came back to the chair. "What?" he said.

"What's a wheel man?"

"Driver of the getaway car. He doesn't go in. He stays at the wheel, where he also serves as the lookout. A most important gear in this kind of machinery. Trouble?—he can drive you right through. Like a horserace, you know? Kentucky Derby. If you're rich enough, big enough, you get the best jockey. Because a great jockey helps the horse. He can get out of a pocket. He can find an opening and drive through to victory. Same goes with a wheel man. In the event of a chase, your wheel man is your last resort. A great wheel man can drive you through to safety. Has to be a guy with cool, with nerve. Glendo'll pick the best—a guy with a proven record on the right side of snap judgments. A guy with a bellyful of guts. In New York there are maybe five-six like that, the top-of-the-ladder boys."

"Name them."

He laughed. "You challenging me?"

"Let's see how good you are, Mr. Wilson."

"Show you how good I am, Mrs. Kearney. I'll name two. It'll be one or the other."

"Name."

"Bobby Morton.   Jake Orin."

"How would I know?"

"What?"

"If you're right—or if you're wrong."

He looked at her. "You'll know."

She had to look away from his eyes. "How will I know?"

"Whoever he is, he's going to die on the job. When you die on a job like that, your name shows up in the newspapers."

She stood up. She went to the bar. She poured more Scotch into her glass and drank. Put down the glass. Did not shiver, but found breathing difficult. Breathed through her mouth, lips parted. But stayed with it. Persevered. She was the helper, selected. Barney Wilson's right-hand man.

"All this," she managed to say, "for the next President of the United States."

"You will be Mrs. President," Barney said.

"Electronics," she said. Staying. Persevering. "The electronics man?"

"He shears through barriers, unlocks doors, handles the telephone wires, discovers the alarm system and cuts it off. And the third of the unholy trio—Mr. Jackhammer. The stash is in concrete. They have to drill." His left hand held the cigar. His right hand picked up the glass. He drank it all down. The glass banged down on the end table.

"What about you?" she said.

"Me?"

"You. What do you do? What next?"

"I sit, I wait, I listen, I watch. I have tails on Armin and Dwyer. Glendo's going to have to put Armin together with the action guys. If necessary, I'll put tails on them, rig bugs where they live, where they work. My hunch, none of that'll be necessary. No pressure on them. A straight deal, no opposition—the esteemed Mr. Carleton Armin is the front man. The operation, the concentration—Tower Stadium. The job —get in there and get out with the stuff. My hunch, I'll get my information just sitting on my ass. Like I'm doing right now."

But he got off his ass. She watched as, cigar clamped in

teeth, he strode to the UHF receiver, took it up gently, placed it gently in a suitcase, and locked the suitcase. And changed. Almost instantly. As though he had locked that hard part of his personality into the suitcase with the tape recorder. He took the cigar from his mouth. His eyes were Barney's eyes, the eyes she knew. His smile was Barney's smile to her, a lover's smile.

"Hungry?"

"I haven't eaten."

"Want to go out for a dinner?"

"Whatever you say."

"I have steaks here. I'll make a salad."

"Whatever you say."

"Can you stay over?"

"Who's going to stop me?"

"Will you stay over?"

"In your present mood—would you want me to stay over?"

"I would want you," he said.

13

T H U R S D A Y. November 13. Carleton Armin in a yellow cab going downtown to Lower Manhattan. Smoking a cigarette. Realizing suddenly. The thirteenth. Thirteen. He is not a superstitious man. But the sudden realization produces a chortle.

"Wha'd ya say?" says the cabbie.

"You superstitious?" says Carleton Armin.

"Superwhat?" says the cabbie.

"Thirteen," says Carleton Armin.

"What the fuck, sir?" says the cabbie.

"Thirteen. Today's the thirteenth."

"Hey. You wanna know something? You're right."

"You superstitious?"

"Oh, *that's* what you said," says the cabbie.

"What I said," says Carleton Armin and litters the New York streets, further litters, by flicking the butt of his cigarette out the open window.

"No sir, I ain't," says the cabbie. "Except like Friday. I mean like Friday the thirteenth. I am not superstitious. But I don't spit against the wind neither, if you know what I mean. You know what I mean, sir?"

"What?"

"Friday the thirteenth it don't fall too often. When it fall, I don' go out in the hack. You know what I mean, sir?"

"What do you mean?"

"I mean I take off the day, stay home. Who needs it to spit against the wind, you know what I mean?"

"Where do you hide?"

"I don' hide. I stay home. Like in bed. Maybe fool around a little extra with the old lady. But don' get me wrong. Not superstitious. Like a black cat, or don' cross under no ladder, or a broke mirror—y'know? But if it's like once in a while Friday the thirteenth, who needs it to spit in the wind? Y'know what I mean?"

"I know what you mean."

The cab, at ten minutes to twelve, stopped in front of Nicola's Grotto on Bleecker Street. Carleton Armin paid the unsuperstitious cabbie and tipped him liberally.

"Thank you, sir. Very much."

"Think nothing of it," said Carleton Armin.

"Thirteen," said the cabbie. "But it ain't Friday. So don't let it get you in your mind."

"I won't let it," said Carleton Armin.

"Good luck to you, sir."

"Thank you," said Carleton Armin.

The cab went away and Carleton Armin went into Nicola's Grotto, a spacious restaurant, the best in the neighborhood, already busy with noontime lunchers. A smiling maître d' greeted him.

"You are alone, sir?"

174

"Alone."

"You wish a table for one?"

"I wish to see Mr. Glendo."

"The senior or junior?"

"The senior."

"You have an appointment?"

"I do."

"Just one moment, sir."

The maître d' went away and came back with Nicola Glendo, dark, tall, bald, immaculately attired. Nicola said, "Mr. Armin, a pleasure."

"I've an appointment."

"I know. Please, this way."

Nicola led Mr. Armin to the rear of the restaurant and through a door to a corridor that took them past the kitchen to another door. Nicola opened that door, stood aside, and Armin entered a large room. Behind him, the door closed softly.

It was a living room with heavy drapes and a Persian rug. The furniture was massive, Mediterranean, the fabrics of gold and green brocade. In the center of the room, a huge mahogany table with carved claw feet; over the table, a Tiffany lamp. At the head of the table in a thick armchair, a thickset man—who courteously rose to his feet and came toward his visitor.

"Carlo. Of honor to receive you."

He was an old man, but he walked with a strong stride. He was a large man with sloping shoulders and a huge paunch. He had a full head of pepper-and-salt hair, and a scraggly walrus mustache. The face was wrinkled, leathery, but young dark eyes, under shaggy eyebrows, gleamed like beads. He embraced his visitor, kissed him. A mephitic odor issued from his mouth, but Carleton Armin did not wince.

"*Figlio*. You are well?"

"Fine. And you, Don Antonio?"

"Eccellente. Come, sit down, my son. We will have the lunch."

They sat at the table, the old man in his huge armchair. Behind the armchair, within reach, a mahogany lowboy supported, among other items, a telephone with many buttons. Don Antonio turned, touched one of the buttons, and almost immediately Nicola appeared. The seated men ordered lunch and Nicola himself served as waiter.

A ritual meal, and Carleton Armin knew the rules. He was an honored guest: one does not disturb the host with mundane matters of business. They talked, pleasantly, of many things—of the revered Don Vito Arminito (may the Lord rest his soul), of Carleton Armin's wife and her charities, of Don Antonio's grandchildren and great-grandchildren. They talked about foreign affairs, and about domestic politics. Don Antonio was very strong for the young Senator from New York as the next President of the United States.

Then Nicola cleared the table, leaving only a bottle of wine and two glasses. Don Antonio reached behind him, opened a box, produced a gnarled black cigar, and lit it. He sat back in the armchair, smiled with yellow teeth.

"So, Carlo *mio.* To what does an old man owe the honor?"

"It is a matter of my father." Armin realized he was speaking a stilted English and realized why. It was an unconscious change in the style of speech; the reason: a conscious deference to the old man in the armchair. "The man who went away with my father—he has recently come out."

"The man Dwyer?"

"You have a remarkable memory."

"Grazie."

Now Carleton Armin told what Simon Dwyer had told him. The stash. Ten million dollars in two suitcases. In a concrete wall behind the wood paneling in the board room under the stands of Tower Stadium. He told that he could pinpoint the exact site. Told about the death of George Ralston, and the marked blueprint now reposing in the safe in his office.

The old man smoked his cigar. "It is of deep pleasure that you trust me with your information."

"You are Don Antonio, a man of honor, a friend of my father. I would trust you with my life, and my wife's life, and my children's lives. If I would not trust *you* with information —then *I* am nothing, a worthless."

"*Sì. Grazie.*" The old head nodded. "The father is dead. There is only one child, the son. The father's money belongs to the son. It is your money."

"My father promised one fifth to the man Dwyer."

"I know you will honor your father's promise."

"Yes. My father wrote it in his own hand."

"Tower Stadium. You are the chairman of the board."

"God, you don't miss a trick."

"To miss tricks—one would not live as long as Don Antonio. So, Mr. Chairman. The Tower Stadium. There is the private police, the inside guards—*i guardiani*—the security. No?"

"Yes."

"Tell me of the security."

"It is complicated."

"Tell the friend of your father of the complications."

Carleton Armin told the friend of his father. "On days when the stadium is in action, like for a Sunday football game, the security staff is augmented."

"Augmented?"

"Increased. There are one hundred men. Many of them trained for crowd control, in case of fights, riots, that sort of thing. On Sundays there are at least sixty thousand people in the stands. And a great deal of money in the till. And on

Sunday the banks are closed. So that money remains over until Monday.

"Then on Monday the security staff is reduced to thirty-six men, mainly as guards for the money. On Monday the money goes to the bank."

"So," the old man said. "We have Sunday. We have Monday. What is—on Tuesday?"

"Tuesday. Generally an off-day."

"How many—*i guardiani?*"

"Twelve."

"So small." The yellow teeth showed in a smile. "I am surprised so small."

"Even smaller."

"Oh? So?"

"Twelve guards, but divided into groups of four. Each group works an eight-hour shift. Eight in the morning to four in the afternoon. Four in the afternoon to midnight. Midnight to eight in the morning. They are sufficient. We have learned by experience."

"Tell Don Antonio of the experience."

"What is there to steal in an empty stadium? The seats?"

A chortle, deep in the chest. *"Sì. Vero."*

"They are there only in case of mischief. Perhaps kids; stupid little vandals. But the alarm system takes care of that. The outside gates are wired. Any tampering with a gate, that immediately registers on an electronic scanning board in the guard room, and the guards know precisely where anybody out there is fooling around."

"Ah, the electronics. It is a magic I do not comprehend. But, my son, there must be more, no? A further alarm system?"

"You are wise."

"I am old. So?"

"Yes. In the guard room there is a second system. Pressure

178

on a white button produces a silent alarm at the Holmes Protective Agency and, at the same time, at the police precinct house."

"How often has this been used?"

"It has never been used."

The shaggy eyebrows came together in a questioning frown. "You can explain this, Mr. Chairman?"

"Don Antonio, for some reason, a sports stadium is like a religious temple. Only a kook would desecrate it. In our present civilization, Don Antonio, there is a veneration for the athletic people. Today's football heroes are, somehow, like yesterday's saints of the church.

"We have learned by experience. There has been no desecration at Tower Stadium. An occasional crazy kid, an occasional bumbling drunk—but nothing of any importance."

"The church of the sports," the old man said.

Carleton Armin lit a cigarette and moved into the heart of the matter. "Don Antonio, there has *never* been a professional assault on *any* off-day stadium—no matter how poorly guarded. What sense? What could they gain? What purpose for professionals?"

"*Sì. Capisco.*"

The old man leaned back in his armchair. He closed his eyes. He was silent for long moments. He seemed asleep.

Then, his eyes still closed, he murmured, "It will be a Tuesday. I do not care of other days. A Tuesday night. We have four guards there at night. They are, by now, lazy. In all the years, nothing has happened. There has been no professional—how did you say, *figlio?*—assault. Never the assault on the church of the sports."

His eyes opened, he sat forward. "Four guards who are guarding nothing. But *we* must have the best. It is a simple job, but dangerous. Because, whoever they are in there—*they* are professionals."

"Yes. Yes, they are."

"Three," the old man said. "Three can do our job. But the best. And therefore expensive. They are going, against armed guards, for ten million dollars."

"They must not know of ten million dollars."

"They will not know of ten million dollars. They will know of two satchels. But they must know they are going against four armed *guardiani*—professionals against professionals. It is not a simple holdup, it is not a simple burglary. They are going—to meet guns. And they must be told. They must be told they can be killed. Therefore—for the best—*we* must be fair. For the best, we must pay—big." He smoked the black cigar. "For the best—and for them to know what they go against—fifty thousand dollars a man."

Carleton Armin did not argue. For the best, he did not argue. For the recovery of ten million dollars, an expenditure of one hundred fifty thousand dollars was cheap.

"Whatever you say."

"I have said."

"I accept."

"Three men," the old man said. He poured wine, sipped. He puffed the cigar. "For the concrete—Joe Stroner. For the wires—Frank Lander. For the wheel—the best in the United States is Bobby Morton. But this Bobby I do not completely trust. A feeling of the soul, if you know what I mean."

"I depend on you, Don Antonio."

"The Bobby is a loner, a bachelor. The best, but a wild one. Could look in the satchels. Could kill his own people and run. Not the Bobby. Will be Jake Orin for the wheel. Yes, we have it the three. Legit. Businessmen. Married. Two with children. Stroner, no children, but *moglie* for which he is crazy. You will have it ready, Carlo, a down payment. I will come to that, the amount. Down payment. If a businessman gets killed, it is insurance for *la vedova,* the widow. You understand?"

"Whatever you say."

"They will come here. Don Antonio will speak. Then he will send them to you. In between, Mr. Chairman, you will think. To prepare a plan."

"I have already thought. I have specific plans."

"Specific?" The grimace was a query.

"I have plans. I have the blueprint. I will have diagrams of the alarm systems. And I do have an overall scheme for the specifics of the action."

"Specifics of action." The bright eyes were proud. "Speaks beautiful, my Carlo, son of Don Vito. So? For when? You have it the plan for when?"

"I wished to discuss that with you."

Don Antonio laughed. "Carlo *mio,* the son of the father. He knows it how to please an old man. To give importance. So. Let us discuss, *per favore.*"

Carleton Armin punched out his cigarette. He stood up, took his wallet from its pocket, took a sports schedule out of his wallet. He went round and laid the schedule on the table in front of the old man. Don Antonio looked without glasses: the don did not need glasses to see.

"Today is Thursday," Armin said. "The thirteenth." He pointed. "This is the football schedule for Tower Stadium." He leaned over the seated man, and together they studied the schedule. "Twelve days from today," Armin said. "Tuesday, November twenty-five."

The old man chewed his cigar. "One month later—it is exactly Christmas."

"Tuesday the twenty-fifth. On Sunday the twenty-third, a football game. On Monday the twenty-fourth, the security staff is still augmented. But on Tuesday the twenty-fifth, there is nothing. The security is back to skeleton. Twelve men, split into four-man shifts. So—that night. After midnight. The old guard is gone, the new ones are settled in. Let us say—one o'clock in the morning. Your people hit the security room, overpower the guards. After that, how long should it take?"

"An hour. Let us give more. They will be out by—the most —three o'clock. So. Now they have the satchels. What do they do?"

"They bring them to me. One of them brings the suitcases up to me at my apartment. My wife is in Europe. I will be there with Simon Dwyer."

"Alone with the Dwyer? Ten million dollars?"

"Don't worry. I'll arrange for security."

"Yes. He does not worry. You are the son of the father. Go now to sit, *per favore*. So I can look on you when we talk it the finish."

Armin replaced the schedule, pocketed the wallet, returned to his chair. The old man smiled, somehow benevolently.

"We must speak now—how is the word? Logistics. You understand it the word—logistics?"

Armin grinned. *"Capisco."*

"I will have them—*tre*—here tomorrow. I will speak. I will warn and they will know. There will be *tre* to be trusted —hundred percent. When you wish them? For discuss— specifics of action."

"First thing next week."

"Monday?"

"Monday's fine."

"Where?"

"My office."

"Che ora?"

"One o'clock?"

"Sì. Lunedì. L'una." Smoked his cigar, stroked his mustache. "So. Now. How is it the word? Yes. Logistics. On Monday you will have it sixty thousand cash. For each man,

twenty, down payment. Then you will tell, discuss—specifics—the action. Then they will do *le preparazioni,* the beginning, the preparations. Then on the Tuesday, the twenty-five, they will do. Then will bring it the satchels to the apartment. You will pay it ninety thousand—balance for the work. He pays, they go, and all is clean all around. If you wish now—ask questions."

"Just—can I trust these people?"

"He does not trust them. Trusts me. You trust Don Antonio?"

"With all my heart."

The old man stood up. Carleton Armin stood up. The old man came round and kissed his mouth.

"Go now. Others to come. It is not to worry, Carlo. For this matter the friend of the father is servant of the son."

"Grazie."

"Prego."

On Thursday when Barney Wilson called Lyle Carter, he was told of Armin's visit to Nicola's Grotto on Bleecker Street, and on this Thursday Barney ordered the procedure reversed. No longer would he call. Hereafter Lyle's people were to call directly to Barney Wilson with whatever they had. From nine to six they were to call at this number—and he gave Bernard Brown's telephone number on Wall Street. After six, no matter the hour, if they had information, they were to call Barney Wilson at home. If they missed him, they were to call again and keep calling till they got him.

"Right," said Lyle Carter.

"Thank you," said Barney Wilson and clicked off.

It was moving. It was moving up. Moving toward crux. He had known from the tape of Armin's appointment with Tony Glendo. Now Lyle's people had verified the fact that Armin had kept the appointment. Crux. The beginning of crux. From here on out it would be a lonely vigil: the full concentration. No sex, no love, no nothing: only the job. No Kathy, no Josh, no Arthur Upton. Nobody. Only Barney Wilson. Happily, gleefully, moving in on the job of work.

14

A T F I V E T H I R T Y on Thursday, Jake Orin started
closing up shop at Nero Car Rental on Merrick Road
on Long Island. Nero was a form of anagram of his last
name. When he had opened the business he had decided to
call it Niro—his surname with the letters reversed. He had
said the name to the lawyer who drew the papers, but on the
papers it had come out Nero. "That's what I thought you
meant," the lawyer said. "Nero. The guy that fiddled. The
emperor of Rome."

"Emperor. Yeah, hell, why not? Leave it Nero."

Now at five thirty in the bathroom of Nero's he was wash-
ing up. Jake the businessman. For which he had to thank
Frank Lander. Nine years ago—Jake was twenty-six, a hard
boy, a muscle, strictly a wheel man—Frank had said, "You
make plenny loot, but you got no cover. A smart guy covers,
and you are smart. Stop pissing it away on the booze and the
broads and get yourself a business. Like that you got your

loot legit, and the Feds won't fuck you away on no income-tax rap."

He grinned at the mirror in the toilet of Nero's—Jake the businessman. Thirty-five years of age, tall, dark, and handsome. Married now seven years, with two kids at home. And here we got Nero Car Rental—a girl at the switchboard, and a good-looking bookkeeper (which I sometimes throw a bang), and a college-graduate fairy which is the salesman on the floor. But we close at six o'clock sharp, because at six fifteen Jake Orin has dinner with the wife and the kids. In his beautiful home in Valley Stream—ten minutes from the place of business. An eight-room house with a big yard in back and a very high fence. The fence had been trouble because on the other side of the fence, in a lousy little four-room cottage, there had lived a young guy and a young gal, and when the fence went up, the young guy had come around to the Orin house. "What the hell you think you're doing?" the young guy said. "You can't put up a fence like that. Eleven feet. It's a violation. You're blocking my sun."

"I'm giving you privacy, prick. And it ain't costing you a dime."

"Now you look here, wise guy. You take it down, or I go to the authorities."

Jake hit the young guy and broke his nose, and five minutes later the young gal was in the Orin house, screaming. "Animal! Oh, you're not going to get away with this. We'll go to the District Attorney. We'll put you behind bars. My brother's a lawyer."

"Fuck your brother."

"Animal!" She rushed at him. *"Animal!"*

He hit her in the mouth and broke four teeth, and half an hour later the cops came, and they all went down to the precinct house, and the young couple swore out a complaint for assault and battery, and the next day Jake went round to the four-room cottage and laid a gun on the living-room table. "You show up for that hearing," he said, "and you will be fucken dead. Do I make myself clear?"

Nobody showed up at the hearing, and the complaint was dismissed, and two months later the young couple sold the cottage to an old couple who moved in with the fence and did not complain, and Mr. Orin was a pleasant and peaceful neighbor.

Now he came out of the bathroom, washed and combed, and at six o'clock he locked up and drove in the Caddy to Valley Stream, and kissed his wife, and kissed his kids, and sat with them at the table for dinner, and the phone rang.

"What the f—" He looked at the kids, smiled. He said to his wife, "Always in the middle of eating. Must be one of your bingo girl friends. If it's for me—tell them he ain't home."

She answered on the kitchen extension. She listened, nodded, said, "Just a moment." She laid the receiver down carefully and went to her husband. "For you," she said.

"Jeez, din I *tell* you—"

"It's Mr. Glendo."

He stood up. "I'll take it in the bedroom," he said, and ran up the stairs.

On this Thursday, Frank Lander changed from his coveralls at a quarter to six. Frank Lander—proprietor of Horatio TV Repair Shoppe on Horatio Street in Greenwich Village. He knocked off at six, but the shoppe remained open until midnight—in the charge of Harry Manley, the night manager. Four years ago the night man had been Al Haley—until Frank Lander discovered that Haley had a side business going: Al's TV on East 38th Street. He did not discharge Haley, but one day Haley did not show up for work on Horatio Street. He had been found in the back room of Al's

TV, with his face very blue. He had been strangled, and his neck was broken. That was when Harry Manley had been elevated to night manager and had been made privy to certain confidential information.

"He was humping me," Lander told Manley. "Putting the boots to me, running this Al's TV on Thirty-eighth. I got friends who don't like it the boots to me. So Haley goes to his fucken Maker and you are the new night man. All I ask, don't never try to hump me. I pay you good—I pay the best. You get worried with the inflation, ask for a raise. You got trouble at home, you need a loan, anything—tell me, talk to me. The one thing I can't take, it rips me in the gut—just don't never try to hump me."

Harry Manley never tried to hump his boss because he knew a bit about his boss's background. As a young man Lander had been a crack repairman, a troubleshooter for New York Telephone. Then the company found out that Lander was doing tap-work for outside parties, and fired him. Then Lander went to California, where he mixed with some very hard people. He was arrested on a murder knock, but was acquitted because at the trial the prosecution's evidence got turned around. Then he came back to New York and opened up the Horatio TV Repair Shoppe. Today he was forty-four, a pale man, very strong. Family man. Lived in a swell apartment on East 72nd. Two kids away in college, one kid, the daughter Debbie, still at home.

Now Frank, out of his coveralls and in his civvies, slapped the back of his night man. "Don't let them give you no wooden nickels, kid."

"Right," Harry said. "Good night. Take care."

Frank Lander went out to his Caddy and rode up to 72nd Street. Parked the car in the inside garage, took the elevator to the sixteenth floor. Used his keys to enter the apartment, hung hat and coat in the foyer closet, and his daughter ran to him and kissed him.

"Hi, Dad," she said.

"Hi, Deb," he said.

"How did it go this livelong day?"

"I didn't take no wooden nickels."

In the living room his wife kissed him and he kissed her.

"You got a call," she said. "You're to call back."

"Sure," he said, "but not till I'm good and goddam ready. First we eat. I'm hungry."

"No," she said. "It was Mr. Glendo."

"Oh," he said, and quickly went to another room and closed the door.

On this Thursday, at ten after five, Joe Stroner in the Caddy was tooling up the West Side Highway. Having quit, promptly at five, Stroner Construction Corporation on Tenth Avenue and 43rd Street. He wore neither hat nor coat, but the heater in the car was going. He was still in his working clothes, smelly and sweaty, because it was Thursday, and Thursday was one of his fucking days with his remarkable wife. She knew nothing whatever of his outside activities.

Nobody knew, except those who had to know. Because those who knew could be, however unwittingly, dangerous. He remembered Johnny Mack. Now, so long after, remembered Johnny Mack. Joe Stroner. In the expensive Caddy. Driving the long drive to his lovely little home in a corner of the Bronx—Throgs Neck. Thinking about Johnny Mack, a good guy and a good worker, but, the way it turned out—dumb.

Once, long ago, Joe Stroner had had a partner in his modest construction business, a smart man, an honest man, and a damn good businessman: Felix Ginsburg. So there had been this contract for an outside job, and Johnny was the helper.

So Joe goes to Detroit for final instructions, and Johnny, the dumb bastard, takes it into his mind to talk to Felix, the partner, believing the partner is a part of the operation. And Felix, who is smart, pumps the shit out of Johnny, who is dumb, and then when Stroner came home, Felix took him into the office for a talk.

"We must split," Felix said. "You buy me out—or I buy you out."

"Which way do you want it?"

"I buy you out."

"Right," Stroner said. "Let it rest for a few weeks, and then we pick it up. Okay?"

"Okay," Felix said, and then he had said, "Look, Joe. I want you should understand. What you personally do is not my business. I know nothing about."

"Thanks. You're a good man."

That week the operation was done, with Johnny the helper, and the next week Felix Ginsburg was shot to death outside his apartment house, and that same week Johnny Mack was found in the driver's seat of a parked car with five bullet holes in back of his head. What must be must be. Felix had to go because he was an outsider who had inside information. And Johnny Mack, good man, good helper, had to go because he was just too goddam fucking stupid.

Which is why Astrid Stroner, remarkable wife, knew nothing of outside activities. Knowing, the very knowing, is already dangerous. What you do not know cannot hurt you, and Joe did not want his wife ever to be hurt. He loved her, he was crazy about her, his remarkable fucking wife. She was his age, forty-six, and as big and beautiful as ever. Big. Joe Stroner was a large man, bulky, florid; he weighed two hundred thirty pounds, most of it bone and sinew. But his wife—almost—matched him. One hundred and ninety, that Swedish goddess, and she carried it like a Swedish goddess. Hell, she was only three inches shorter than him; his goddess was five foot eleven. And built! Christ! None of that hundred and ninety was fat; all of it was strong, firm, hard, glistening white flesh. Married twenty-five years and the fucking was better than ever. Three days out of every week they fucked like mad; Saturday and Sunday it was nice clean fucking, with showers and stuff, but Thursdays it was dirty fucking, and he loved it, and had taught her to love it. On Thursdays he did not shower back at the plant; and on Thursdays she cleaned the house and did not bathe. On Thursdays it was dirty fucking, filthy, smelly, stinking, animal fucking, and they loved it, they both loved it.

Now at Throgs Neck he pulled the car into the garage, went round to the door. He did not use his keys. He rang the bell. He wanted to see her when she opened the door. He kept ringing. Finally, she opened. In a pale green housecoat. Her long blond hair hung loose. Her face, without makeup, was perspiring. He kicked the door shut. He plunged a hand into the housecoat and grabbed a huge hard tit. She laughed. He kissed her, his tongue deep in her mouth. He took her to the bedroom, tore off the housecoat, tore out of his clothes, threw her to the bed. She kissed him, bit him. He turned her over, kissed the cheeks of that bountiful ass, reamed her asshole. The phone rang. He released her. She turned over, lying on her back, the curved white body gleaming in sweat. The phone kept ringing.

"Shit," he said. He took up the receiver, barked, "Yes?" Then more softly, "Oh. Yes." He listened. Then he said, meekly, quietly, "Yessir. Yes. I'll be there." He hung up.

"Who was it?" she said.

"Nobody," he said, and parted her sturdy thighs and rammed himself into her.

15

THEY ARRIVED SEPARATELY on Friday, Lander at a quarter to three, Stroner at ten to three, Orin at four minutes to three: their appointment was for three o'clock. Nicola placed them together at a square table at a side of the room. It was an off-hour: it was not busy. He served them white wine in small glasses. Wine. Not whiskey. In small glasses. They would be cold sober when the old man wanted them. At three thirty Nicola received his buzz, went to the men, said, "Okay," and led them through.

"*Grazie,*" the old man said to his son.

"*Prego,*" the son said and went away.

Don Antonio was seated in his armchair at the head of the table. Near him were a bottle of wine, a glass, and an ashtray. For all the rest the table was shining, bare. No glasses for the visitors, not even ashtrays, and for these visitors the old man did not rise.

"*Buon giorno,*" he said. "Sit."

They sat. Respectfully. They did not speak, they did not smoke. They were killers, murder was integral to their work, but they were each acutely aware that they were rank amateurs as compared to the smiling, pleasant-faced old man with the walrus mustache. This was Don Antonio Glendo, man of honor, man of his word, a man who could be kind and thoughtful and gentle, but do not ever cross him because he could produce death more quickly in more ways—

"*Signori.*" The don wet his lips with wine. "We have to do. A nice job. A big payday. Now, *per favore,* you will listen very careful." He spoke slowly. He told of the date, and told of the details of the job at Tower Stadium. Told of the four guards. Told that the boss of the job was Carleton Armin. "He is banker. A fine *galantuomo.* I know since a little boy. Now is Carleton Armin. Was once Carlo Arminito, the son of Don Vito Arminito, rest in peace. Was the good friend, Don Vito. So. On Monday you will go to *il signore* Armin. It is Armin Building on Wall Street. You will be at one o'clock. *Il signore,* it is the chairman of the board of the Tower Stadium. He has it blueprint, diagram, all. He will lay out for you everything. He will give—specifics of action." The old man reached back to the lowboy. He lit a gnarled black cigar. Eyes gleaming, he looked from one to the other to the other. "So? We understand?"

Lander said, "Just, if you please, Don Antonio."

"What is?"

"You mentioned big pay. Please, how much?"

"Fifty thousand dollars. Each man."

Orin smiled. Stroner nodded.

"Fair enough," Lander said.

"It is to remember, you go against guns. I have told—four guards, lazy, they will not expect. And I have the best—Joe, Frank, Jake—the best. Should be *facile.* But. When guns, can happen. To get killed." He tapped the middle finger of his right hand against his chest. "Is here Don Antonio Glendo," he said proudly. "He have picked special—Joe Stroner, Frankie Lander, Jake Orin. So, also, he have arranged it with the money. On Monday, one o'clock, in the Armin's office, my special people, he will get, each one—like down payment—twenty thousand dollars. It is to give to the *moglie.* It is like—how you say?—the insurance. For the wife in the house, the missus. If goes wrong, you know?" He smoked the cigar, chuckled. "Will not go wrong. So. The night, the *martedì.* You do job, you get satchels. You bring to apartment of the Armin. He gives balance of money. Ninety thousand cash bucks. *Finito!*"

"Goddam fair enough," Stroner said.

"Is also fair the other way."

"What other way, Don Antonio?"

The old man put the cigar in the ashtray. He leaned forward in the armchair. The gleaming eyes gleamed differently. The thick voice was thicker.

"What is in satchels—for you, you, you"—a finger pointed at each of them—"not your business, not your job. You take from Tower Stadium, you bring to Armin apartment— that is it the job, nothing else. No funny business, no fuck around. Fuck—is dead. You are dead. Also—more dead." The finger pointed at Stroner. "The blond *moglie*—dead." The finger pointed at Orin. "The *moglie,* the two kids—dead." The finger pointed at Lander. "The *moglie,* the boy in the college, the girl in the college, the girl in the high school—all dead." He leaned back in the armchair. Took up the cigar. Smoked. Smiled. The bright eyes gleamed pleasantly, paternally. *"Scusi, amici. Mi dispiace.* Is necessary, one time, to say the bad words. Is not necessary for special—for Joe Stroner, Jakie Orin, Frankie Lander. But is necessary—any time, anybody, even special—to say *once* the warning, to remind." He looked toward Stroner, the oldest of the trio.

"*Scusi,* Joe. You will not be dead. The big blonde *moglie,* she will not be dead."

"You betcha," Joe Stroner said.

"So. Is now all. *Finito.* You will go to the Armin on Monday, one o'clock."

Glendo stood up. The others stood up.

"Is one more little thing." The don stroked his mustache, smiled yellow teeth at Joe Stroner. "The night on the job, you go in like one o'clock. By three—should be finished."

"If we hit at one, we'll be out way before three," Lander said.

"So," the don said, still looking at Stroner. "Joe, you know my number in my house. It is this a personal matter to me— a job for the dead Vito Arminito. I will be waiting to hear. So. The job it is *finito.* So before the delivery to the Armin, you will step in some place and you will call me in my house. You will tell me all is well. Then I will be able to sleep."

Stroner braced his huge shoulders. "You will get your call, Don Antonio. If not"—his mouth opened wide in a deprecating smile—"all your boys are dead."

"We will not be dead," Orin said. "This job is a wrap-up. Could be other people will be dead—but not your boys, Don Antonio."

"You will get your call," Lander said. "Before three o'clock."

"*Grazie.*"

"Don't mention," Lander said.

Don Antonio Glendo stood tall. His gaze at Frank Lander expressed his feelings for Frank Lander: dirt. "I will mention," Don Antonio said. "You are not a companion of the heart. You are a worker for pay. It is something to understand."

"Yessir," Lander said. Lamely.

"*Ciao,*" the old man said.

"Ciao," Joe Stroner said.
"Ciao," Jake Orin said.
"Ciao," Frank Lander said.
"Buona fortuna," said Don Antonio Glendo.

Early this Friday, November 14, Ollie Dwyer drove Simon Dwyer to Connecticut (with permission from the parole officer) to visit his sister. A short visit. Mrs. Hulett served tea, then took them to her bank vault and returned Simon's manila envelope. The Dwyers drove back to Queens, and there Simon Dwyer transferred the envelope to Ollie's vault.

On this Friday, Barney Wilson, with lunch sent up, spent the entire day, nine to six, in Bernard Brown's office, and the UHF receiver, talking most of the day, gave him nothing. Gave him legitimate Carleton Armin financial business. Gave him the fact that Suzy Buford would be in New York for the weekend. And Lyle's people, over the phone, gave him the same load of nothing. Simon Dwyer's wife had driven him up to his sister in Darien, Connecticut. Sister took the Dwyers to her bank. Simon came out carrying a manila envelope. Back home, the Dwyers brought the envelope to Mrs. Dwyer's bank vault. And Mr. Carleton Armin, carrying a briefcase, had also gone to a bank today—downstairs to the vaults—and he had then returned to his office. That was it.

At six o'clock Barney Wilson went home. Cooked and ate a dinner of spaghetti and meat balls. At ten o'clock, to Bernard Brown's apartment. Listened to the tape, erased, returned the receiver to the bedroom commode. Back at home, a call from one of Lyle's people: Armin was out on a date with Dolores Warren. Well, hell, good for Carleton.

Drank bourbon. Watched a late movie on the TV.

At one o'clock he went to sleep.

196

16

W EEKEND COMMENCING Saturday, November 15.

Kathryn Braxton Kearney and Joshua Fitts Kearney, at home in Chevy Chase, host and hostess at a brilliant weekend party attended by political VIPs. Kathy would prefer to return to New York on Sunday, but Barney has instructed that she remain at Chevy Chase until further notice.

Weekend commencing Saturday, November 15.

Carleton Armin and Suzy Buford—but no contact most of Saturday. He had called, and called—nobody home. Finally, at seven o'clock she answered.

"Where the heck have you been?" he said.

"I'm hungry," she said.

"Me too," he said. "Where would you like to eat?"

"How about Monsignore? I love the food, the atmosphere, the strolling musicians."

"Right. I'll make the reservation. Pick you up in half an hour."

"No. I'll meet you there. Seven thirty? At the bar?"

"You all right, Suz?"

"Just fine."

"You sound—a little dippy."

"Woman's prerogative."

"Seven thirty at the bar," he said.

When he arrived at seven twenty-five, she was already there. The maître d' gave him a smile that was all teeth. "The lady awaits," the maître d' said. He led them to an excellent table. He loved Mr. Armin, who was an old customer and also a generous tipper. But he loved Mr. Armin even more because over the years Mr. Armin had given him some damn good tips on the market.

At their excellent table they ordered cocktails, ordered food, and over the cocktails he said, "Where've you been all day?"

"Home."

"Home?" A querulous squint. "I called. A lot."

"I know."

"You—know?"

"I wasn't answering the phone."

"Weren't— Why the hell not?"

"Tell you later. When we get back to the apartment."

He was Carleton Armin. Lifelong ladies' man. Aware of the vagaries of the female of the species. Therefore he did not press. He grinned, raised his eyebrows, cocked his head to a shrug of shoulders—but did not press the point.

They ate—the wine was champagne. They talked, chatter, but, somehow, all evening, stiffly. They came home to Central Park West at twenty after ten, and immediately he realized a change was in the offing. He did not have to be an oracle to divine the change. There were bags all over the place—packed bags.

"What the hell is going on?"

"I'm moving out."

"Moving where?"

"I'm getting married."

"You are getting—*what?*" He tried, valiantly, to conceal elation.

"Carleton," she said, "you know you love it."

"I know only—I love you."

"God, I admire. The bullshitter's bullshitter. Carleton, you're beautiful." She kissed him.

"Who?" he said. "Where?"

"West Coast. Los Angeles."

"How old?"

"He'll be thirty-five in January."

"That's good. At least, *that's* good. Another old guy like me, you don't need."

"I don't, don't I? Do I?"

"What's his racket?"

"Lawyer."

"Lawyer." A shrug of expressive Italian shoulders. "Eh. How's he fixed in the money department?"

"Rich. Very rich."

"Very rich is very good."

"Rich by inheritance, and rich by work. Oil wells in the family."

"Oil wells is very damn good."

"A brilliant lawyer with an excellent practice. A gorgeous mansion in Beverly Hills. We're getting married the day before Thanksgiving. I've already quit my job. We're going to have a lot of babies."

"A lot of babies is the way God wants."

"Yeah, God," she said. "Whatever is here is all yours. For your next girl."

"Next girl," he said sadly. "There won't be a next girl for a long time."

"Of course not," she said and laughed and kissed him. "Carleton," she said. "Two years. Two—in a way—wonderful years. You've been good, sweet, charming, beautiful. But we've had our time, haven't we?"

"No," he insisted.

"It's over, dear friend. Wish me luck."

"Buona fortuna," he said. *"Auguri."*

"Thank you. I leave tomorrow. For good and all. It's been something. Really. Two crazy years. The growing up of Suzy Buford. The education of Suzy Buford. The—"

"Tomorrow's Sunday."

"All day."

"Today's Saturday."

"All day."

"There's all night in between."

"Doesn't ever miss a trick, does he?"

"I love you."

"Yeah."

"Let's go to bed."

"Yes," she said. "Last time."

Weekend. Barney Wilson. Lonely, lousy weekend. No trips to deserted Wall Street. Trips to Bernard Brown's apartment and quick-listens to the nothing-crap on the tape in the commode. But this is the job, and you have to stay close, because the fat is in the fire. Something is going to happen.

When? Goddam, when?

17

MONDAY. Monday morning. Promptly at nine, Barney Wilson in Bernard Brown's office. Jacket hung away, tie pulled down, shirt collar open. Smoking the fucking cigar and listening to Carleton Armin's fucking financial crap and bored to fucking tears. But this is Barney Wilson here. Once a spook in the CIA. He knows. In his time, he has learned to cope. You sit. You do nothing. You eat down ennui like a dog eats down the afterbirth placenta. In cloak-and-dagger there *are* high points. There are the moments of crazy danger, the insane moments of jagged hazard. The life-fulfilling, self-proving, peak moments of high adventure. But in essence they are—moments! Overall, in the long term, there are the other moments, the cumulative moments that can go to days, weeks, months; that can lump together like the wild cells of cancer in the crippling disease of boredom. You have to watch out for that sickness. If the boredom catches up with you—give up. If your attention begins to waver—get a replacement, because you are a detriment. Barney Wilson here, long in experience. Once head of the division, Deputy Director for Plans. Barney knows: The chief virtue of an effective undercover agent is his stubborn capacity for abiding patience.

At noon he called down for lunch. Poked at the food, ate without appetite. Sat in his fancy swivel chair and listened to the receiver talk.

The gentlemen appeared at one o'clock, and Ron Seely, as instructed, immediately ushered them to the sanctum sanctorum. Three well-dressed gentlemen, one of them quite handsome. Seely held the door open, and the gentlemen entered, and Seely closed the door, and Armin stood up and locked the door.

"Carleton Armin," he said.

The pale man said, "Frank Lander."

The one with the steam-shovel shoulders said, "Joe Stroner."

The dark one said, "Jake Orin."

"Please be seated."

They sat. Armin opened the steel-blue safe, took out a leather briefcase, and from the briefcase he extracted three letter-size envelopes and gave one to each man.

"Please count your money, gentlemen."

While the gentlemen counted, Armin returned to his swivel chair and laid the briefcase on the desk.

When the gentlemen were finished counting, Armin said, "Satisfactory?"

"We are at your service," Stroner said.

"A simple job," Armin said. "Tower Stadium. Four guards —guarding nothing—in the guards' room. They should be easy to take. I mean"—he smiled—"they won't, quite, be expecting you."

202

"Consider them taken," Stroner said.

"Then, in the board room, you drill through for the suitcases. I assume Don Antonio told you."

"He told us," Stroner said.

"I assume he told you when."

Orin said, "The night of Tuesday, November twenty-five. We hit at one o'clock in the morning."

"Now then," Armin said. "Blueprint." He took the marked blueprint from the briefcase. "Who's the blueprint man?"

"Me," Stroner said. He stood up and went to the desk. Lander went with him. They studied the blueprint as Armin explained, his finger moving. ". . . and here the cashier's office, and along here the various other offices, and here the guards' room, and here the board room. Now here—that little red X —that's where you drill. Behind that concrete—the suitcases."

"Beautiful," Stroner said.

"What about the alarm system?" Lander said.

Armin drew sheets from the briefcase, parchment sheets with intricate diagrams. Lander studied them carefully, and now there was general discussion of the alarm systems—the scanning board in the guards' room, the white button that could touch off a silent alarm to the Holmes Agency and to the police precinct house. Armin said, "There are similar white buttons in the other offices."

Jake Orin joined in none of it. He sat sprawled in a leather easy chair, smoking a cigarette. Now he said, "Mr. Armin."

"Yes?"

"The don he said you were gonna give us, like, the game plan."

"Yes, game plan," Armin said. "Now, gentlemen. The entire grounds of Tower Stadium are enclosed within heavy-aluminum, spike-topped, chain-link fences, twenty-four feet high. All the gates in these fences are thoroughly but separately wired. Tampering does not set up a general alarm. Tampering with a gate *does set* up a buzzing in the guards' room, and the appropriate spot lights up on the scanning board. Thus the guards can quickly get to whatever drunken fool or crazy kid is bumbling around out there—but without undue, unnecessary howling sirens. The *gates* are wired, but, of course, all those miles of heavy, spike-topped fences are not wired. Now then."

Armin pulled the blueprint near, and his finger was moving again. "The westerly fence at the rear of the stadium runs six hundred yards, and it fronts upon nothing. Across the street are empty lots and broken-down, boarded-up, abandoned buildings. Quite desolate there. The street is dark; there's only one dim lamplight at the far corner. So, if I may —my suggestion." He looked up at them, grinned. "You can, of course, reject my suggestion. You're the professionals. Me —I'm not even an amateur."

"My money's on you," Stroner said.

Armin was back to the blueprint. "Here." His finger pointed. "You cut a small wedge in the fence. Sufficient for you to get through. Of course, you'd have to know, you'd have to see—"

"Mr. Armin!" Jake Orin again, languid in the easy chair. "Mr. Armin," he said and his grin was arrogant. "Like you said, Mr. Armin, you are nothing. We are the pros. It will all be checked out, in advance, in the daytime."

Carleton Armin kept his temper. They *were* the pros, but, even more, they were Don Antonio's people. And what was at stake here—only ten million dollars.

"Don't mind Jake," Stroner said. Joe Stroner was an old-timer, and he was going to earn fifty thousand dollars, and he didn't want a young prick like Jake Orin to fuck up the deal. "He shoots off with the mouth," Joe Stroner said. "He's still wet behind the ears."

"Fuck your mother," Jake Orin said.

"I don't even listen to him," Stroner said.

"Best wheel man in the business," Lander said.

"*Your* mother too," Jake Orin said.

"How about Don Antonio's mother?" Armin said.

"What?" Jake Orin said. "Wha—?"

"Mr. Orin," Armin said, "I wouldn't want to complain about you to Don Antonio. Or would it please you if I did?"

"Okay, okay," Jake Orin said. "I am just a young prick who shoots with the mouth. Please don't take no offense. Make believe I ain't even here."

"Right," Frank Lander said. "You ain't even here."

No reply from the glowering Jake Orin. He smoked his cigarette.

"Mr. Armin," Joe Stroner said. "Please take up where you were at. I apologize for the prick. He ain't used to good company."

Jake Orin dumped the butt of his cigarette into a stand-up ashtray. His eyes were hot, but his mouth stayed shut.

Carleton Armin's finger was on the blueprint. "You've cut through. You are here—within the outer grounds. But the stadium itself is a concrete fortress. There are many entrances to the stadium proper, but those are all huge steel doors with heavy bolt-locks. And, as Mr. Lander was able to ascertain, that alarm system is different. Anyone tampering with *those* doors is already within the premises; not some idiot fooling around at the outside fence-gates. Bells ring, sirens scream, and the scanning board in the guards' room comes alive.

"Further, and as an added protection—that alarm cannot be cut off by slicing through any single wire. Each door, with a separate alarm system, is interconnected with the alarm systems of the other doors. The turn-off is internal. Many separate switches must be pulled inside the guards' room."

"Just a minute," Jake Orin said.

"Here we go again," Stroner said.

"No, serious," Orin said. "Mr. Armin."

"Mr. Orin?"

"The don, when he told us, he told us about the changing of the guards. Three eight-hour shifts. Right?"

"Right."

"The old ones go and the new ones come. Doors have got to open. So? Do they have to cut off the whole fucking works for that? And like what about if one of the inside guys wants to go out? Like for a fast blow-job with some broad parked out in a car or something? They don't figure to have to pull a zillion fucken switches. I mean, one of them guys just steps out to get his cock sucked. Man, them guys that make them alarms, they ain't no dummies born in fourteen-ninety-two or something. Them guys know how to figure angles."

"In a way he's right," Lander said.

"He's entirely right," Armin said.

"Like how?" Joe Stroner said.

"Here." Armin's finger at the blueprint. "There is this one door—this door in the north corner. The alarm system at this one door can be operated externally and manually." From the briefcase he produced three keys, and then the finger was again at the blueprint. "Now, here. Around the corner from that north door—a metal box set in the wall. The box contains nothing—except a keyhole." The finger, off the blueprint, pointed. "This small key opens that box. This one— this long thin one—fits the keyhole inside the box. You turn it all the way to the right and you shut off the alarm system of that one particular north door. You withdraw the key and lock the box. The north door can now be opened without alarm. And this key—the big one—it opens that steel door. Once inside, whoever has the keys, he locks the door. Then he uses the small key to open the metal box on the inside. Slips the long thin key into the interior keyhole, turns it all the way to the left, and the alarm system is on again."

"Beautiful," Lander said.

"I cannot be deprived of these keys. In view of what we intend to occur, I must be able—whenever in the future called upon—to present my keys to whoever may be properly investigating. And in view of what we intend—there will be investigation."

"Hey, the don din tell us wrong," Jake Orin said. "This Mr. Armin—this is no dummy. Smart in the head."

"Thank you," Armin said.

"No sweat," Lander said. "I will take the keys. I will make duplicates. And I will bring you back your keys before five o'clock."

"I presumed that that was what would be done."

"He presumed," Jake Orin said. "Hey, I'm really beginning to like you, Mr. Armin."

"Thank you," Mr. Armin said.

"Mr. Armin," Joe Stroner said.

"Mr. Stroner?" Mr. Armin said.

"Like—I'm curious. How *does* it work—the changing of the guards?"

Armin leaned back in the swivel chair. He took a cigarette from a pack. Orin jumped up and lit the cigarette.

"Thank you," Armin said.

"Think nothing of it," Orin said. "My pleasure."

"How does it work?" Stroner said.

"When the new ones come," Armin said, "the old ones are expecting. Regular hours, you know? The new ones rattle the outside fence-gate, and it shows on the scanning board in the guards' room. One switch turns off that alarm system. Then one of the old guards goes out for the new complement through the north door, that manually operated steel door. He escorts them in, and then one of the new ones escorts out the old ones. He locks up, and all the switches are on again."

"Yeah, beautiful," Lander said.

"In the bag," Stroner said. "In my humble opinion, this

is a piece of pie. We hit the joint at one o'clock. It don't figure for more than an hour—hour and a half the most. Then we deliver them valises to you, right? Your apartment."

"Four Hundred East Sixty-seven. Twenty-three-C. If you please, just one of you. The doorman will know, he'll be expecting a man with two suitcases. Not unusual. I'm in the money business, gentlemen. There are times when negotiable securities are delivered at odd hours. Yes, Mr. Stroner. Delivery for delivery. I will have the bags, and you—or which of you delivers—will have ninety thousand dollars in cash." Armin stood up. "That should do it, gentlemen. All clear?"

"Just one thing," Lander said.

"Mr. Lander?" Armin said.

"Mr. Armin, Don Antonio has give us the office on you. One hunnert percent. So we ain't worried about the ninety thou. What *I* am worried—it's them bags. We don't know what's in them bags."

"Precisely," Carleton Armin said.

"Believe me, we don't wanna know. What I mean—we don't want nuthin to happen to them bags after delivery, y'unnerstand? I mean if something gets fucked with them fucken bags after delivery, the don can figure maybe we pulled a *shtick*. If the don figures like that, it can be fucken unhealthy for us, if you know what I mean, Mr. Armin."

"I know what you mean. But nothing will happen because nobody knows about any of this—except us. So the don would be correct. If anything did happen, it *would* happen because one of you tried to pull off a *shtick*. I'm sure nothing will happen. On my part—for your protection and mine—I intend to take precautions. I shall alert several of my own security people. Once the bags are delivered, my people will remain with them for the rest of the night. In the morning, the contents of the bags will be properly disposed of."

"Hey," Jake Orin said. "This Mr. Armin is a Mr. Armin. Man, lemme tell you. No grass grows under *your* tires."

"Thank you. Any further questions, gentlemen?"

"I think we got it all," Lander said and took up the keys.

"Like you are already in the bag with them fucken bags," Orin said. "You got them as good as if right now."

"Goodbye, Mr. Armin," Joe Stroner said. "See you the night of the twenty-fifth."

Barney Wilson.

In the office of Bernard Brown.

Flips off the tape recorder. No more need.

We have it. We have it all. They go in on the night of the twenty-fifth. Today's the seventeenth. Plenty of time. For the new preparations and the canceling of the old. A glance at his watch, a quick grin. Buttons his shirt collar, pulls up his tie, slips into jacket and topcoat, and out to the bank. There he closes out the Bernard Brown account. Takes ten thousand dollars in cash, the rest in a cashier's check made out to Barnabas F. X. Wilson. Then back at the office he dials the Carter Agency, gets through to Lyle.

"Call off your dogs. The job is finished."

"You're the boss."

"I want the bill."

"When?"

"Now."

Lyle laughed. "How about sooner?"

"Don't you want to get paid?"

"I do."

"I'll be up there within an hour."

"You'll have your bill."

"Nothing in writing. A verbal bill."

"Right. Verbal bill."

"Thank you very much," Barney said.

He unlocked the desk, took his bag from the closet, and transferred the stuff from the desk. He cleaned up the office: nothing much to clean. He slipped into his topcoat, took up the bag, went down for a cab, and waved goodbye to Wall Street.

At the Carter Agency on 57th Street, he chatted briefly with Lyle, paid his bill in cash, and went home. There he emptied the bag, and took it with him to Bernard Brown's apartment. Placed the UHF receiver in the bag, cleaned up (nothing much to clean), took up the bag, went down for a cab, and waved goodbye to 67th Street.

At home he endorsed the cashier's check, filled in a deposit ticket, slipped the check and the ticket into a mail-envelope, licked on a stamp, went out to the chute in the corridor, and mailed the mail. And did a little jig out there by the chute. End of Bernard Brown. No more Bernard Brown.

Back in the apartment he called Dr. Michael Boysen at his office at 900 Fifth Avenue. A secretary—or a nurse or whatever—answered. Naturally. Doctors do not answer their phones.

"May I talk to the doctor?"

"Doctor's busy."

Naturally. Doctors are always busy.

"Will you tell him, please, Barney Wilson."

"You wish him to call you back, Mr. Wilson?"

"I wish him."

"What is your number, Mr. Wilson?"

"He knows my number."

"Thank you, Mr. Wilson."

"Just a minute."

"Sir?"

"When?"

"I beg your pardon?"

"When—will he call back?"

"Oh. I can't quite say, sir. I would say within an hour."

"Would you—or somebody—tell him, now, that I called?"

"Yessir. We will do that, sir."

"Thank you."

He hung up, made a bourbon and soda, thought about Dr. Michael Boysen, and liked what he thought. A good guy, Dr. Mike; a crazy guy, damn valuable. Each to his own: we all fit within the niche—or the grave—that our unconscious has dug for us. Dr. Michael Boysen was a GP who in his time had done a hell of a lot of good work for CIA people in need of emergency repairs. This particular doc happened to fit that particular niche. First off, Doc Mike had an innate spirit of derring-do. Next, he was a damn good doctor and absolutely trustworthy. And third, and most important, he was in love with money—especially the kind of money he did not have to report to the IRS. Dr. Michael Boysen was a proven commodity.

It did not take an hour.

The phone rang in ten minutes.

"Barney, how are you?"

"Very sick. It hoits me here."

"You? Nothing ever hoits you. With patients like you, doctors would starve."

"When doctors start starving, we're at the millennium. I want to talk to you, Mike."

"You're talking to me, Barn."

"Wanna talk to you personal."

"Hang a minute." A murmur. "Let's see now. My last appointment—five." Louder. "How about six o'clock?"

"Where?"

"Here."

"You got a date, Doc."

At six o'clock Barney Wilson, equipped with cash, rang the bell at 900 Fifth, waited many minutes, rang again, and then Dr. Michael Boysen opened the door.

"Were you napping, Doc?"

"In the bathroom. You caught me in the middle of a piss."

"Hope you shook it all off."

"I didn't." Boysen grinned. "This here is a patient who's hoiting."

"What I'm going to lay on your desk—hoits. Me. You it won't hoit at all."

"This way, Mr. Wilson."

The doc was fifty, looked forty. Lean. Tall. A tucked-in stomach. Blond hair, smiling eyes, a ruddy complexion. Young. Must be one hell of a bull with the women patients.

Barney followed him to the consultation room. There the doc opened a cabinet and produced medicine. A bottle of bourbon, a bottle of vodka, two glasses.

"No ice?" Barney said.

"Please! This is a doctor's office."

Barney laid a thousand dollars on the desk. "Tuesday. Next Tuesday night, the twenty-fifth. Will you be available?"

"What time next Tuesday night, the twenty-fifth?"

"After one in the morning."

"I'll be home. In bed with my wife."

"Will you be available?"

"For the wife?" A grin.

"For me." An acknowledging grin.

The young eyes danced. "What do you have cooking, Mr. DD/P?"

"A private job. Could be I'll take a bullet. Maybe more than one. If so, not a job for a hospital. Can be very embarrassing—in a hospital a patient with bullets."

"Yeah, I've heard."

"If I take bullets, I'll call you—if I can. If I'm in too bad shape, someone else will call. If I'm dead—I won't call. But, possibly, someone else might."

The doc poured a small vodka.

"Well, here's to you," he said and drank.

212

"If I don't take any bullets at all"—Barney pointed at the desk—"then the fee is for being available. Will you be available?"

"I will be available."

"Thank you, Dr. Boysen."

"Not at all, Mr. Wilson. Have a drink."

Mr. Wilson had a drink. "I hope you earn that fee for just staying in bed with your wife."

"That could mean—you're dead."

"The way I mean it—no bullets."

"I would love it. A thousand dollars for sleeping with my wife, I would love it. On the other hand, I would hate to lose my favorite patient."

"I don't intend for you to lose me."

"I'm all the way with your intentions."

Now Barney poured. A short vodka for the doc, a not-so-short bourbon for himself. "Well," he said, "here's hoping nobody calls you on the night of the twenty-fifth. Here's hoping you've earned yourself a freebee."

"Correction. Here's hoping that nobody calls me because nobody's accumulated a bullet."

"Right you are, Dr. B. Here's hoping."

He ate a steak at Moriarity's. With salad, a boiled potato, and green peas. And coffee and a chunk of coconut pie. And paid, and went out, and into a cab, and home, and called Kathy in Chevy Chase. "Darling!" she said.

"Mr. Man around?"

"You kidding?"

"Where?"

"At a stag dinner for the Senator from Oregon."

"What's his schedule for tomorrow? Afternoon, tomorrow?"

"I—don't know."

"Whatever it is, it's canceled. Tell him that when he comes home. We have a meeting, important. Tomorrow, twelve o'clock noon. You, me, The Man, and Upton."

"Where?"

"Your house. Chevy Chase."

"I'll be glad to see you. Lord, it's been so darn long."

"Yeah. Can't talk. Got things to do. See you tomorrow."

Hung up and started the packing. Not much packing. The two UHF receivers and the picklocks. There was nothing else that had to do with the preliminary preparations. He donned his topcoat—then went to the bar. He filled a flask with bourbon, stuck the flask in a pocket of the topcoat. Picked up the bag, locked up, took the elevator all the way down to the garage. His car was a black compact Mercedes, a four-door sedan in its paid-for space in the garage. Opened the trunk, laid in the suitcase, locked the trunk. Unlocked the driver's door, got in, started the motor. Pulled out, braked the car at the garage door. From the glove compartment he took out the remote-control contrivance, and pushed the button. The garage door rolled up, and the Mercedes rolled out.

He drove all the way, without stopping for food or coffee. He nipped from the flask. On the road he stopped here and there where a station was open and gas was available. He arrived at his home in Georgetown in the dead of night. He opened up, put the car in the garage. He took the bag into the house, and took the contents of the bag up to the attic. Set away the receivers and the picklocks with other stuff up there in the attic. There was other suchlike stuff in the attic. Hell, why not? Barney Wilson here, once with the CIA. Barney Wilson, DD/P.

Downstairs in the bedroom, he stripped off clothes and showered. Went to bed. Set the alarm of the clock, and pulled up the covers. Slept like a newborn baby, sweet and peaceful. No dreams, no nightmares. Slept like dead.

18

A T T W E L V E O ' C L O C K N O O N they were gathered
again in the house in Chevy Chase: Big Four. Bar-
ney told his story and they listened, rapt. He told it all without interruption and when he was finished Kathy said, "Dear
Jesus, Lord."

"It's all mine now," Barney said.

"You and who else?" Upton said.

"Me alone."

"Now just a minute."

"All the minutes you like, Professor."

"Assault on Tower Stadium. Three professionals. And you
say: you alone. I respect your high regard for yourself, but
you must respect what's at stake here."

"I respect," Barney said.

"How—alone—can you possibly handle it?"

"I know precisely how I'm going to handle it."

"I asked how?"

"If you don't mind, I'd rather not discuss it."

"Why in hell not?"

From inside his jacket Barney produced a silver cigar case (Kathy's gift). From a side pocket he brought out a gold lighter (Kathy's gift) and snapped flame to a long thin cigar.

"Mr. Maestro," he said to Upton. "Mr. President," he said to Kearney. "Gentlemen, you are lawyers. Certain criminal acts may be involved in the rescue of the tape. I believe—correct me if I'm wrong—that if I disclose such criminal acts and you discuss them with me, then you yourselves are already guilty of a crime. True or false?"

Kearney smiled. "Technically, yes."

"Such discussion would render you—accessories before the fact." Barney grinned toward Kathy. "How do I sound, Mrs. Man? Sufficiently pompous? Sufficiently legalistic?"

"Leave me out of this."

"No, you I'm leaving in."

"Now just a minute," Upton said.

"Professor?"

"Cockiness becomes you, Mr. Wilson. You're our adventurer; you *are* our cocky boy. And we've never interfered in your matters; left it all to you. But this time it's different. This one is it! If you fail, *there are no more matters!*"

"I'm aware, and I agree. Which is the reason there can't be even the slightest taint. J. F. Kearney *must* not be involved. Nor you. Simply, I don't want you people mixed up in anything that's even faintly criminal."

"Professionals, you said. Three professionals. And on the other side—you alone."

"I'll do it."

"But if you don't—"

"Then I retire," Kearney said.

"You're not going to retire, Mr. Man."

"Three against one," the old man said. "That's bad odds.

Barney, you're CIA. You know people, trustworthy people."

"There are no trustworthy people. Not on a deal like this."

"People who can help, who can reduce the odds. People—"

"Mr. Maestro, there ain't no such people. Christ, I'm back to the beginning again. My job—that tape. The reason I'm after that tape—is to prevent blackmail. If I bring in people, they'll know what I'm doing, and once they know what I'm doing—*they* can blackmail. That's the amateurs' game—frying pan to fire."

"But what about professional odds? Three against one?"

"What I intend—the odds are in *my* favor."

"And what I'm asking—what do you intend?"

"We keep going round and round the mulberry bush."

"I'm afraid I must insist. I believe that in this particular matter—"

"I don't give a damn what you believe."

"Now, look here—"

"Hold it!" Kearney raised his hands. "Let's just settle down, please. Arthur," he said, "you know my instincts, my form, my direction. I believe in the delegation of authority—provided the delegate has the full confidence of the believer. We're a team, but we each have our function, and we *must* believe, one in the other." He pointed a finger at Barney. He said slowly, "I want that tape. I don't care how you get it—I want that tape."

"You'll have it."

"You believe you can do it alone?"

"Practically alone."

"Practically?" Upton said. "Now what does that mean—practically?"

"His job however he wishes," Kearney said.

"Thank you," Barney said.

Kearney sighed. "Whoever the leader and no matter the cause—delegation of authority is a major precept."

"This is my husband, folks." Kathy applauded. "He is it. The divine, the selected. Who else in all this world can deliver a full political speech in one sentence?"

"Thank you, my dear," Kearney said.

"She'll be my helper," Barney said.

"Who?" Upton said.

"Kathy," Barney said.

"Are you drunk?" Upton said. "Have you been drinking?"

"Cold sober," Barney said.

"Then what in hell?" Upton said. "You just stated you were Barney Wilson alone. No old friends from the CIA, no cohorts, no accomplices. So, now—*Kathy?*"

"Not an accomplice," Barney said. "But I'll need somebody near—one of *us*—in the event of emergency. Not you." He pointed the cigar at Upton. And pointed the cigar at Kearney. "And certainly not you. Tomorrow, I want Kathy to go to New York, to Sutton Place, and stay there till after November twenty-five. But you two—I'd like you out of here. Out of the States. During the hot period, far away. Australia, or something. Can you arrange Australia, Mr. Maestro?"

Arthur Upton went to the bar. The first one of the Big Four, the old man. Poured a gin and drank. Smiled.

"In December," he said slowly, "the British Foreign Secretary is coming to the U.S. Unofficial visit—guest of Senator J. F. Kearney. Those arrangements have been made." He smiled toward Kearney. "We can nail that down—*I* can nail that down—and the press people will play it up." He smiled toward Barney. "Suppose Senator Kearney, and party, flies off to London on Thursday. For a quick visit to England—and a hint of personal talks with the British Foreign Secretary."

"King Arthur, the image maker." Barney bowed.

Kearney said, "We'll return on the morning of the twenty-sixth."

"Sutton Place," Barney said. "Your house in New York."

From the house in Georgetown, Barney called Nate Hanna Lingle in Baltimore, Maryland.

"I need a thing, Nate."

"Right. Come tomorrow. Four o'clock."

"What's the price these days?"

"Three thousand."

Barney whistled. "Used to be fifteen hundred."

"Them days are gone. Ever hear of inflation?"

"I've heard."

"You buying?"

"See you tomorrow at four," Barney said.

And so on Wednesday, Barney drove toward Lingle's Sporting Goods Store in Baltimore, Maryland. Lingle's was a three-story building wherein one could purchase anything from a basketball to a hockey puck to a fishing rod to a hunting rifle to the complete equipment for a safari in Africa. Nate Hanna Lingle's vocation was merchant, but his avocation was something else again. He was a learned gunsmith, a superb artisan who custom-created exquisite firearms for rich and proper gun-lovers who could afford to ride an expensive hobby. But his masterpiece, although for the rich, was not for the proper. He called it the Hanna Special and he supplied it to the upper crust of the underworld, and to such of the upperworld as Barnabas F. X. Wilson. It was the most efficient lethal instrument that Barney had ever handled, and it was the favorite weapon of the CIA spooks. The Hanna Special was a lightweight submachine gun, snub-nosed and built along the lines of an M-16, but it contained its own silencer, a noise-suppression device constructed within the armature. Pressure on the trigger of a Hanna Special produced a continuous sequence of high-velocity bullets but with scarcely any accompanying sound. A gorgeous weapon.

At five minutes to four Barney locked the car in the parking lot, entered Lingle's, shook hands with Nate, and went with him to the private quarters on the third floor. There the transaction was consummated and Barney emerged from Lingle's with a fully loaded Hanna Special innocuously wrapped in thick brown paper.

In New York on Thursday morning he visited Bloomingdale's for less deadly purchases: a gray blanket, a heavyweight black wool suit, a black turtleneck sweater, a pair of black sneakers, tight-fitting black gloves, a suit of longjohn underwear. He met Kathy for lunch, then went home with his package, unwrapped it, and put the things away. At one thirty he left the apartment, took the elevator down to the basement garage. He backed the car out of its slot, drove to the garage doors. Took the remote-control appliance from the glove compartment, touched its button, and the garage door rolled up. He rode through and behind him the door came down and locked automatically.

Timing himself, he drove up to the 59th Street Bridge, and across, and thence at an even pace to the Deaver Hotel in Jackson Heights, Queens. The Deaver, within winding roads, sprawled over two acres of grounds, a series of contiguous cabins. He knew the place, but he had not been there in a long time: not since Kathy. It was a good, solid, clean, well-kept motel, and, once registered at the Deaver and given a key, the guest (and companion) never again encountered the lobby, the office, or the desk clerk. You go with your key to your specified ground-floor cabin, park your car outside it, and privately enter for whatever your dalliance.

He arrived at the Deaver in thirty-five minutes. From the garage of the apartment on 30th Street to the Deaver Motel in Jackson Heights: thirty-five minutes. He did nothing at the Deaver. He entered at one end, drove through the winding roads, came out at the other end, and, again timing himself, continued to the Tower Stadium in Flushing. The time from the Deaver to Tower: thirty minutes.

Reconnoitering, he drove slowly along the rear street of Tower Stadium by the high, westerly, chain-link fence: truly a deserted area. He made a right turn, and a little way up the other street—a flaky, boarded-up warehouse with a long, narrow drive-ramp, asphalt cracked and pitted: that would be the place to park the car. He did that now, as though in rehearsal. Turned off the ignition, pulled the key, and strolled around the corner to the street with the westerly fence. Deserted. It was bright daylight, sunny November, but not a soul in sight. Of course. What soul? Who would want to *be* here? There was nothing here. Blank. On one side a high, spike-topped cyclone fence. On the other side, old, filthy, closed buildings: rotting, crumbling, vermin-infested. Smiling, he strolled. He could see the outer walls of the stadium, far in, perhaps a quarter-mile from the westerly chain-link fence. Strolled, grimly smiling, observing sharply. The street lamp, at the other end, was a great distance away—therefore Armin's people would work the job from this end. He crossed the street and inspected among the ramshackle abandoned buildings. A rat scurried across his shoes. He kicked at it and the rat ran. Christ, look at that bastard. Big, fat, with a thick tail. Where in hell do they get the food to fatten up like that? And then here—perfect. A slanting, peeling, falling-down house, but with a deep, dark, dirty, angled-off entranceway. Perfect! He knew, now, exactly how he would work *his* part of the job. And there was the rat again, sitting there, looking at him. Christ, you're a real fat bastard, aren't you? He found a stone, threw it, and the rat disappeared. He stood still for moments, waiting, curious. The rat did not come out again.

Hell, rat, we all have got to live, huh? In the great overall scheme of things we all must have a purpose. What's *your* purpose in the scheme of things? The rat did not come out to evince reply, and Barney shrugged, sighed, strolled round the corner, and got into the car. He drove home at an even pace.

19

F RIDAY. Morning. Carleton Armin. A call to Simon
Dwyer. "Would you like to come in for dinner, Simon?
I've been working. You know?"

"I didn't call to inquire. I felt that whenever—"

"Whenever is shortly, my friend. I'd like to acquaint you—"

"Just a moment, Carleton." A silence. Then Dwyer said,
"Why don't you come here for dinner, Carleton? Ollie's just
dying to cook a meal for company. You know—*italiano.*"

"Yes." Armin laughed. "I accept. Damn good idea. You
know Carlo, the man of the grand appetites. Gourmand,
gourmet." He laughed again. *"Porco. Porcello.* Ask Ollie
what that means."

"Six o'clock, Carleton? Is that all right?"

"Love it."

"See you at six, then?"

"Splendid, my friend."

*　　*　　*

Carleton Armin came with a hamper containing six bottles of champagne, only one of which was drunk during the dinner—a leisurely, expansive, succulent, old-fashioned Italian dinner (with many courses and home-baked bread)—and after the dinner, old-fashioned Italian Ollie discreetly removed herself and left the men alone, and Carleton opened a second bottle of champagne, and drank, and informed Dwyer in detail of the proceedings that would produce ten million dollars in Armin's apartment on the night of Tuesday, November 25.

"You'll be there with me," he said. "You'll pick me up at the office and we'll go out to dinner. Then to my apartment, you and me. We'll be alone. Marion's in Europe. You'll tell Ollie that you're sleeping over in New York; that you have important business with me in the morning."

Armin lit a cigarette, drank champagne. "We will receive the suitcases, and I will turn over ninety thousand dollars in cash, ready for them, prepared in advance." Suddenly he threw his head back and laughed. "Can you imagine—if we open those bags and find them stuffed with nothing! God, a *joke!* All that careful planning, an expenditure of a hundred and fifty thousand—"

"They will not be stuffed with nothing," Dwyer said quietly. "They will be stuffed with ten million dollars."

"I've arranged the security. Night work. Four armed guards, professionals, but in civilian attire. They'll be at the apartment of my personal secretary. We will get our delivery. We will divide the money in accordance with my father's wishes. Then I'll call Seely—he's the secretary—and the guards will stay with us the rest of the night. In the morning two will go with you to your bank, two will go with me to mine. And so our deal will be done. *Finito.*"

*   *   *

London, England. Saturday evening, November 22. Joshua Kearney awaiting harlots in a dimly lit room in a quiet hotel. Drinks Scotch, chuckles. There in a drawer of the maplewood dresser repose the wig and the mustache: a black-haired mod-cut wig and a thick, black, curved-down mustache. Arthur insists that during these anonymous comings and goings Josh wear the wig and the mustache; Arthur would prefer that Josh wear the wig and the mustache during whatever the diversions—but who in hell can wear a wig and a false mustache while throbbingly engaged in sexual calisthenics? Of course he understands the demands of Arthur the king-maker. This is Joshua Fitts Kearney here, Josh the vaunted junior Senator, Joshua Fitts the next President of these here United States: you don't screw it all up because the carnal aberrations require the ministrations of two (two!) paid prostitutes. But, actually, as both he and Arthur know, there is no risk. Coming and going, he *does* wear wig and mustache, and is therefore unrecognizable, but once in the room and the lights low—what difference? Suppose he *is* recognized by the frolicsome doxies—so what? What harm can doxies do? In political circles there have always been naughty rumors—going all the way back to Mr. George Washington, reputedly a formidable fucker, a slave-owner who continued his lusty extracurricular activities even after his convenient marriage to a widow lady named Martha who had more money than Mr. George could ever accumulate in all the rest of his life. In sexual matters—unless there is a wide-open scandal—politicians are safe. The opposition does not press in sexual matters. On both sides, there are libidinous peccadilloes. Therefore the tacit *quid pro quo*—*you* don't talk about *my* thing and I don't talk about yours. And Joshua Fitts Kearney's thing had the *least* basis of probity—no platform of respectability. There were no affairs with married women, no affairs with noble unmarried ladies high in the echelons—

no *affairs* at all. Only simple combat with paid prostitutes, and paid prostitutes—however sad the fact—have no status whatever in civilized society. The poor, rich, beautiful bastards, they are the nadir: used by the best and despised by the most. So, even if ever recognized, what risk to Joshua Fitts Kearney? Who takes the word of a whore, trying to lift herself in the oldest profession, trying to make character by asserting that she has screwed this British Member of Parliament, or that Croesus of a Greek shipbuilder, or that there American who figures to be the next President of the U.S.A.? Nobody believes. That kind of word wafts around the world, interminably. Without proof, absolute proof, *proof positive,* nobody believes. It is the law of the land in every land: the credibility of a prostitute is virtually nil. Sad the fact and unfair, but nobody believes a whore.

A knock now. A gentle tapping.

In the dimly lighted room Joshua Fitts sets down his glass, flicks a quick look at the mirror, and goes to the door.

New York, New York. Saturday evening, November 22. Carleton Armin and Dolores Warren. They have attended a private screening of the newest touted film (new and touted are synonymous)—a film financed by one of Armin's corporate clients. And after the film, dinner at "21," and there he continued to tease her about the surprise in store.

"What? Please. I'm dying."

"Soon," he said.

"When?"

"After dessert."

"I know. A present. You've another present for me. Dearest Carleton. A crazy present in your pocket."

"This present is too big for my pocket."

And so, after dessert, he took her to the apartment on Central Park West, led her through, showed her, and she stared, and admired, and loved it, and then in the living room she stared at him, the long dark witch's eyes quizzical, and she said, "So? Is it your present that you're moving out on your wife? Are you moving in here?"

"*You're* moving in here."

"I am—*what?*"

"Sit down."

She sat. He went to the kitchen, to the refrigerator, where there was lying-down champagne. He opened a bottle, and came back to her, with the bottle and two goblets. He poured, for her and for him. He drank. She did not drink.

"Our time has come," he said.

"Our time for what the hell?" she said.

"Listen to me, please." He sipped champagne, put down the goblet. He paced. His voice was deep, serious. "I love you. That's number one. Okay, let's put that aside. Let's put me aside, but not you. You. You're a kid, you're a baby, but you're one hell of a terrific talent. I know, because I've inquired. You're going to make it, and you're going to make it big. The only thing that's *really* holding you back—bread. Bread and butter. You have to eat, and buy clothes, and pay the rent—and that keeps you quivering around at the loose ends. Okay. From here on out—that's over. You'll be able to devote yourself entirely to your talent, your career—no more headaches about bread. You're going to live like a lady. No more Perry Street. This is *your* apartment—my office pays the rent. And my office is going to do more. Starting Monday, you're on the payroll of Carleton Armin, Limited. Consultant, researcher—who in hell cares? My accountants'll figure out the proper title. Five hundred bucks a week. That should set you out in the clear. Full devotion hereafter to the career."

He stopped in front of her, smiled down at her. "In the history of talent—people get breaks. I'm your break. Carleton Armin, patron of the arts. I'm old. You're young. I'll get my credit when I'm dead. One day when you're big—big!—and you write your biography, you'll tell about Carleton Armin, who believed in you, who paved your way and paid your way, who set you out on your own—no aches about bread. Full devotion. The talent free and clear."

"For how long?"

"Until you can pay for all of this on your own. I promise you. I promise, by God." He leaned down, kissed her forehead. "I beg you to believe me."

"I believe you."

"Thank you."

She was weeping, but smiling.

"Remember Mama," she said.

"I remember Mama."

"I don't sell."

"You can't sell because I'm not buying. I'm giving."

She stood up and went out of the room. He waited, but she did not return. He went looking and found her in the bedroom on top of the bed, naked.

"Opening night," she said.

"Beg pardon?" he said.

"Am I of the theater?"

"You're of the theater."

"So." That small witch's smile. "Opening night."

"Opening—"

"The cunt, Mr. Armin. Dear lover, you've had me in every hole except the holy hole. Tonight Dolores Warren loses the cherry. Tonight she gives up the fruit of the loom."

"Who wants it?"

"Me. *I* want it. Come here to me, Carleton. Please come to bed."

New York, New York. Saturday evening, November 22. Barney Wilson and Kathy Kearney. A play on Broadway, and then lamb steaks in the Russian Tea Room, and then home to Sutton Place, where she put him up in a guest room.

Kissed him. "Sleep well, darling."

"Where you going?"

"Unwell. Sort of, the last day."

"So? Who cares?"

"Want to tidy up a bit. I'll be back."

He undressed, went to bed. The lights were on, but he dozed off. Slept and dreamed, a peculiar dream, partially a nightmare. He dreamed that the Kearney plane, upon arrival at Kennedy, suddenly tilted over, exploded, and burned. He could see the flames, hear the explosions; in his dream he could smell the odor of burning flesh. They were dead, all dead: Josh, Upton, the crew, everybody. And then, after a proper period of mourning, Kathy Kearney married Barney Wilson. A solemn ceremony. A church wedding—

She was touching his shoulder. He awoke.

"My gosh," she said. "You were making terrible sounds."

"A crazy dream. They were in the plane—"

"Just a moment." She slipped out of her robe and into the bed. "Yes, tell me."

He told her. She looked at him.

A catch in her voice. "Wishful thinking? Wishful dreaming?"

"No. Not the first part. I don't wish him dead. But the second part—" His grin was crooked. The dark face looked young; that strong face, somehow vulnerable. "What *would* you do?"

"Exactly what you dreamed. What else?"

He took her in his arms, kissed her, held her.

They talked, for a long time, before they made love.

20

S HE DID NOT see him on Sunday.

As per his instructions, she visited friends on Sunday. And on Monday, as per instructions, she remained at home attending to her chores and duties as lady of the house. He had promised he would call her at four.

On Monday he drove out to the Deaver Motel. Parked and went in and was smiled upon by a sleek-haired young man. "Yessir," said the sleek-haired. "What can we do for you?"

"I want the best cabin available."

"Yessir, you got it."

"Want it for four days. Today, tomorrow, Wednesday, and Thursday." Two extra days in case there were bullets in him.

"Yessir, four days. That'll be two hundred and forty dollars."

Sixty dollars a day in this nothing joint. The sleek-haired bastard has upped the price and will probably pocket some of those bucks. Because what sucker takes a room for four days in the Deaver Motel, which is strictly a quick-shack hostel, the usual suburban happy humping grounds? But Barney is in no position for discourse or protestation. He pays the money, signs in as John Gross, and accepts the key.

"Cabin Seventy-four," said the sleek-haired young man. "When you go out of here, it's to the right. Then when you come to the fork, you make a left. It's all the way down."

"Right," Barney said. "Thank you."

He followed directions, parked within the white-painted lines outside No. 74, went in for inspection, and was pleasantly surprised. The sleek-haired bastard had done all right by John Gross. It was a good-sized room and it contained all the appurtenances: a bolted-down color TV, a bolted-down radio, a big bed with a plump mattress, a small refrigerator with solid ice cubes, two easy chairs, a chest of drawers, two wooden armchairs, a coffee table with a pitcher and glasses, bed lamps and ashtrays on little tables on either side of the bed. The bathroom was spotless: a shiny-clean bathtub and a purple-tiled stall shower.

He went out and traveled until he found a liquor store and returned with purchases that completed the room: a bottle of Scotch for Kathy and a bottle of bourbon for him. Then he drew the venetian blinds, locked up, pocketed the key, and drove home.

He called her at four o'clock: precisely the time he had told her to expect his call. He could easily have gone over to Sutton Place. He didn't because he did not want any witnesses to associate them at this period. She answered on the second ring.

"Hi," he said. "Guess who?"

"No idea." She laughed.

"Listen. You'll meet me at eight o'clock. A restaurant in

Chinatown. You'll take a cab down. It's the Hong Gung. Thirty Pell Street. I'll be waiting in a booth. If you don't see me, ask the front-guy for John Gross. I'll have told him I'm waiting for my date. Okay?"

"Whatever you say."

"I've said. See you later."

He was there at a quarter to eight. He told the front-man he was John Gross expecting his date, a beautiful blonde. The front-man grinned, nodded, showed him to a booth. He ordered a bourbon Manhattan, and then at five to eight she was there in the booth with him. She ordered a martini and they perused the menus. He said, "On the appetizer stuff, whatever you like. For the real thing, I suggest the sliced beef in oyster sauce."

They ordered, they ate.

"Tomorrow," he said. "Tomorrow's our day. Tomorrow we cast our vote for the President."

Her hands were cold. "Yes," she said.

He told her about the Deaver Motel in Jackson Heights.

"Tomorrow evening at ten o'clock. You'll meet me at the southwest corner of Thirtieth and First. I'll be there in the car, waiting. You'll come by cab. You'll dress warmly, you'll wear gloves. Very important—wear gloves."

"Barney, please. I don't understand all this cloak-and-dagger. Why in heck am I here in Chinatown? Why did I have to see people on Sunday? Why did I have to stay in all day today? Why must I meet you out on the street tomorrow? And what's with a motel in Jackson Heights?"

"I can get killed."

"No."

"I don't want you mixed in it. If I get killed—you know nothing. Last time you saw me was Saturday night. Even tonight here—who knows? You were home. Who can say different? Your old people, your caretakers, they retire early. And for tomorrow—same deal. If something happens to me, if ever you're questioned, you don't know from nothing—you were home in bed."

"Nothing will happen to you. Please, nothing will happen to you."

"Nothing will happen to me." He grinned that crooked Barney grin, and around it the dark face was happy. "But just in case—we must provide for eventuality. Therefore the Deaver Motel. For this job, that will be home base. I will leave from there and I will, I hope, return there. And there at the Deaver, you will be the point of contact."

"Point—for what?"

"I can come back—bleeding. Bullets make holes. You can't go to a hospital with bullet holes, because like that you get cops. Cops ain't good—for me, for you, for Mr. Man. Therefore, no hospital. If I can, I go to the Deaver. I go to you at the Deaver."

"Me." The hands were freezing. "What can *I* do?"

"You call the doctor."

"Who? What doctor?"

"Dr. Michael Boysen. He's worked before on this sort of stuff. I've talked to him, he knows. Doesn't know what this deal is all about, but he knows I can get holes in me. If I come back with holes, you'll call him and he'll come. This is his number. I don't want you to write it down. I don't want writings. I'll say the number and you'll remember it." He said the number. Then he said, "Say it to me."

She said the number.

"Say it again."

She said the number again.

"You'll remember?"

"In all my life I'll never forget."

He laughed. "Okay. Enough for tonight. I'll see you tomorrow at ten. For now, would you like another drink?"

"Absolutely," she said.

He waved to the waiter and ordered new drinks.

21

T UESDAY. The day. November 25. Exactly one month away from Christmas, the birthday of the Christ Jesus, Son of God, Man of Peace, Apostle of Redemption. This day, a month before the celebration of the birth of the Lord Jesus, it is ugly, wet, cold, sodden. All this raw day the skies have been low, dull, heavy. The weather prediction is for sleeting rain late this night.

9:35.

Barney Wilson naked in his apartment. Pulls on the heavy longjohns. Black wool socks. Black turtleneck sweater. The pants of the black wool suit. The black sneakers. The jacket of the black wool suit. The black gloves. Already in the apartment he is perspiring. Wraps the Hanna Special in the gray blanket and goes down to the basement garage. Opens the trunk of the car, lays in the blanket-wrapped package, slams the trunk shut. Round and into the car. Starts it up, backs it out from its slot, touches the button of the remote-control device.

The garage door rolls up. The Mercedes rolls out.

9:55.

Double-parked. Motor quietly idling. Southwest corner of First Avenue and 30th Street. He sees the taxi stop. Kathy comes out and the cab pulls away. He leans over and opens the passenger door. She gets in and closes the door. Wearing a cloth coat and a pants suit. And gloves.

He smiles. "Hi."

"Hi. You look very handsome."

"Yeah, I shaved for the occasion."

Shifts into gear. They drive up First Avenue toward the 59th Street Bridge.

10:00.

Carleton Armin and Simon Dwyer in the drawing room of the duplex on 67th Street. At the center of a cocktail table, in an envelope, $90,000 in cash. At the corner of the cocktail table, an open bottle of champagne.

Armin sets down a long-stemmed glass, smiles. "How do you feel, my friend?"

Dwyer is not drinking. His return smile is wan. "As well as can be expected—when the heart is in the mouth."

"Nothing to worry, Simon. Our project is in the best of hands." Crosses to the phone and calls Ron Seely. "How goes it?"

"They're here, but you'll never guess what they're doing."

"What are they doing?"

"Playing Monopoly. The four of them. And me on the outside, I'm the umpire or something."

"Right. Talk to you later." Armin hung up. "Our guards are playing Monopoly there."

235

"Do you have a Monopoly?"

"No."

"How about some gin? Gin rummy."

"Yep, you bet."

He got out the cards, the pads, and two pencils.

They sat at a table. "What stakes?" Armin said.

"Whatever you say."

"Five cents a point."

"Are you crazy?"

"Sane as rain."

"Five cents a *point!*" The eyebrows knitted, but the wan smile had more mirth. "I'm not one of your banker friends."

"Probably richer."

"Me?"

"It just won't come through to you, will it?"

"What?"

"Tomorrow morning you're a millionaire."

10:38.

The Mercedes noses to the curb within the parallel parking lines in front of No. 74. Barney locks the car and they enter the cabin. Clicks on the light, secures the door, tosses the key to the top of the chest of drawers. "I'll leave it here. Don't want that key on my person. If things go wrong, the cops would find it on me. They'd crash in here, and you'd be linked. Can't have any of *that,* can we?"

She didn't answer.

She removed her gloves, slipped off her coat, and hung it away.

"Is it hot here? Or—"

"Hot. Damn hot."

"I—I'm nervous." She was pale.

"Of course you are. You wouldn't be human if you weren't."

236

He pulled off his gloves, took off his jacket. He made a drink for her, Scotch and water with cubes from the refrigerator. For himself he poured a bourbon, a good shot, and gulped it down. One shot. Any real drinking would be *after* the job. He looked at his watch—still plenty of time. He had specially selected this see-in-the-dark wristwatch: luminous white hands and numbers on a black face. He paced, chatted of small things, the weather. She was sitting in one of the easy chairs, and most of the highball was in her. The color was back in her cheeks, the blue eyes were glittering.

"Feeling better?"

"Yes," she said.

"My money's on you." He laughed. "I know my people. You're strong. You're a rock. Any *real* emergency—my money's on you."

"Thank you," she said.

He looked at the wristwatch. "Okay. Final instructions. I should be back about three, perhaps before. I'll ring. You'll look through the peephole before you open. If I've got holes, if I'm in bad shape, you'll call Boysen. He'll come and patch me up. If I'm unpatchable, you'll turn me over to the doc and he'll drive me away in *his* car. Then you'll take my car, drive it back to my garage, leave it there, and go home. For the world—you were home all night. Clear?"

"Yes."

"The thingamajig that opens my garage door—it's in the glove compartment. And remember to wear your gloves; we don't need you fingerprints on the thingamajig or the steering wheel or whatever." He took up his jacket, shrugged into it. He turned to her: his voice was soft. "If I die here, you'll tell the doc to take me out in his car and dump me somewhere. Those are my orders. He knows about such matters. In his time he's dumped other such sudden cadavers out of his MD car in the dead of night. As for you, same

237

instructions. You'll leave in my car and you know nothing from nothing." He pulled on the pliant black gloves. "Just one more thing. If I'm not back by five, call a cab and go home." And now the Barney grin was wide. The face was happy. The dark eyes smoldered. "Cheer up, sweetheart. None of it is going to be. I'm coming back with two suitcases and no holes." He waved. "Wish me luck."

She ran to him. They embraced.

"Good luck," she whispered.

"Yeah. Lock up after me."

Outside in the raw wet night, he opened the trunk, took out the wrapped submachine gun, closed the trunk. In the car he laid his package on the floor in the rear. He started the motor, backed out, and glided off. On the way toward Tower Stadium he punched the radio button to a news station. He heard political news, murder-and-mugging news, and the weather. It is thirty-five degrees, the man said, and there is rain and sleet on the way. He flicked off the radio. He glanced up through the windshield. No stars, no moon. A dark night. A dirty sky, heavy, ominous. A cold, wet, rotten night—perfect for Tony Glendo's boys. But also perfect for Barney Wilson.

11:37.

Barney Wilson. Drives up the bumpy ramp of the boarded-up warehouse. Turns off the motor, turns off the lights. Darkness. Sits, waits, letting his eyes grow accustomed. Then out of the car, opens a rear door. Bends in, unwraps the Hanna Special from the gray blanket. Closes the door, trudges silently on sneakered feet around the corner, a dark figure in darkness. Finds his recessed, angled-off entranceway, and enters it deeply. Places the submachine gun a distance behind him, and sits. Should a prowl cop come along, he will sprawl out on his belly, a sleeping derelict. But who in hell could possibly notice him?—black-dressed in blackness. And what cop would be prowling an utterly deserted area on this cold, wet, filthy night? It is cold, but Barney Wilson is not cold. He is wearing thick longjohn underwear, gloves, wool socks, a heavy wool turtleneck, a heavy wool suit. He sits, feeling his blood pumping. Happy, restraining excitement. This is it, the job, the contest finally at peak. Christ, I love it. The thrill. The weird rapture. The animal at surface, atavistic. Animal. Out on the hunt. Hunting the hunters. If you win, you have meat. If you lose, *you* are the meat. Animals hunting. A contest. At stake—your life. Christ, what could be more beautiful, what greater thrill! Once more, so rare, you are at point of pinnacle. Life or death: an exquisite rapture.

Barney Wilson in darkness. Sitting. Waiting.

12:25.

Guards' room in Tower Stadium. Four men. One of them —as the others know—has had a rough day. A fight with the wife, a debilitating afternoon at the Deaver Motel with a girl friend, and then a fucken fight with the girl friend. Jacketless, his gun in the holster strapped to his belt, he is dozing on a couch. Jacketless, guns in holsters, the other three are playing pinochle at a table. It is a lousy tour of duty, a weight-gaining sinecure of a tour of duty: nothing ever happens. You play cards, or you watch the fucken TV, or you doze—but you are always goddam snacking from the goddam icebox. What in hell else can you do during eight long hours of nothing—except watch TV, or sleep, or play cards, or eat? Always eat. Boredom generates appetite. They are all overweight, but one of them is really fat. And now the fat man is roaring.

"Jeez, Freddie," he shouts at a pinochle player. "You're dumb. I mean you are really fucken stupid! I mean that kinda bid—"

239

A groan from the couch. "Jeez, can't you hold it down?"

"Fuck you," is the fat man's retort.

"Jeez," Freddie says to the fat man. "How come you get meaner and meaner? Suppose it wuz you tryin' to ketch a nap? Would you like people hollerin'? Like do unto others, you know? Ever hear of the Golden Rule?"

"Sure. If you got the gold—you rule. Okay, come on. Deal the fucken cards."

12:34.

The street by the westerly fence of Tower Stadium. A long black station wagon enters the street, rolls slowly to the darkest area, the farthest distance from the lamplight.

Barney Wilson up on his haunches. A glance at the luminous hands of the wristwatch. The bastards are early. Sure. Smart. They are taking advantage of this wet, cold, dirty night.

12:36.

Jake Orin at the wheel of the station wagon. Parks at the curb, pulls the brake, turns off the ignition, turns off the lights. He is wearing a black suit and a black, thick-knitted stocking hat pulled down over his ears. On his left, a carbine. On his right, Joe Stroner wearing gloves, a jump suit, and crepe-soled shoes. On Stroner's right, Frank Lander wearing gloves, a jump suit, and crepe-soled shoes.

"Here we are, gents." Orin's voice was placid, unruffled, unexcited. "All yours now."

From the big button-pockets of the jump suits—ski masks. Stroner pulled his on and sat there. Lander pulled his on, opened the passenger door, went round, lowered the tailgate of the station wagon, reached in, and brought out an enormous bolt-cutter. He shouldered it, like a soldier with a rifle, and trotted to the chain-link fence. From the station wagon he

240

was covered by Orin with the carbine and Stroner with a .45 automatic.

Lander worked quickly, sundering links, snipping downward, vertically, for about five feet. Then he reversed the bolt-cutter, pressed the rubber grips against the severed fence, and a sufficient wedge was open. He returned to the wagon, tossed in the bolt-cutter, and pulled out a valise.

Orin said, "Okay, Joe. Start haulin' ass."

Stroner quit the front seat, went round to the tailgate. He climbed in and came out with a huge, lumpy duffel bag.

And now, suddenly—rain. The promised rain was upon them; heavy, sleeting, streaming rain. The masked men shuffled through the rain, Lander with the valise, Stroner with the duffel bag. They pushed through the open wedge of the chain-link fence, disappeared into the streaming darkness, and Orin was alone in the driver's seat of the station wagon, the carbine on his knees. This was the part he hated. The doing nothing. The sitting. Waiting.

Silently a dark figure. Sidling in the pouring rain. Crouched, a black figure impossible to see in the black rain. Furtively creeping along the left side of the station wagon. Then a submachine gun is raised and bullets stream through the rolled-up window and Orin falls from view. Barney races round, snatches open the passenger door, looses an additional volley. Pulls out the inert man, drags him to the tailgate, and hoists him in. Removes the stocking hat from the dead head.

And now it is Barney Wilson, the black hat pulled down over his ears, who is sitting in the driver's seat, the Hanna Special in his lap. Orin's carbine is now on the seat beside him; Christ, it's enough to make you want to laugh. *Two* submachine guns. We're a goddam arsenal. He sits there in Orin's seat, thinking the thoughts that Orin would be thinking. Cops. What else? Unlikely—no question about it. What cops would be dumb enough to prowl in this deserted area?

241

And in this weather, not only improbable but virtually impossible. Virtually. A weasel word. It leaves open a tiny speck, a modicum of possibility. Christ, it would be just too bad. For the cops. The surface amenities are far submerged now. You're an animal, atavistic, and the first law of life is self-preservation. You would have to kill in order not to die. There would be more bodies in back of the station wagon. Innocents. Not the prey of the hunt. Jesus, no. Please, no. He prays there won't be cops. He *knows* there won't be cops. He sits. In the driver's seat.

Outside the rain pelts fiercely.

12:51.

Lander and Stroner. At the steel door in the north wall. Around the corner from it, three feet in: a small, square, gray metal plate with a tiny keyhole. Lander uses a pencil-flash for illumination. Unlocks the metal plate. Inserts the long thin key, turns it all the way to the right. Withdraws the key, locks the box, returns to Stroner waiting with the bags outside the steel door. Now Lander utilizes the third key, the large one, to unlock that door. Replaces the keys and the pencil-flash in separate pockets of the jump suit; separate pockets so there is no clinking. They take up the bags, enter, close the door, but do not lock it.

Stroner has a full-size flashlight, but it is not necessary. Little yellow night lights burn in the corridors of Tower Stadium. On crepe-soled shoes they proceed along a corridor, then descend two flights of stairs, make a left turn, and then a right turn into a long corridor with many doors. They know precisely where they are going. Outside the guards' room, they set down the bags, unzip the top of the jump suits, reach in, and pull .45s from shoulder holsters.

*　　*　　*

12:56.

Guards' room. Three men at a table playing cards. A fourth is dozing on a couch.

The door bursts open. Two men in ski masks, grotesque, dripping wet—flashing huge black pistols.

"Freeze! Don't fucken move!"

The card players remain motionless. But the sleeping guard, abruptly awakened, automatically reaches for his gun.

Stroner shoots him in the head.

The guard topples from the couch.

"Up!" With his free hand, Stroner points. "Over there. You three cocksuckers, over there by the wall. Spread your hands on the fucken wall. And don't try no tricks. You try, you're fucken dead."

The guards comply. While Stroner covers him, Lander plucks their pistols from them. Lays the pistols away, stoops to the man on the floor, examines. Stands up, looks at Stroner.

"This one is a doornail."

"You guys by the wall—you heard? Your friend was stupid, he is fucken dead. So don't none of you get stupid. Unless you're looking to get dead. Okay. Now lay down on the fucken floor. On your bellies."

The guards lie on the floor on their bellies. Lander goes out, comes back with his valise, opens it. He handcuffs the the guards' wrists behind their backs. He shackles their knees, shackles their ankles. Winds friction tape around their heads and over their eyes and over their mouths until nothing is exposed except the holes of their noses for breathing. He closes the valise.

Joe Stroner. Frank Lander. The black .45s are back in the holsters inside the jump suits. They drag the guards along the corridor to the far end, the board room. That door is locked. Lander goes back for his valise. Takes out picklocks and opens the door. Flicks on the lights to a large wood-paneled room that features an immense, thick-heavy, rectangular, walnut library table surrounded by walnut armchairs. Goes out for the valise. Stroner goes away for his duffel bag and comes back with it.

They drag the guards into the board room. From the valise, more chains. Lander shackles each prone guard by his shackled feet to a different leg of the refectory table. If the bastards pull, they'll be pulling in different directions. Next, from the valise, a cutter for the phone wires, and then delicate instruments that disconnect the wiring of the push-button silent alarm. Lander's work is done. He draws back a walnut armchair, sits in it, smiles inside his ski mask, looks up at Stroner.

"All yours, baby."

Joe Stroner opens the duffel bag for the electric jackhammer; plugs it into an outlet. He has studied the blueprint: he knows exactly where to drill. It is short work. In fifteen minutes he has opened a hole, sees the suitcases, pulls them out. Finished. The job is done.

They leave everything—except the suitcases they came for. They are professionals: none of their stuff is traceable. They flick off the lights, close the door of the board room. The guards cannot do a thing. If they pull, they will be pulling one against the other. They cannot communicate: their mouths are sealed by friction tape. Even if somehow they learned to pull together: so what? They could drag the heavy table to the door, but it is too big to be pulled through. Nothing. They are helpless. They will remain in the board room, blind, gagged, handcuffed, and shackled, until in the morning they are rescued by the new company of guards.

1:32.

Barney Wilson in the station wagon. He has the motor on.

For the windshield wipers to work, so that he can see. He sees. They are still within the stadium grounds, two ski-masked men, each with a suitcase, coming toward the open wedge of the chain-link fence. A quick glance at his wristwatch, and a thrill of anomalous admiration. Christ, you have got to hand it to them: that whole damn job done within an hour. He slides across the seat, opens the passenger door. The men come through the fence, come near, and the submachine gun delivers its hail of soundless bullets. The men fall; the suitcases drop from dead hands. He leaps out and completes the work with a spray of bullets to each head. The rain washes away the blood.

Lays the machine gun in the car, on the seat beside Orin's carbine. And back in the rain pulls the dead men, first one and then the other, to the station wagon. Hoists them in, and they join Jake Orin. Flips off the knit-wool stocking hat and tosses it in. Closes the tailgate, runs round, takes out the Hanna Special, slams shut the passenger door. Picks up the suitcases. The submachine gun under one arm, he trots around the corner to the Mercedes. He places the suitcases and the Special under the gray blanket in the rear, climbs into the driver's seat, starts the motor, backs out, and takes off. For minutes he drives slowly, without lights. Then, on a good piece of road away from the scene, switches on the lights. Drives skillfully, at even pace, the windshield wipers rhythmically thumping. Done. Job done. This job is done. Mr. Man is in the clear. The sins of the father will not be visited.

22

A T F I R S T she had been uncomfortable and then somehow—perhaps thanks to the Scotch—comfortable.
The very fact of a motel had made her uncomfortable; she had
never before been to a motel. Not even in the loose years, the
running years, the years before Barney, never a motel. There
had been apartments, there had been discreet *pieds-à-terre,*
there had been country homes, there had been hideaway cot-
tages, there had even been charming suites in fine hotels—but
never a motel room. Somehow the very word—motel—had
conjured up a cheapness, a tawdriness, a sleaziness.

Not true. Not true, here. It was quite a nice room, and
quite nicely furnished. But the heat! The heat had made her
uncomfortable. They were just *too* kind to their guests. The
darn heat kept pouring from the radiator without let-up, and
there was no way of turning it off. She had tried. She had
stretched out flat on the floor and had peered under the radiator shield for the handle, the screw, the turn-off thing. There

was no turn-off thing, and it had made her laugh, because if there is no turn-off thing, there is no turn-*on* thing. A dictatorship, by God. Big Brother. We are taking care of you, good people. It is cold November and we are giving you heat —so what's your complaint? My complaint, Big Brother— I want my rights, my privileges. And she had laughed again. Rights, privileges. Political philosophy in the Deaver Motel, Cabin 74. Microcosm. Criticism of benevolent dictatorship in Jackson Heights. I want my rights, my civil rights, my civil liberties. I am the people. I want to be able to turn on or turn off as I wish, when I please—

Experimenting, she had learned—as others in far-off places in far more important matters—to cope with Big Brother. She had opened the windows; they were darn good windows, storm windows, screen-protected. And for a while it was good— the fresh air was cooling. But then it had got cold, despite the pouring radiator heat—cold and wet. So she had closed the windows and was hot again, and had taken off clothes and opened one window several inches and thus had made her compromise with Big Brother in Jackson Heights. Without clothes, and with one window open several inches, she had achieved a balance: the temperature was satisfactory. Not all her clothes. In panty hose and bra, she was finally comfortable in No. 74. Physically comfortable. Mentally, of course not. But the Scotch, in small imbibations, did help. After all, he *was* Barney Wilson, once the chief spook of the CIA. She tried not to worry. Barney the formidable, Barney the indomitable, he knew what he was doing, he *had* to know. He had made provisions for dire possibilities, but that did not mean he expected dire possibilities. In any adventure one must provide . . .

She had watched a talk show on the TV, and now, lying on the bed, she was watching an old film with Gable and Lombard, and the bell rang, and she looked at her watch:

247

twenty after two. She swung off the bed, ran to the door, looked through the peephole, and there he was, big as life, the dark face beaded with rain, but he was smiling, that big Barney smile, a triumphant smile. She unlocked and opened and he came in—carrying two suitcases. He set them down, locked the door, grabbed her, and kissed her.

"God, you're all wet."

"Yep," he said and released her. "We're in the bag, luv. No bullet holes, no Dr. Boysen. I'm yours in one piece. Say hello to Barney."

"Hello, Barney."

He ripped off his gloves, tossed them away. He crossed to the bourbon on squashy sneakers squirting water. He poured and gulped, poured another and gulped; poured a third drink and gulped it down. He took off his jacket and hung it on the back of an armchair, switched off the TV. He pulled out of the turtleneck sweater, threw it on the radiator. He sat, undid the sneakers, kicked them away, pulled off the wet wool socks, stood up, took the socks to the radiator. He zipped open his trousers, removed them, laid them on the radiator. Went into the bathroom and came back with a Turkish towel. Wiped his face, wiped his hair, wiped his feet, threw the towel away. He seized her, kissed her, held her. She laughed.

"What the hell?" he said.

"Look. There. In the mirror."

He looked, and laughed. Perpendicular lovers, embracing. The man in ridiculous longjohn underwear, the woman in ridiculous panty hose and bra. He broke from her, somehow roughly. Pointed at the suitcases.

"We did it, luv. He's in the clear."

"How? How did you—"

"Not your business. That's none of your business." He went away from her, picked up the towel, did a knee-bend by the suitcases, wiped them, flung away the towel. Still squatting on haunches, he looked up. "Ever see ten million dollars? In cash? Have you ever looked at ten naked million dollars in cash money?"

"No."

"Let's hope it's there. And let's hope—the other thing's there."

The suitcases were heavily strapped, but not locked. He undid the straps and laid back the covers. Money! Packages of money! Packages and packages of money, money! One-thousand-dollar bills. In bank-wrapped packages of fifty. The brown strip around each thick package stamped: *$50,-000*. Two hundred neat, bank-wrapped packages. Ten fucking million dollars. Ten million!

"Lord," she said.

"Jesus," he said.

"God," she said, and somehow, strangely, she was sexually excited.

He was sitting now, on the floor, cross-legged.

"Wanna know something?"

"What?" she said.

"I'd like right now, this minute, to get laid."

"Me too."

He grinned up at her. The crazy, handsome, big-toothed, white-toothed Barney grin. "Rain check," he said. "We're working. There it is." He pointed. To a corner of one of the suitcases. To a tape recorder in a corner of one of the suitcases. "There it is. What could have destroyed an innocent man. What could have taken away from us—me, you, everybody, the people—the right man, the best damn man as the next President of the good old U.S.A." He was on his knees now, a reverential posture, a religious posture, as he took the tape recorder, tenderly, from the suitcase.

He stood up with it and placed it, tenderly, on the coffee table, and sat on the floor again and looked at it.

"Japanese," he said. "An expensive job, the best, the most expensive. The Nipponese," he said and laughed. "They made the best way back then; they still make the best." He bent to it, opened it, examined. "Everything in order, tape and all. It can go by batteries, it can go by electric current. He was smart, that old boy, that Don Vito."

"Why?"

"Removed the batteries."

"Why was that smart?"

"Leakage. In ten years there could be leakage, and that kind of leakage could spoil the tape." He stood up. "Would you like to hear?" he said. "The sins of the fathers?"

"Yes."

"How Mr. Man's father—the illustrious Earl Kearney—shaped up a bribery deal?"

"Yes." She sat in an easy chair and crossed panty-hosed legs.

He plugged in the recorder. He reversed the tape to its beginning and then set it going. He sat in a hard armchair and listened. He had never heard the voice of Mr. Justice Otto Yoder, nor the voice of the Mafia don, nor the voice of old Earl Kearney (always on the tape respectfully addressed as Mr. Kearney). But as Barney Wilson listened, his spine grew cold, and a strange, fierce, thin pain stabbed at his rectum. He had never before heard any of these voices, but he *had* heard one of these voices, and he sat in the hard armchair and listened, spine cold, rectum hurting, his tongue a lump in his mouth, sat listening until he was certain: definitely, absolutely certain.

Whoever had been the fucking father: that was not the father there on the tape. That was the son: whom Barney Wilson damn well knew. That was not Earl Kearney, whoever had been Earl Kearney. That was Joshua Fitts Kearney. That

250

was Joshua Fitts Kearney there on the tape, smoothly, corruptly arranging the bribe.

"Son of a bitch!"

He was on his feet and stood over the seated woman. Behind them the tape kept talking.

"That's Josh," he said.

She did not answer.

"Did you know Earl Kearney? You knew Earl Kearney."

"Yes."

"That's not Earl Kearney. That's Josh there."

She did not answer. Her lips were pale.

"Kathy, Jesus, please. Am I crazy?"

She looked up at him. Saw, for the first time, tears in his eyes. This strong man, this strongest of men: tears in his eyes.

"Not crazy," she said.

"That's him there."

"Him."

"Say it. Say it for me. Say who's talking there. Say the whole, full, fucking name."

"Joshua Fitts Kearney," she said.

He ran from her. In the longjohn underwear, ran from her. To the tape recorder and switched it off, and he turned toward her, and she saw a different face, not the handsome face she knew, a face distorted, contorted, ugly in wrath.

"The son of a bitch!"

"Barney, easy."

"Oh, the fucking son of a bitch."

"God. Please. You. God, you know him, really know him, better than any of us. A strange one. He's a strange one, Barney. A secretive man."

"But not with me. I didn't believe—with me. Christ, he could have told me. He could have told *me* this fucking truth."

"How would you have reacted? Would you have—"

"I don't know. I don't, really, know—" Dazedly, shook

his head. "All I can say is this." But he did not say. He went to the bed, sat on the edge of it, knees spread. Elbows on knees, hands clasped, head down. He sat like that, head down, silent, for many minutes. And when he looked up at her, the face was handsome again, and the dark eyes were clear of tears. His voice was soft.

"If you want loyalty—you have to give loyalty."

"I understand."

"No, you don't understand." The voice hardened. "I believed in the man. I killed for the man. Tonight. Three people. Dead."

"Don't tell me. Please don't tell me."

"We can all kill. Depends on the balance; what we believe in." He sighed. "We are all capable of killing." He pointed a finger. *"You* can kill—depending on the balance."

In the easy chair, she shuddered.

"We kill animals," he said, "in order to eat their flesh. In the higher form of killings, people kill people"—he laughed —"for the good of commonweal. Hell, if early on someone would have assassinated Hitler—it would have been good for the commonweal. Take Jesus Christ. He *had* to be killed, because without that killing there would be no resurrection. As St. Paul said—no resurrection, no Christianity." He rubbed a hand across his mouth. "I killed because I believed in a man. I killed"—his smile was awful—"for the good of the commonweal. Turns out I was wrong. Turns out I killed for a deceitful bastard. A liar. The worst kind of liar. A liar who lies to his own. To his own—"

He stood up. He glared at her.

"Did *you* know? The truth about that tape? Did he tell you? Did—"

"Are you crazy? God, if he didn't tell *you!"*

"Yes." His eyes tightened in a squint. He shook his head. "I'm sorry." His hands clenched. "You see what happens

252

once the rot sets in. Spreads. So damn quickly. Like—like plague. I'm sorry," he said, and walked, paced, the hands still fists. "As of now, I'm no longer working for the bastard. If I can't have loyalty, I can't give loyalty—simple as that. And, more complex, he can be dangerous. To me. In my line of work, when you learn you can't trust the boss, then you take a nice long walk—out!—while you've still got the legs to walk on. I'm going to make damn certain about the legs. That, now—that's imperative."

He stopped walking, stood with his back to her. She saw his hands unclench. Then he turned, went to her, looked down at her. "He threw us the bullshit. Well, we're going to rub his nose in it. Do you love me?"

"Yes."

He reached down, took her wrists, pulled her up, lifted her bodily, carried her to the bed. Tore off the panty hose, jolted penis into vagina, and they made love, furiously, savagely, brutishly, the woman's breasts enclosed within a brassiere, the man dressed in longjohn underwear. And then they lay, supine, side by side, and the man was talking, quietly, but the voice was not the voice she had known for so long, a different voice: flat, cold, hard.

"Our problem was money. No longer a problem, no more problem. We own a fortune—ten million dollars. We own it, and he can't do a thing about it. Because I've got him where the hair is short. Tomorrow morning I make a copy of that tape. And I take it—with ten million bucks—to my vault. Then I'll bring him the original—me alone. Not you. You'll stay at my apartment. I'll give him his tape, and I'll give him my story. Mr. and Mrs. J. F. Kearney—they're going to have a nice, quiet, civilized divorce. Then, in time, Kathy Kearney and Barney Wilson are getting married. And if he doesn't like it, he can lump it. He'll just have to wish us luck. Because there isn't a fucking thing he can do about it. No revenge, no punitive reaction, no reprisals against an employee who committed murder because he believed in his employer. Our beautiful Mr. Man, in consultation with King Arthur, will quickly come to the proper decision. Blessings upon ye—will be the decision. Because the bastard will damn well know that if I leak that tape, he's finished, he's done, he's all washed up. He might plead that we postpone—"

He got out of the bed. "He's lucky I'm not vindictive, lucky I don't leak it anyway, just for the fuck of it. Hate," he said, "a holy emotion. Hell, like religion. There's no one more religious than a convert. Well—for a friend—there's no worse enemy than the friend's friend converted to enmity." He padded barefoot to the tape recorder, unplugged it, laid it in tenderly, strapped the suitcases. He looked up and the voice was Barney's again: warm, resonant, sardonic, lively.

"Okay, me love. Let's start getting dressed."

They left the key, the Scotch, and the bourbon, and went out to the black night, the ceaseless rain. He unlocked, and she snuggled into the passenger's seat. He gave her the Hanna Special, placed the suitcases on the floor in the rear, and covered them with the blanket. Then up front in the driver's seat, he punched down the door buttons, leaned over and kissed her ear. He patted the gun.

"Keep it, like, on your knees under your coat."

"Yes."

"When you carry that kind of money, you ride it shotgun. These days there are even muggers on wheels. You stop for a light, you can suddenly have company. You'll keep your window as is, rolled up. Trouble, I'll handle it, but be sure you slip the shooter to me." He kissed her again, laughed. "If I get scrambled up, *you* use it. Nothing to it. Just point it and squeeze the trigger. There won't be any sound, nothing to startle you. Built-in silencer. Point it, squeeze it. The bullets fly and the people fall."

He drove in the dark wet night. She sat slumped, gloved hands holding a submachine gun. They crossed the bridge, turned left, rode along deserted streets. When they arrived, he looked at his watch. Forty minutes from the cabin in the Deaver Motel to the garage in the apartment house in Kips Bay. He parked the car in its slot, switched off the engine, unlocked the doors.

"You all right?"

"Yes."

"For the elevator, we'll wrap our pea-shooter in the blanket. I'll carry the bags. You'll carry the baby in the blanket—just in case we happen to meet somebody in the elevator. Okay?"

"Yes."

The dark eyes were happy, laughing. "I mean it ain't quite proper for people in the up-elevator to be riding with a hunk of naked artillery. Hell, we meet somebody, they can die of a heart attack, right? Come on out with that thing, sweetheart. Wake up. Move the gorgeous ass."

She came out with it, held it quite competently. He yanked out the bags, put them on the concrete, and reached in for the blanket.

"Okay." The Barney grin. "I'll wrap. Gimme."

She gave him. Point-blank at the face. The grin was suddenly smashed teeth. The nose seemed to dissolve. The eyes were holes. He dropped, and she pointed it down, and more bullets entered the dead body.

She dragged him, and the blanket, to a corner, laid the submachine gun on him, and covered all with the gray blanket. Then the numb, stiff-legged journey back to the car. There she shoved in the suitcases, slammed the doors. Climbed into the front, started the motor, backed out, shifted the gear, moved forward, and was confronted by the locked garage

255

door. For a moment—panic. She sat numb, her foot rigid on the brake, a scream howling inside her. Then remembered. Glove compartment. Remote-control thing. She got it out, touched the button, and a murderer's prison opened. The garage door rolled up to the freedom of streaming rain.

She drove. The wipers thumped, her heart thumped. Her toes were cold. Her hands in the gloves were ice. Her mouth was dry. She rolled down her window, gulped the cold air. Drove. Sutton Place. Double-parked by the house. The November street was pouring rain. No people. Nobody. Darkness. Running now, out of the car, to the downstairs gate, the side gate. Fumbled for the small purse in a pocket of her coat. Found her keys. Opened the gate, and then in the alcove under the entrance stairs, removed one glove, felt for the lock of the basement door, discovered it, opened the door. Ran back to the car, pulling on the glove. Reached in, tugged at the bags, drew them out, and carried them—so *heavy* now—to the tiny foyer beyond the basement door. Placed them on the foyer floor, locked the door, locked the gate, ran back to the car. Must get it away. Must get his car away from here.

She drove, westerly. The wipers thumped, her heart raced. Drove, her hands and feet icy cold. At Third Avenue, a right turn and up Third. 60th Street. 70th. No people, no traffic, but she stopped, dutifully, at each red light. 75th. 80th. Enough. It is far enough away. Near 86th there was an open space by a fire hydrant. She parked, turned off the lights, shut off the motor, dropped the ignition keys on the seat, got out, slammed the door. Up there at the corner of 86th, a lit-up all-night cafeteria, the rain showing in gleaming stripes. Near the cafeteria—the canopy of a funeral parlor. She sloshed through the rain to the canopy, waited under it, and when she finally saw a cab with its dome lights lit, she ran out to the street and waved. The cab stopped and she got in.

"Where to, ma'am?"

"Not yet. In a minute."

"Right on. Take your time, ma'am."

He slapped down the flag of the meter. She could see him faintly through the dirty, bullet-proof, plastic barrier. He wore large wire-rim glasses; he had a beard and long hair.

She sat, her knees tight, her shoulders hunched, wet, cold, thinking, desperately thinking. She must not give him her address: they write that down on their trip card. They write down where they pick up the passenger and to where they take the passenger. Barney will be found in the Kips Bay apartment garage. His car will be found on Third Avenue near 86th. It would not do for a trip card to show that a lady was picked up at Third Avenue and 86th and driven to the house on Sutton Place—not when the lady of that house is very well acquainted with Barney Wilson. No, that would not do at all.

"Plaza Hotel," she blurted.

"What? Where?"

She could not hear him clearly.

"Plaza Hotel," she shouted through the small mesh screen.

"Right."

He took off with a lurch. He drove as though drunk, or stoned. She held on for dear life, but said nothing, not a word. Just held. He crossed lights, he made wild turns, but then at last they were there, Plaza Hotel, and she paid through the aperture in the plastic divider, got out, and the cab screeched away.

Emptiness. No one to greet her, no doorman, thank God. He is somewhere inside, safe from the rain. She walked, quickly, down Fifth Avenue. Alone. Cold. Wet. Frightened. To 57th Street. Turned left. Crossed Fifth. And walked. Madison. Park. Lexington. Alone in pelting rain. Third Avenue. And look there!—a man. On her side of the street, coming toward her from Second Avenue. A burly man in a raincoat, his left hand swinging free, his right hand holding a bulge inside the raincoat pocket. A mugger? God, no. Please, no. But what can she do? They are alone on the street. If she runs, he'll run after. And where can she run! Don't run. Hold on to yourself. Walk. Walk strong. And when he comes, smile at him, seductively. You're a prostitute, a street-walker. But what insane prostitute would be walking the streets, deserted streets, at this hour on this dreadful night? No matter: you're an insane prostitute. If you smile at him, at least you'll be face to face. You won't get a mugger's arm, from behind, that can crack your neck. Smile, and see what he wants. Money? You have money in your purse, and you're wearing an expensive wristwatch, and a diamond marriage ring. But suppose he wants more? Me. My body. Rape. All right. Do whatever you want, but don't hurt me, please don't hurt me.

When he came to her, she smiled at him, but he passed her without a glance, absorbed in whatever his own dilemmas. And she was sobbing now, struggling to walk faster in the drenching rain. Second Avenue. First Avenue. Stumbling. Panting. And finally Sutton Place, and down to the gate. Unlocks it, and into the alcove under the stairs, and locks the gate. And she stood there, for minutes, her forehead against the cold iron of the gate. Then she pulled off the gloves and stuffed them away. Felt, with trembling fingers, for the lock of the basement door. Inserted the key, opened, entered, closed, flicked on the yellow light, and she was home. She was home! And had never this night been out of her home. Barney had told her, instructed her, prepared her, protected her, and the old couple, the caretakers, safely in the cocoon of their own apartment, could never say otherwise. Kathy Kearney, all this night, had been peacefully asleep.

She pushed the button for the elevator and it came down to her. Its interior illumination was sufficient. She clicked off the yellow basement light, carried the bags into the elevator. Upstairs in her bedroom, her clothes dripping, she first—first of all—placed the suitcases in a closet. Then she undressed, spread her clothing to dry. Naked, shivering. Into the bathroom for a long hot shower. Then, in pajamas, to the bar of the recreation room for Scotch. She drank it like Barney drank bourbon. Straight. Small shots, gulp after gulp. But, unlike Barney, she grimaced as the burning liquor struck at the base of her throat. And then in the kitchen, coffee. A slice of ham on a piece of toast, and coffee. And then back to the bedroom and out of the pajamas and into bed. Sets the clock for nine thirty, switches off the light, lies in darkness, but cannot sleep. The mind moils, but she fights it. She thinks black. Her system for sleep: she thinks black. Thinks nothing: black, blank, blackness, absence of light, nothingness, a trick she has learned from a famous, faddist psychologist, a form of self-induced hypnosis. But tonight it is difficult. Of course this night it is difficult. Turns, twists, struggles with pillows. In time she will sleep. She knows she will sleep. . . .

In the Armin apartment the gin-rummy game was long forgotten. The cards were still on the table, and the pads with the score. And there were plates on the table, and cups and saucers: Armin had served chicken sandwiches and coffee. Simon Dwyer had been the winner in gin—three hundred forty-two dollars—and Armin had smilingly proclaimed him a lucky man. Now the lucky man lay resting on a couch. Occasionally his eyes moved to Carleton Armin smoking cigarettes in an easy chair. There was a stubble of beard on Armin's face, and a deep furrow between his eyebrows. Occasionally Armin glanced at the man on the couch, but did not speak to him. Nor did Dwyer speak to the man in the easy chair. For a long time now, they had had nothing to say.

259

Then the phone rang, shrill in the silent room. Armin sprang to it. Dwyer looked at his watch: 4:17.

"Hello?" Armin said.

"It has fail, *figlio mio.*"

"What? Beg pardon?"

"I am in my house, I wait. I have told—to call me in my house when the job it is finished. He will come the call—it is the promise—by three o'clock sure. Is three o'clock, nothing. Half past three, nothing. So I call up my Nicola. I tell he should go out there, take a look around. He goes, and we know. By the west it is cut the fence. By the west, on street, station wagon. In station wagon Jake Orin, Joe Stroner, Frank Lander. Shot with bullets. All dead. My men for the work—*tre*—all dead. We cannot take back money from the missus. Would be wrong, would be without honor. They have work, our men. No success—*successo*. They have work, lose life in the work. We must leave the money, the insurance, with the missus. If you wish, I will return you the money."

"No."

"Then you must lose it that money."

"Yes."

"A good son of Don Vito. You are of honor."

"Thank you."

"In *la vita,* there must be sometimes fail. He has happened, this time, to us. So. Fail. *Finito.* For now is over. I go to sleep. Tomorrow I begin. Maybe find out why fail, why it has been without *successo.* Maybe find out, maybe not. I am of sorrow. *Buona notte, figlio mio.*"

"*Addio. Grazie.*"

He clicked off, dialed Ron Seely.

"Tell the men to go home," he said and hung up and turned to Simon Dwyer, who was sitting now, his feet on the floor, his hands gripped to his knees, his face cocked upward, the eyes blinking, questioning. Quickly, succinctly, Carleton

Armin answered the questions. He told Don Antonio's story. Then he opened his arms and did a correct, courteous, graceful little bow. "We're out of the box, my friend. And I am out sixty thousand dollars in cash." He smiled within the dark stubble of beard. He said, "We tried."

"Do you think—Don Antonio? The old badger game? Sucked you in and then turned it around? You know him far better than I. Do you think—possible?"

"No. Impossible. Not Don Antonio."

"Then—what?"

Armin lit a cigarette. "One of those mechanics shot his mouth off. Perhaps too much to drink one night—who knows where's the chink in anyone's armor? Or maybe one of them told his wife and the wife tipped her lover. They were getting big money—therefore those bags figured for a real heavy payday. So parties unknown killed them and pulled off a hijack. And there isn't one damn thing we can do about it."

"But—Don Antonio—"

"He'll set out his lines, perhaps pick up some information. If so, there'll be more dead bodies. Revenge. A form of satisfaction. But that satisfaction won't produce the money. Different if there were *things* in those bags. Things have to be fenced. Once the word was out, nobody would fence; in fact, the don would fast learn who was trying to do the fencing. But the stuff in the bags wasn't things. Cash. Ten million dollars in cash money. It's going to disappear. It's going to spread out and get swallowed up. *Finito.* Out of the box. We tried. We lost. Nobody's always a winner."

"God." Dwyer's head sank. He wrung his hands. "Ten years in prison, waiting, hoping. God, what am I going to do?"

"You're going to come up off the floor, you're going to come up punching."

"I'm old."

"To hell with old. You're in good shape, good health.

You're going to come to work for me. And it's not charity. I'm not throwing a bone to my father's friend. You're a money brain, a tax brain, a CPA. We're going to put that valuable brain to legitimate use, and at a damn good salary. A thousand bucks a week, and that's for starters. You'll probably wind up with more because you'll probably be entitled to more. So? What say, Mr. Dwyer?" A harsh laugh. "This is a hell of a time for a business proposition, but one time is as good as another. So? What say, sir?"

The old man looked up. Gratefully.

But he could not speak. He was weeping.

23

SHE AWOKE from the turmoil of a dream to the consternation of the pealing alarm. She reached out to it, could not find it, finally found it, turned it off, and lay back, in limbo, not asleep but not yet awake. Lay deep in a notch of pillow, eyes closed, awakening, remembering. Crossed her arms over her breasts, held herself, shivered. Sat up, touched a button of the radio to the news, and listened to sharp-quick staccato reports of another lethal night on the killing grounds of New York City. Two policemen ambushed at 134th Street and Seventh Avenue: one dead, one wounded. A seventy-six-year-old woman raped, robbed, and strangled in her apartment in Bedford-Stuyvesant. A man found shot to death in his garage at 333 East 30th Street. A man found beaten to death in the hallway of a tenement at 221 East Fifth Street. A security guard murdered during a robbery at Tower Stadium. A cab driver found shot to death in his taxi on Brook Avenue in the South Bronx. Three men found shot to death in a station wagon in Flushing, Queens. A stockbroker found shot to death on 57th Street and Third Avenue, a gun in his hand, apparently a suicide—

She switched it off, showered. Looked in at the bags in the closet. Put yesterday's clothes in a hamper—to be sent out for cleaning. Then she dressed in casual sweater and slacks and went down for breakfast.

The phone rang at 11:40. She suspected it was Josh from the airport. It was Inspector Harold V. Grover, attached to Police Headquarters. Harold was an old friend; she had known him since the time of her marriage. He had been Captain Grover then, a protégé of Earl Kearney, but he had risen to inspector under the sponsorship of Senator Joshua Fitts Kearney: he was Josh's man in the NYPD. At public functions—at any time in New York City when Josh required protection from crowds or cranks—it was Inspector Grover who automatically acquired the assignment. She had always liked him, bluff, rubicund, with keen blue eyes and a deep, hearty voice.

"How are you, Kathryn?"

"Quite well. Yourself?"

"Fine. Is the Senator there?"

"No. As a matter of—"

"Called his office in Washington. They told me he was returning from England today—to New York. They said he was due this morning."

"That's when he's due, Harold."

A gruff chuckle. "Yes. When you're flying over the ocean, you never know what kind of weather you have to buck. When he comes—as soon as he comes—would you please tell him to call me? Important. Rather important. I'll be waiting for the call. Thank you, Kathryn."

*　　*　　*

They came home at twelve thirty, Joshua Fitts Kearney and Arthur Upton, to Kathy Kearney awaiting them in the lower drawing room.

"Hi, people."

"Hail, person."

"How was the trip?"

"Rough," Upton said.

Kearney said, "How was last night?"

"Call Harold Grover. He phoned about—an hour ago. Said for you to call back as soon as you come. Said important. Said he's waiting for your call."

"I asked you—"

"He said for you to call as *soon* as you come."

Impatiently, he flung away from her. Crossed quickly to the phone, dialed, got through.

"Harold? Josh Kearney here."

"How are you, Senator?"

"Kathy said you called."

"I've got some lousy news."

"What?"

"Barney Wilson."

"What about him?"

"Dead."

"What?"

"They found him this morning. In the garage of his apartment house. Rather peculiar circumstances. I'd like to come see you, Josh."

"When?"

"I'll leave immediately if it's all right with you."

"Yes. Of course." He hung up slowly, frowning, deathly pale.

Upton said, "What's the matter?"

"Barney Wilson. He's dead."

"Oh my God!"

Kearney went across to the woman, took her arm roughly. "I asked you. What about—"

"Your precious tape"—she shook free—"safe and sound. Two suitcases from Tower Stadium. In my closet upstairs."

"Christ, thank God."

"Barney Wilson," Upton said. "Grover. Did he tell you— the circumstances?"

"Found dead in his garage."

"How—what—"

"He'll be here shortly. He's on his way."

"But what happened?"

"Dead. Garage. That's all he told me. Goddamn—"

"Gentlemen," Kathy said.

"Do *you* know?" Upton demanded.

"How in hell would *she* know?"

"Would you like a drink, Arthur? You look like you can use—"

"Please. A bit of gin."

"Josh?"

"Scotch."

She went to the bar, poured gin for Arthur, Scotch for Josh, and sherry for herself.

Inspector Harold V. Grover, burly, blue-eyed, sharp-eyed, arrived in the company of a tall young man.

"Lieutenant Powell," he said. "Lou Powell, Homicide South. Wilson is Lou's case."

Kearney said, "A drink, gentlemen?"

"Not me," Grover said.

"No, thanks," Powell said.

"Tell the people, Lou."

"Yessir." The tall young man took a notebook from a pocket. "Garage. Three-thirty-three East Thirty. Body discovered at seven forty this morning. By a tenant of the prem-

266

ises, a multiple dwelling. Squad car arrived at seven fifty. Officer Garth. Officer Lopez. Lopez called it in to Communications. Communications gave to Homicide South, Detective Paul Donovan in charge."

Powell looked up from his notebook and his eyes met Kathy's. She smiled. He smiled, a thin smile, polite, perfunctory. He was a serious young man with serious brown eyes and a conservative haircut. He wet his lips and returned to the notebook.

"The body was found under a blanket. Cause of death, bullet penetration. Eight bullets in the head, eleven bullets in the torso. The murder weapon, a submachine gun, was found beside the body. No identification on the person of the subject. The superintendent identified the subject as Barnabas Francis Xavier Wilson, a tenant of the multiple dwelling, Apartment Eleven-F. In Apartment Eleven-F, Donovan verified the identification. In the apartment, further investigation disclosed that Mr. Wilson was a vice president of Kearney Computers. At this point, Donovan called in to Homicide for a superior officer."

Upton said, "Why?"

The serious young man closed the notebook, smiled his thin smile. "The Police Department is no different"—a shrug —"from any other business. Donovan realized the subject was a big shot. With a big shot, if you make a wrong move, you can get jammed up with the brass. Therefore, for your own protection, you move it up in rank. You lay it onto a superior officer. I'm the superior officer."

Kearney frowned. "If *you're* the superior officer—then why's Inspector Grover here?"

"Senator," Grover said. "Let him tell it his own way."

"Yes, I'm sorry," Kearney said.

The tall young man strode to Kathy at the bar, looked at her glass. "Is that sherry, Mrs. Kearney?"

"Sherry," she said.

"May I—would you, please?"

"Certainly."

She poured a sherry and he drank a bit of it, a touch at his lips. "We did our things," he said. "Cop things. Medical Examiner, photographs—all the necessary. Then the body was removed to the morgue, and at nine thirty I went to Kearney Computers. Talked with the president, Mr. Dwight Hickey. He verified that Wilson was a vice president—salary, seventy-five thousand a year. But he told me that Wilson had been detached from service at Kearney Computers. Temporarily out on loan. As a political aide to Senator Kearney. That's when I called it in to Inspector Grover."

"Why?" Upton said.

And now, for the first time, the young man's smile was open.

"Same reason as Detective Donovan," he said. "The moving up in ranks, the shifting of responsibility. Who needs trouble, who wants to look for trouble? The vice president of Kearney Computers was over Donovan's head. The political aide to Senator Kearney was over *my* head. Inspector Grover —as is very well known in the department—is a good friend of the Senator's, an old friend, a dear friend. In a sense, I ducked out from under. Just as Donovan laid it onto me, so did I lay it onto Inspector Grover."

"Smart." Grover laughed. "Lou Powell over there, one of the new breed, a college-educated cop. By the way, who's Bernard Brown?"

"Who?" Kearney said.

"Bernard Brown. Which of you knows a Bernard Brown?"

The sharp blue eyes moved from Kearney to Upton to Kathy.

They all answered. None of them knew a Bernard Brown.

"Who's Bernard Brown?" Kearney said.

"Back to Lou Powell," Grover said. "It's still yours, Louie."

"A strange case, a peculiar case," Powell said. "And Mr. Hickey's disclosures made it even more peculiar."

Irritably Senator Kearney said, "Disclosures? What disclosures?"

"Last summer, in July," Powell said, "Mr. Wilson came to Mr. Hickey at Kearney Computers. He asked Hickey to get him an office down on Wall Street. But under an assumed name—Bernard Brown. And under an assumed profession—travel agent. And under an assumed address—Mr. Hickey's address in Scarsdale. And he asked Mr. Hickey to get him an apartment on East Sixty-seventh Street—under all those self-same conditions. In August, Bernard Brown moved into an office on Wall Street. In October, Bernard Brown took over an apartment on the upper East Side. Today a corps of experts—police experts—fine-combed that office, fine-combed that apartment. Found nothing. Found no connection between Bernard Brown and Barnabas Wilson. So now, if you please." And the serious young man finally seriously drank. He took up the glass, drank down all the sherry. "If you please," he said. "Can any of you help us? Why did Barnabas Wilson become Bernard Brown? Why the office downtown, the apartment uptown? Anything? Any idea at all?"

"Absolutely no idea at all," Senator Kearney said.

"Just a minute," Upton said. "I don't know if you gentlemen know. Barney Wilson was a bigwig with Central Intelligence—"

"We'll come to that," Grover said.

"We know," Powell said. "We know from papers we found in his apartment. It's one of the reasons we're here—"

"My turn," Grover said. "Go give yourself another sherry, Louie. My turn now. What I'm going to tell you, lady and gentlemen, is going to make this case so much more strange, more peculiar." He pointed a finger at Upton. "I think you said it, Arthur. I think you just said it all."

"What did I say?" Upton said.

"Listen, please. All of you. Listen to strange, listen to peculiar." Grover passed a hand through his hair, shook ruddy jowls. "Last night, at about one o'clock, there was a robbery at Tower Stadium. And for that robbery the same words apply —strange, peculiar. Two ski-masked men burst into the guards' room—four guards. They killed one guard; they blindfolded, gagged, and bound the other three. Then, in the board room, they drilled through a wall, to some sort of vault, a cache. We have no idea what was in that vault. But we must assume it was valuable treasure since the thieves, quite evidently, were skilled professionals. Are you with me? Are you following me?"

"Not quite," Upton said.

Grover grinned. "This morning, at about eight o'clock, three men were found dead in the rear of a station wagon near Tower Stadium. Two were in ski masks, the third in normal attire. The men in the ski masks were wearing jump suits, and the security guards definitely identified them —by size, configuration, and attire—as the Tower Stadium robbers. Presumably the station wagon was the getaway car, and presumably the man in mufti was the wheel man. But no treasure was found in the station wagon. So, again, presumption. Hijack. Thieves stealing from thieves."

Senator Kearney said, "Harold, you're losing me. What the devil does that have to do with—"

"Ballistics," Grover said. "The submachine gun that killed Barney Wilson—is the same submachine gun that killed the thieves in the station wagon."

"Are you crazy?" Upton demanded. "Are you trying to say that Barney was a thief mixed up in some sort of hijack?"

"No. Not a Barney Wilson. Not a vice president earning

270

seventy-five thousand dollars a year. Not a political aide to Senator J. F. Kearney. Not a man of the caliber of Barney Wilson. Not a man who was the chief of the spook department of the CIA. I think that's our answer, Arthur, and therefore we're never going to get any real answers."

Kearney said, "You're still talking in riddles."

"No riddle. I called the CIA, gave them the facts. They denied any knowledge whatever. They stated—as if I didn't know—that Barney had resigned five years ago. But we all know that the CIA does reach back when an ex-employee fits for a certain special assignment. And we also know that Central Intelligence is not going to confide in the local gendarmes."

"Yes, true," Upton murmured.

"And the local gendarmes are going to play it close to the vest—because we're looking for the killers of three in the station wagon, and if we get them, then we'll also have the people who killed Barney. Thus Wilson is just another murder in New York City, and by tomorrow he'll be yesterday's news."

"Been in touch with the next of kin," Powell said. "Parents in Lincoln, Nebraska. The father's ill. The mother asked if we could ship the body—"

"I'll take care of those arrangements," Kearney said.

Their conversation became a distant drone for Kathy Kearney at the bar sipping sherry. She was free and clear, as was Josh, as was Arthur: they were out from under, free and clear. The way it had worked out, the submachine gun and all, there was not the faintest possibility of complicity. The authorities were seeking professional thieves who had murdered professional thieves (and had also murdered Barney Wilson). It would go down as another crime, open in the police files and forever unresolved. . . .

She heard Harold Grover.

"Goodbye, Kathryn. Sorry we had to disturb you."

"Not at all."

"Good day, Mrs. Kearney," Powell said.

And then the policemen were gone, and they were alone in a dreadful silence. After a time Kearney said quizzically, "I hope—I mean—are you sure you have those bags up there?"

"God, aren't you the son of a bitch!"

Kearney looked to Upton. "What the hell's the matter with *her?*"

"Easy now," Upton said. The old man. The patriarch. "Easy does it," he said soothingly. "We're all of us tight." He smiled. "Or is the modern word—uptight?"

Kearney turned to her. "Please, if they're up there, will you—"

"Up there," she sang. "The bags, the bags, two bags full. One for my master—"

"Would you get them, please?"

"At once, oh master."

She entered the elevator.

Upton, facing Kearney, had his back to her.

"Barney Wilson," he said. His mouth was slack, his voice tremulous. "I cannot understand. Can you? I mean—if he brought out the bags—if she has the bags—then it was accomplished, it was done. Then how—why—dead? What reason? Who—"

"Me," she called. "Me. I killed him."

And touched the button and the elevator closed.

At the bar, Joshua Fitts and Arthur Upton. Scotch for Joshua, gin for Arthur. "She's crazy," Joshua said. "Her entire attitude—from the moment we came home."

"Can you blame her? We've been away, out of it. A fantastic emergency, and the burden on her. She and Barney—"

272

"Did you hear? Did you hear what she said?"

"A joke. When you're tense you make jokes, macabre jokes. That I *can* understand. She's shaken, no question. So are you, so am I. And we've not been in it. She's been *in* it."

"Yes," Kearney said. "Yes, of course."

He drank his Scotch. Upton drank his gin.

She returned, lugging the bags. She laid them on the floor, unstrapped them, threw back the covers. Upton peered down at the stacks of money, whistled. She lifted out the tape recorder and, as Kearney reached for it, she veered away from him.

"I want that," he said.

"Sure you do, you son of a bitch."

"What the hell's going on?" Upton said.

She placed the recorder on a table, inserted the plug into an outlet. Her voice was sly. "Don't you want to hear it, dearest husband?"

"I—I'd prefer to hear it alone."

"I'm afraid I can't grant you that privilege. Because I've already heard it. So did Barney Wilson. And now King Arthur must hear. So that he can know who in hell you really are."

"What in hell?" Upton said.

She switched it on. She reversed the tape to the beginning, then let it play. And as it talked, she watched Arthur Upton. She saw amazement transfigure his face, saw the face pale, saw an old man grow older.

"Recognize voices?" she said.

"Enough. Goddam, enough!" Kearney ran to the recorder, closed it off. He looked at Upton, looked at her, looked back to Upton. "I—I'd hoped—I had hoped never to have to admit . . ."

A squint, pale. A squint within the wrinkles of old eyes.

273

"Why you? Why would you do this? Why would you stoop to filthy bribery? You?"

"Him!" Her voice cracked, but she held on, straining against hysteria. "Him, the lying bastard. Not the father. The son. Not Earl Kearney. But Joshua Fitts Kearney."

"Ten years ago," Kearney said.

"Him. Him. The lying bastard."

"Ten—"

"Him!"

"Let him talk," Upton said.

"Talk, son of a bitch. Talk."

He talked, Joshua Fitts Kearney. Told about ten years ago. Told about the beginnings of desire for politics. Ambition. The nomination in his congressional district was wide open. If he could obtain the nomination, his election was a virtual certainty. But Vito Arminito was the power; Vito controlled the political boss. With Vito behind him, the nomination was his. With Vito opposed, it would pass to another. The opportunity was at hand, the golden opportunity. Therefore he had gone along with Vito in the bribery scheme, because Vito in jail was still the political power, and Vito—word of honor—had promised him the nomination. But J. F. Kearney had never dreamed that Vito Arminito was insuring the action by recording the proceedings.

"Liar. Lying bastard," she shouted. "He *never* tells the truth. Perhaps even right now he's lying. But he's stupid. I tell you—stupid! Because there comes a time, by all that's holy, when you *must* tell the truth. He was after this goddamned tape—it could ruin him. Wasn't *that* a time for the truth? To us? The Big Four? But he held out, didn't he? God, this monster would lie on his deathbed to a priest. But for once, this once, his lies came home to roost. And I saved him. I saved our beautiful paragon of virtue. This once his lies could have murdered him. As they did murder Barney Wilson."

"What?" Upton said. "What? How?"

Hysteria stemmed, she stood tall. She stated her piece, confessed unashamed. Barney was her lover, a marvelous lover—she loved him. And she knew that Josh knew about Barney and her, just as Arthur knew, just as she knew that Joshua Fitts, no lover at all in bed with his wife, was the kinky lover of paid prostitutes. And then she passed from love, lover, husband, bed, and told about Barney's work on behalf of Joshua Fitts Kearney. Told about the prospective hazards, the standby doctor, the instructions in the event of his death, the room at the Deaver Motel in Jackson Heights. Told about Barney's return from Tower Stadium, the inspection of the suitcases, the casual curiosity, the playing of the tape. And told about Barney Wilson's reaction: shock, chagrin, disgust, disappointment—and rage.

"Wrong," she said to her husband. "You don't tamper with a man like Barney Wilson. For certain games there are certain rules, Mr. Man, and when the game entails the risk of life, then the primary rule of the game is honesty. Barney played by the rules. Not you. You didn't. You withheld the truth—and created an enemy implacable. I remember his exact words: *'If you want loyalty, you have to give loyalty.'* You did not give loyalty, and so he no longer owed loyalty, and right then and there in the Deaver Motel it was over. He considered *you* a potential danger to *him*. And therefore he turned it all around. He quit the team. He was on his own."

And she told of Barney's proposition: the embezzlement of the cash, the duplication of the tape, the wife walking out on the husband, and her eventual marriage to Barney.

"And there wasn't a damned thing you could do about it. Because in his vault he would have the trump card—a copy of that tape. And I agreed to all of it, everything. I would leave you and marry him. I acceded. I pretended to accede."

"Pretended?" Upton said.

And now, haltingly, she told of the murder, and told why. Ambition. The perennial, perpetual, age-old story: ambition. First Lady of the Land; wife of the President of the United States. For that, for the prospect of that, all else is expendable, all else must be sacrificed.

"I agreed. I pretended to accede—otherwise he would have been *twice* traduced. Rage upon rage—it would have been all over for us. He would have—immediately—exposed that tape, no doubt, no question whatever. I knew the man better than either of you, better than anyone else in this world. He wasn't a politician, not Barney. Not one for the twists, the tricks, the chicanery. His nature was essentially straight and simple. Your friend, Mr. Kearney, had become your enemy—and he was beyond compromise. There could not be two ways. It was either the death of your political career or the death, literally, of Barney Wilson." She shuddered, her arms rigid at her sides. "What I did, I did with little risk—no risk at all. He had arranged to keep me out of it, to keep me unconnected. He himself had arranged my full protection."

The old man stared at the woman standing there, somehow a figure of dignity, tall, erect, the wan face composed, but her eyes showing her torture, and her contempt, for them, for herself.

"So here we are," she said. "Without glory, but intact. Here we are, narrowed down; despicable but intact. Here we are again the Big Three, Mr. President."

Arthur Upton crossed to the tape recorder. He started it up, touched the ERASE button, and watched as the machine wiped away the possibilities of disaster. He was visibly shaken by all he had heard: connivance, deceit, bribery, mendacity,

276

adultery, armed robbery, and multiple murder. But in his lifetime he had heard it all before; the experiences of a lifetime had taught him of the myriad private machinations that boil, churn, gestate, and converge to produce the public man. And this man, quite purely, this public man, J. F. Kearney, had evolved as the best man for the highest job. In comparative youth, he had indulged in an act of corruption—and had striven to keep it undisclosed. We make mistakes: we are all human. But thereafter, rising in public life, he had proved himself, over and over, time and again. Of course he had his foibles—God, who hasn't?—but he also had marvelous strengths, a fervid dedication, a quintessential drive for good. And now, at the brink of catastrophe, the woman had snatched him from destruction by the *ultimate* act of corruption—murder! And she had not done it for him. For herself. For *her* ambition. But fate works its ways. He was unscathed, politically unharmed, and as President he would continue to develop. It has long been demonstrated that the right man grows with the office, and this man was the right man. . . .

Arthur Upton shivered, moved away from the quiet whirring erasing disaster. He came to them, an old man showing his age, frowning, fatigued, desperately tired.

"I don't envy you, Kathy. I—me—I could not live with what *you* will have to live with for the rest of your life. On the other hand, may I offer a philosophy?" He smiled, small, a crooked little smile, tentative. "What you did—you did for yourself. Without aura of sacrifice, no martyrdom. You did for ego need, personal aggrandizement, lust of ambition. But sometimes a wrongful act wrongfully impelled, an evil act, egregious, horrendous—sometimes, somehow, it can result in benefit, it can transcend, it can produce an overall good." The smile disappeared. The wrinkles about his eyes were deep and dark. "God moves in mysterious ways." And now, before addressing Kearney, he did what she had never seen him do before. Slowly, quite reverently, he made the sign of the cross on his body. Then he said, "You were finished, Josh. Done for. Destroyed. Demolished. And suddenly you are whole again." He sighed, his voice trembled. "You can thank your lady for that miracle."

"Yes. I thank you," Kearney said simply.

She stood there. She said nothing.

Then she turned from them and walked out of the room.

Henry Kane

Henry Kane has written novels, short stories,
screenplays; he has been published in virtually every
language. A man of frightening energy, a native
New Yorker, a volatile man of high humors
and black despairs, Kane has been described
by *Esquire* magazine as "author, bon vivant,
stoic, student, tramp, lawyer, philosopher, a
master of the massé shot on a pool table."